The Midlife Pact

1

Sherri Egan slid the casserole dish into her oven just as she heard the knock on the door.

She skipped to her front door. She hadn't seen her son, Tanner, in almost a month. She missed him now that he had a life of his own. *Why'd he have to go and grow up?*

She snickered as she unlatched the door, expecting his shiny face to be on the other side.

She took a step back, cringed, as her ex-husband Burt stood there instead.

"Hi, beautiful."

She hated that name.

"What are you doing here, Burt?"

Burt stepped over the threshold, pulling her into a hug, leaving a wet kiss on her cheek. "Is that a way to greet your favorite husband?"

She dabbed at her cheek with the back of her hand. "Ex." As she shut the door behind him, she added softly, "You always seem to forget that part."

Of course, he didn't hear her. Or maybe it was selective hearing.

"What brings you here?" She tried again. "Tanner should be here any minute."

"Tanner's coming?" That seemed to get his attention.

"Yes. For dinner. I thought that was maybe why you showed up too."

Right after their divorce, she'd invited him frequently to dinner, trying to keep their father/son relationship strong. He rarely showed. And when he did, it was usually for a quick visit, something that always disappointed Tanner. She'd finally given up.

"I won't stay long then. I don't want to intrude," he trailed off.

Now she knew something was on his mind. "You can stay if you like." She didn't want him there, but she didn't want him running out just when Tanner arrived either.

"No. Really. I have to be someplace." Burt looked at his watch, scowled.

"Burt, what is it? I can see you have something on your mind."

"I just wanted to talk with you about a new venture I've found."

"Shit, Burt, really? More money?

"You haven't even heard the idea."

"I don't need to. How many things have I paid for over the years?"

"But this isn't just paying off a bill. This is an opportunity. And it's the best I've seen. It's a sure winner. I know I have something here. Besides, how do you know I'm asking for money?"

"You always ask for money."

"I can't help our paychecks have never been equal. I can't help your parents left you a windfall while mine left me nothing. This isn't about me; it's about creating something for our son."

Sherri went eyebrows up, squinting at him. "Really? You want to go *there*? You're going to bring my parents' death into this? And our son? Since when are your ventures ever about our son?" She could go on and on, but what was the point?

He brushed his hand through the air, as if to say she wasn't listening. "I'm only doing this for Tanner."

"You're doing this for Tanner? Will you be leaving this new venture in your will? Will this add money to an account you can leave in his name?" She moved closer, eyes narrowing. "Of course not. You're doing this for you. You always do this for you. You spend more than you make. You go through new ideas like water. If you'd plan a little better, maybe you wouldn't buy things you didn't need. If you'd just get a better job instead of trying out new schemes, maybe you'd have enough to run with this idea on your own." She tapped him on his chest with her finger. "Instead of using *my* money."

Burt moved closer, trying to look her in the eye.

But Sherri was through with that. She was tired of his plans, tired of his requests for more.

If she'd stopped and added up how much she'd given him since their divorce, she knew she'd be shocked.

Which is why she'd never dared do the math.

"Burt, look, I've given you more than enough. Don't you think it's time to stop? Can't you do something else that doesn't require funding? Why not take a budgeting class instead?"

He didn't even flinch. He ignored her sarcasm, and kept right on talking. "I could. But I've always wanted to start something and leave a legacy. For Tanner. You know that. It's why you married me."

That was true. She'd been a dreamer right out of college. That's what appealed to her when she'd first met Burt. He'd been a dreamer too.

It was only after they were married that she discovered she was a doer. Him, not so much.

He'd drifted from job to job, trying to *find himself*. And after two decades of marriage, the only way he could find himself was to do it alone. Or so he'd said.

Oh, that had bugged her. Driven her crazy.

She'd invested more than twenty years in a marriage, worked hard to make a home, and he just walked off to discover something more?

She hated him for it.

Now, five years later, he still kept showing up at her door. She'd find it easier if he'd walked away and just kept looking.

Whenever she thought she'd moved on, he'd turn up on her doorstep.

Always asking for money.

Always looking like the sexy, handsome man she'd married all those years ago.

She had a weakness for him, she knew it. He'd aged well. It's why she listened when he asked. And boy, did he ask.

A thousand for this. Five thousand for that.

She'd been the saver in their marriage too. So she'd always had plenty to share.

That was her problem. She always gave. To keep peace.

For Tanner.

She looked at the clock on the wall. She knew he'd be arriving any moment.

"How much?"

"Just a thousand. I need it for the start-up kit for a health food business I'm going to be representing." He shoved a brochure at her. "When I get it going, I'd love to talk with you and Tanner about it. We can set you up underneath me. That way we can all earn as we go. It's great stuff."

"Just. No." She didn't want to fight. She didn't want to argue with him. She just wanted him out of her house.

She walked to her desk, grabbed her checkbook out of the drawer.

In seconds, she had a check made out to her ex. She ripped it out and handed it to him. "Here."

Then she moved back to the front door. "If you don't want to run into Tanner, I suggest you leave." She opened the door wide and stood to the side.

She'd love it if he argued with her. Told her to close the door, he'd changed his mind, he'd gladly stay for dinner.

But she knew that would never be the case.

"Thanks, beautiful." He grabbed the check from her fingers, kissed her cheek once again, and was out the door.

She might have slammed the door a little harder than she should have.

She might have screamed, just a little.

But she had to. She had to get *him* out of her system before Tanner arrived.

Sherri put the last of the dishes into the dishwasher, added soap, and clicked the dial to the on position.

She picked up her wine glass, filled it with what was left in the bottle. Then she carried her glass to the table, dropped into the chair, and used her fingers to massage her temples.

Dinner had been good. Her son was happy and thriving.

Nothing like his dad.

At least she'd done that right. She'd raised him as a strong, independent person who knew how to take care of himself.

And to *not* ask for help.

In fact, she found he was the opposite, always complaining when she tried to help. It was as if he knew what his dad was like, and wanted to do the opposite of his actions.

Yep, she'd done that right.

She'd been happy Tanner had been late. At least he hadn't seen his dad when he arrived. She'd avoided having to tell him she'd handed him another check, more money to fund his latest business venture.

Chances are he'd never hear it from Burt. It would fail, like all the rest.

Like the *coach* he'd signed with who promised him businesses would pay big bucks to have someone handle their social media accounts for them. The trouble was, Burt himself knew little about social media. He never did get a company to buy into the fact he knew what he was doing.

Or the multilevel marketing program for supplements he'd joined a year before. How many vitamins did one person need? And why would anyone spend that much on so little? Burt had given that program up before he worked his way through the first bottle.

Burt drove her crazy. She wished he'd move far away and just leave her alone.

But all was forgotten when Tanner finally arrived, and she had her son back in her home.

They'd chatted about everything. His job. His new apartment. His new girlfriend, and a promise to meet said girlfriend in a couple of weeks. They'd made a date for dinner; she'd drive up to Portland and take them both out.

She could see in his eyes how much he liked her. She might be *the one.* He'd hinted at that when she'd pressed.

Not that she was one to push him into marriage. Or grandkids.

She was way too young for that.

But still, she was glad he was happy.

You should be happy too, Mom. When's the last time you dated?

Tanner had actually asked her that.

Could it be Tanner was truly an adult, asking about her happiness?

God, she loved that boy.

Even if she didn't want to talk about it with him, he had made some valid points.

She should be happy. She should get a life. She should do what she wanted to do.

She was fifty, after all. Fifty fucking years old! *When had that happened?*

What *did* she want to do? That was always the question. A question she never found the answer too. And she'd been asking it a lot since her birthday.

She gulped down the rest of her wine. She pushed aside her glass and grabbed her iPad instead. She clicked and pulled up a browser window, sat there and sighed.

She stared at the bright colors of the Google logo. *If only Google could tell me what to do.*

Maybe it can.

She punched in "fabulous at fifty." Because she was fabulous. And she was fifty. She wasn't lying.

And there on the very first line was something that caught her attention.

Are you ready for the best years of your life? Then click here and come inside.

Yes, yes she was. She could do this. Maybe all she needed was the right guidance to find her way. Maybe what she needed was right here all along.

A warm and inviting online community, filled with other fifty-year-old women asking the same questions as her.

She clicked. She read. She loved what she saw.

2

"Did you get it?" Sherri was chomping at the bit. She'd waited a full five minutes before calling her BFF, Annette Hinton, who had the nerve of answering with a casual *Hello* instead of being just as excited as she.

"What are you talking about?" Annette asked a little warily. After spending most of her adult life with Sherri by her side, she knew when she sounded this excited, things were about to get crazy.

"The email. Did you check your email? I just sent you something."

"Why don't you text like the rest of us?"

"Because it came in the form of an email. So I forwarded it to you."

"*What* did you send to me?"

"Just check your email."

"I'll have to call you back. I'm in the kitchen and I can't do two things at once on this phone. Let me get to my office."

Annette clicked her phone, grabbed her mug of tea, and strolled through her home, to the front office space. She'd spent the morning cleaning; it smelled lemony and fresh. Just the way she liked it.

She slid into her Herman Miller chair, the one her husband Curt had so thoughtfully given her two years before when she'd decided to start writing for a living. He believed in her; he still did. Too bad the school system paid better than her writing. With bills piling up faster than they could pay them, she figured she'd be teaching fifth grade for the rest of her life.

Ugh.

As she dropped to the chair, she glanced at the portrait she kept on the corner of her desk. It was her favorite, she had three more in various sizes just like it scattered throughout her home. She stood in the middle, with Curt holding her hand on the right. Her daughter Clara held her other hand; CJ, her son, had his arm wrapped around his dad.

Good times. The best of times.

And then the kids went and grew up.

Clara was currently living in Seattle with her boyfriend, zooming up the ladder of a startup that had her working sixty hours a week. She was happy; that's all that mattered. Plus Annette finally approved of her current boyfriend; also another reason to do a happy dance.

Then there was CJ, who'd recently graduated with honors from the University of California. He was currently in Los Angeles, trying to fulfill his dream of producing documentaries. He'd had three jobs in six months; after hours - days - of *conversation*, she'd hoped she finally convinced him that it was okay to start at the bottom.

She rolled her eyes at the thought. Twenty-two and convinced he could do no wrong. She loved that about her son. She also hated it.

Annette jumped as her phone buzzed on her desk.

Well?

Sherri's text message blinked up at her.

Annette tapped her keyboard, bringing it to life. She typed in her password, and let everything come up full screen.

She pulled up her Gmail and weeded through a few messages before she found the one Sherri had referenced.

Fw: Fabulous at Fifty Conference Coming Soon

She clicked. And she scanned.

Hey all you fabulous fifty year olds, are you ready for the second annual partay of the century? We had a blast last year, and this year promises to be even better.

We're here to give you the push you need to take on your next fifty years with magic and pizzazz. We want you to come with hopes and dreams, and leave with new friends, a strategic plan in hand, and more motivation than you'll ever need to succeed.

Whatever your dreams are, we're here to support you.

We'll party like it's nineteen-ninety-nine. We'll motivate you with some of the most amazing speakers around. We'll entertain you with nonstop action and fun.

And when you leave, you'll have a support group of one hundred other fifty-something women who want to see you succeed!

Are you ready to celebrate your age?

Are you ready to make some magic?

Then click this button and get started right now.

It only takes a minute to register. And a few more minutes to book your hotel. Then you can join us for the biggest event of your life.

One that will change your world forever.

Annette clicked. She scanned through the website, looking at photos from the first annual event.

She knew all about this group. Sherri had been talking about it nonstop for weeks. Ever since she'd turned fifty a few months before, and had rather loudly made the declaration that she was going to make big changes in her life, and she was bringing Annette along.

Annette bit her lip. She huffed out a breath.

It sounded good, it did. But she'd been down this road before.

She'd had the dream when she was approaching forty-nine. She'd always dreamed of being a writer. She'd make plans.

She had the freaking chair her husband had bought for her to prove it.

Yet here she was, still tooling away doing nothing with those dreams.

Did she really want to go and *celebrate* all of that with Sherri and a bunch of other fifty-somethings?

Her phone buzzed. She hit accept.

"Yes, you do. This is what we're going to do to get us away from that hellhole they call a job, and put us on track for a better future."

"And what makes you think this group will do that for us?"

"Because we need to get out of our comfort zones. We need to have a reason to make a plan and stick with it. And the sessions they offer look great. It'll give us ideas we can take back with us. And we'll hold each other accountable."

"We will, will we?" Annette knew she didn't sound very enthusiastic. She couldn't help it.

"Yep." Sherri sighed. "Look, I know I've been super excited about this group ever since I found it. I know I've been talking a lot about getting old, and making a change, and all that crap. But I really think this is our time. You've wanted to be a writer forever. We've been talking about *something new* for months. Isn't it about time we did something about it?"

She had her there. Annette tapped her finger on her mouse as she clicked and scrolled.

The more she looked at the photos and the schedule of events, the more she liked what she saw.

Maybe this is what she needed. What *they* needed.

She smiled as she thought back to the first time she'd met Sherri at Apple Creek Elementary school, where they were first starting their careers as elementary school teachers. They were both crazy excited at the prospect of making a difference in kids' lives. They were both filled with hopes and dreams for the future.

Then life happened. And here they still were.

Two of the longest teaching instructors at the school.

They'd seen a lot of changes. Too many changes to still believe they could make a difference. They both loved teaching, and helping kids learn. But the red tape had grown out of control. And they both wanted more … just more.

Between the constant meetings about performance, the write ups when they didn't follow the rules to the tee, and the safety classes they'd had to attend the past few years just in case an active shooter entered their classrooms, they both wanted out.

It wasn't fun anymore.

It was just belittling. Wearing. Treacherous.

A mind-field of parents, supervisors, and regulations had pushed them both way too far.

But there were bills to pay.

Annette still had loans out for both kids' college tuition. The mortgage on the house. The credit card bills they'd used for a vacation. The ever-growing insurance premiums. And the never-ending medical payments from Curt's cancer scare a year before.

They'd be paying off that loan forever at the rate they were going. At least he was okay. But those kinds of bills really made them question if retirement was ever in their future.

Why shouldn't she hope for more?

Why shouldn't she go?

"This works with school?"

"Of course. It's spring break. The conference is two full days, but we'll have to be there the day before, and fly out the day following. San Diego is only a two-and-a-half-hour flight. So we should easily be able to find cheap flights."

"We'll room together?" Annette knew Curt would feel better about it if she saved where she could.

"Yep. I already have the room reserved. And get this; it's a buy one, get one ticket for the conference. They want people to bring a friend. That way you have a support system back home. You're my one. So you're going. It's all booked. We're all set. We just need to finalize the airfare."

"And I need to pay you. *If* I'm going."

"Of course. *When* you say yes."

"You really are confident, aren't you?"

Sherri chuckled. "How long have we been together?"

Annette just shook her head. They'd been fast friends forever. The kind you finish sentences for. The kind you'd walk over hot coals for. The kind you'd say yes to when she already had everything booked. "Okay."

"Goodie! Now you can get your butt over here to help me. I need to know what to wear."

Annette rolled her eyes.

Sherri's taste in clothes was … interesting.

She still thought Crocs with dresses was perfectly acceptable attire.

"You're leaving those ugly shoes at home." Annette shuddered at the thought of the outfit Sherri had picked out for her last date. Luckily, Annette had arrived a half hour before her date did; plenty of time to pull the god-awful shoes off her feet and put her in something sexier.

"But I love my shoes." Sherri whined the way she always did when they discussed her shoes.

"It's me or the shoes."

"Well, when you put it that way …"

"I do."
"Okay, the shoes stay here."

3

Annette dropped her bags of groceries on the counter, backtracked into the mudroom to deposit her things. She slipped her coat into the closet and dropped her purse and keys onto the table.

She flicked on the television and started putting everything away.

She pulled a few things from the fridge and laid them on the counter. She grabbed a pot from the cupboard and a knife from the drawer.

She cut and chopped, making soup for dinner.

She stirred the pot absentmindedly, thinking of all she'd need to do before she left on her trip.

Luckily, with it being just the two of them, there wasn't much to be done. Annette would make sure all the laundry was done before she left instead of saving it for Saturday morning. She'd also double up a couple of meals, to put a few extras in the freezer for Curt to eat while she was gone.

She knew he wouldn't starve. He was a pretty good cook himself, after all. And once their family and friends found out she'd be out of town for a few nights, the dinner invitations would roll in.

He'd be glad she returned just for the peace and quiet of being able to stay home. She smiled at the thought.

She turned as Curt came stomping through the door.

"Leave your boots in the mudroom, please."

"Don't I always?"

"Not when you have things in your hands like you do right now," she teased as she laid her spoon on the counter, wiped her hands on the dish towel, and walked over to where he was standing.

He glanced around at the counter, where dishes were scattered. "What should I do with these boxes?"

Annette took them from him, trying to peer inside. "What's in here?"

As the head of landscaping and maintenance for their local parks and recreation office, Curt was always bringing things home. Their backyard was filled with a little of this and a little of that, thanks to his never-ending supply of plants he received throughout the year.

"I pulled these out when I redid Johnsons Park this morning getting ready for summer. I hate ripping out perfectly good plants and throwing them away. I thought I could fill these into the back corner."

"Well, you better do it quickly. They don't look very good." She moved a couple of them around. They seemed a bit wilty to her. But she always left landscaping to Curt. She'd tried to weed once, and he complained for a week about how she'd tossed aside perfectly good plants. That had been the end of her weeding.

He sniffed as he walked over to the sink to wash his hands. "What's for dinner?"

"The chili you like. I figured it would give us several days of leftovers."

He grabbed a spoon and dipped it into the pot.

"Curt …" She slapped his hand away playfully.

He stuck the full spoon into his mouth. "Mmm …"

He was all up in her face, playing, the way they always did. He grabbed her by the shoulders and pulled her in, planting his lips on hers. "Good," he rolled off his tongue.

They exchanged a look. Together *forever*, and they still had fun.

"Go plant your plants." She swatted at his fingers as he playfully pinched her in the ass.

"What time is dinner?"

"This needs to simmer for awhile. How about in an hour?"

He nodded, turned and went back to the mudroom for his boots.

"Curt?"

"Yes?"

She walked over, leaned against the doorframe. He was down on the bench, tying his shoelaces. He had other things on his mind; perfect for telling him her plans.

"So I'm going to be gone the last weekend of the month. Sherri and I are heading to San Diego for a conference."

"Okay." He didn't look up. "For work?"

"No. It's more of a woman's retreat. It's that group I told you about. The one she joined right after her fiftieth."

"The nifty fifties?" He stood up, stomped his feet a couple of times to put everything in place.

Annette crossed her arms, shaking her head with scorn. "Fabulous at fifty. Nifty fifties? What decade are you living in?"

He slid into his coat, kissed her forehead as he moved around her.

"And this is something you want to do?"

"Yeah. I think it is."

"And we can afford it?"

"Yes."

He leaned on the box, looking at her.

"Curt, yes. I keep up with our finances too, you know. I know how tough it's been lately. This is a buy one, get one, Sherri already has the tickets. We're going to share a hotel room. And it's San Diego. I'm sure I can get a cheap ticket out of Portland."

"Okay." He held up his hands in defense. "I'm just asking. I trust you. If this is something you want to do, do it. I know things have been tough lately. And it might do you some good to get away from it all, even if it is just for a weekend."

"I'd like to tell you about it."

He looked in his box.

She knew that look. He'd only partially listen anyway if she tried to talk with him now. His mind was on his garden.

"Later." She motioned outside.

As he left, she almost thought he sounded giddy as he yelled, "I'll be back in a jiffy. We can talk then."

Annette picked up their bowls and brought them to the sink. She ran water in both, grabbed the wine bottle and headed back to the table. She poured some in his, before finishing the bottle.

She picked it up, swirled, and tasted. Her favorite.

They'd cut back in a lot of areas since the kids went away to college. She'd even lowered her standards a bit on her wine selection. But she loved her pinot, and she'd found this one at Trader Joe's. They'd both declared it to be one of the best they'd found, at least at this price range. So it was their one splurge every week.

She relaxed back into her chair, watching her man sitting next to her talk about his day.

She loved him. She loved hearing his stories. She loved the way he could make her laugh.

His hair might be thinning a bit on top. He might be a little gray around the temples. He had a few more wrinkles then when they'd married.

Because of his job, he was still as lean as ever.

And thanks to his cancer scare, he'd been trying to stay active more than ever.

They'd both changed their eating habits, eating vegetarian most days of the week.

And while many of their friends had either grown complacent with each other, putting up with each other, or flat out hating one another and divorcing, she liked to think they still had it good.

Of course, that didn't mean they couldn't make it better.

She loved him. But things could be a bit … routine.

Quick dinners during the workweek. Friday night out with one of their friends. Sunday was clean-up day, making sure everything was picked up and ready for the coming week.

And at precisely nine o'clock on Saturday night, Curt would look at her, wiggle his eyebrows, and they'd turn in early for the night. That, of course, was his cue for their weekly round in bed.

It was good if not predictable. But what more could two people want after twenty-five years of marriage? She knew most people would give anything for what they had. Sherri had said as much more than once.

Still, sometimes it seemed too regimented. *Was it just her?*

"Do you think we're too predictable?"

Curt set his glass down. "In what way?"

"I don't know. Like in every way. We've worked at our same careers for two decades. We've lived in this same house since Clara was born. I haven't even replaced the dishes," she held up the wine glass they'd received as a wedding gift.

"Comfortable is good."

"Yeah, but don't you ever want more?"

Curt frowned. "After what I went through last year, I value every day."

Annette winced. "Curt, I'm sorry. That's not what I meant."

He reached out and grabbed her hand, rubbing his fingers over hers. "I know it's not. I always know what you're thinking. This is a midlife thing, isn't it."

She gasped, then caught the twinkle in his eye. She bumped her knee against his. "Okay, maybe it is. I don't know. I guess this conference thing really has me thinking."

"About how you want to change things up?"

"Maybe. Did I tell you we have to go through mandatory training again this summer? They're making us take a security class. They're training us on gun safety. If they ever make me keep a gun in my classroom, I'm quitting."

He nodded. "I agree. We've talked about that. You're a teacher, not a police officer."

"I'm fifty. I've never held a gun in my life. And now I have to be trained to potentially someday possibly have one in my classroom? Around ten-year-olds? No way, no how." She could feel the heat rise into her face. Every time she thought about current school conditions, she got flustered. When she thought of what she might be called on to do in the event of an emergency, it was almost more than she could take.

With tears in her eyes, she met his eyes. "I honestly don't know how much more of this I can take. I did this because I love the kids. I want to teach, to help them learn. I didn't sign up for the rest of this crap."

Curt leaned in again, framed her face with his hands. "I know." He pressed his lips softly to hers, lingered.

She reached up and wrapped her hands around his, let her forehead drop to his.

"So why don't you turn to your writing again? I know you've had writers block thanks to me, and the kids, and the …"

She pressed her lips to his one more time before grabbing her glass and settling back into the chair. "I've been thinking a lot about that lately."

"And?"

"And that's one of the reasons I want to go to San Diego." She got up, went into the mudroom and pulled a paper out of her bag.

She unfolded it and pushed it across the table to him, before sitting back down.

"This conference is all about getting your life back. Seems many fifty-year-olds have a bit of trouble with trying to figure out what the hell to do with the rest of our lives."

He chuckled as he picked up the paper and started reading.

"They have four tracks. Saturday morning is self track; you can choose from three different classes on taking care of yourself as you age." She pointed to the descriptions.

"Saturday afternoon is about career; three different tracks again. I like this one here about writing. Actually, blogging. I'm intrigued. All of the women on this panel are bloggers. They make a living out of blogging."

"How do they do that?"

"Hell if I know. But I guess they'll talk about it. That's the one I'm going to take."

Curt's eyes were busy reading down the page. She grinned when she saw him hit Sunday morning's track.

He looked up at her with raised eyebrows.

She pressed her lips together for a moment, stifling her laughter. "It's the love track. It's all about creating better relationships. Women want sex too, you know." She batted her eyes at him.

"Well, we don't need any help in that department." He winked, before returning to the page.

She contemplated his answer for a moment. Yes, they had sex every week. But was it the best sex they could have? She wasn't so sure after reading the summaries. But she didn't want to get into it, not now.

"Sunday afternoon looks good too."

"Yes. It kind of ties everything together. It's a little more philosophical. Supposedly they're going to teach us how to dream bigger. It intrigues me. I'm going with an open mind."

He laid the paper down, then reached over and linked his fingers with hers. "It sounds good. I'm glad you're going."

"You are?"

"Yeah, I am. I know things have been rough. This will do you some good. When was the last time you did anything like this by yourself?"

She thought for a moment. She looked up as she heard him chuckling. "I guess it's been a long time."

"Exactly. I'll be fine while you're gone. And you're going to come back with all of these new ideas."

"Maybe with new ideas for two." She wiggled her eyebrows.

He stood up, put her wine glass on the table, before pulling her up. "Maybe we should practice a little bit more before you go."

She looked at him, aghast. "On a Wednesday night?"

He glanced around, as if searching for someone. "Don't tell anyone."

She mimed locking her lips and throwing away the key. "My lips are sealed."

He walked her back until she butted up against the counter. "Maybe you can part them, just a little," he whispered as let his tongue slip in, exploring.

She let her hands roam until she found what she was looking for, hard and waiting. She pulled away, just for a moment. "If you take me upstairs now, maybe my mouth could widen just a bit more."

God, she loved this man. She loved watching him go from zero to all the way in seconds. The heat that turned his baby blues a smoky color turned her on in so many ways.

"Well, come on then." He pulled her as he flew up the stairs. "We've got things to do."

She laughed. Yes, they did.

4

Sherri pulled into the driveway of the house she'd rented after her divorce. The owners did their part by keeping the place in great shape. She did her part by spending lots of time in the yard. No one would ever guess it was a rental - just the way Sherri preferred it.

She'd never been ready to buy. At first, she wanted to adjust to being single. Then she wanted to wait until her son went off to college. She'd dated a bit; she'd thought maybe she'd find someone and want to find something together. In truth, she was now kind of happy with her arrangement.

If there was a problem, the owners were over almost before she put her phone away. They'd turned into great friends. And she never had to hit the hardware store ever again.

She preferred to spend her inheritance in other ways. Like the Audi TT she put into park. Thankful for the beautiful afternoon, she pushed the button to put the convertible top back into place, before sliding out and visiting her mailbox for the daily round of garbage. She put most of it into recycle, as she turned and waited for Annette to pull in behind her.

"I thought you got lost," Sherri teased.

"My minivan can't keep up with your race car."

"When are you going to trade that beast in? Where's your sense of free spirit? You need something more respectable."

"Like a little red convertible?"

Sherri hooted her response as she led the way to the front door.

She picked up a package, and threw it on the front table, before depositing her work belongings in a chair next to the front door.

Annette knew her place well. The two spent as much time in each other's homes as they did their own. Neither of them had sisters, so they'd adopted each other. They couldn't imagine life any other way. She made her way into the kitchen and put the teapot on the burner.

Sherri pulled two mugs and several boxes of tea out of the cupboard. "Earl Gray or jasmine? I got this ginger peach the other day that isn't half bad."

They each made a selection and dropped the bags into their mugs.

"So how was Curt when you told him?"

"He's Curt. He's happy if I'm happy."

"See? I keep telling you how perfect he is. Not many men would just nod and say okay to whatever you decided to do."

"Then you've been hanging around with the wrong men."

Sherri nodded. "That's why I divorced."

"What about Tony? Didn't you guys have another date this past weekend? You never mentioned it."

"To be fair, all we've talked about is this conference since you agreed to go."

"True. So spill, what happened with Tony?"

Sherry huffed out a breath, before filling both of their mugs with hot water, picking up her mug and sipping. "I don't know. He's nice and all. He's a good guy. It's just he's someone else's good guy. He doesn't excite me, you know? Maybe I should go for a younger guy."

Annette pulled out a bar stool and took a seat. She blew on her own tea as she rolled her eyes. "Now you want to be a cougar? Ready to go for someone like Ryan?"

They both looked at each other, batted their eyelashes, before bursting into a fit of giggles.

Ryan. He was the newest teacher in the school. A thirty-ish fifth grade teacher who could have just as easily gotten a job on the runway in New York. Every female in the school was swooning over Mr Nevins. A lot of the fifth-grade girls were starting to agree.

"Maybe I should go for Ryan. I don't have to marry him. But I bet he could be fun for a day or two or three."

"Yeah, right. You'd never get a word out. You'd simply stare."

"Well if I'm cougaring, maybe we'll skip the formalities and just come straight back here. Then I could *stare* as much as I want."

"Ohmigod! I think you've actually thought about this. Are you fantasizing about *Mr Nevins*?"

"Maybe. A little fantasy never hurt anyone."

"Do I want to know?"

"Probably not."

Annette put down her mug, stood, then pushed in her chair. "On that note, I think we should do what I came here to do. Let's have a look at your closet."

"You really don't have to do this." Sherri looked at her friend nervously. She had sensible tastes. Comfort was always in fashion. Or it would be if she had her say about it. Why wear anything but jeans if you could get away with it? A sweatshirt was best in her mind because it could take you from cool mornings, to messes in the classroom, to a night out with friends when the rain started coming down.

"Yes, I do. You did look at the photos from this conference for last year's event, right?" Annette gave her the stern look that only a mother could give.

"Yes."

"They wore *dresses*. They have a cocktail party Saturday night just so we can all get dressed up. Plus they want us to bring pink along for the group photo. Do you have anything that's pink?"

"I have that sweatshirt ..."

"No."

"Yes, mom."

Sherri trailed behind her friend as they made their way into her bedroom. The two friends worked for several minutes creating a yes pile, a maybe pile, while leaving everything in the "hell, no" section firmly attached to hangers in her closet.

Annette held up a pair of black flats she found deep in her closet, behind two old pairs of hiking boots. "These are a maybe. But just for that long skirt you can wear in the day with your jean jacket."

"Are we really going to have to change clothes all day long? Maybe I should rethink this conference," Sherri teased. She'd wanted this so bad, since the moment she'd found the group online. She'd sworn to herself she'd wear sequins and diamonds if she could get her friend along.

But that didn't mean she had to make it easy for her.

Annette looked right through her as she continued to talk. "I think if we look for a pair of heels, possibly a pair of flats. And a dress for the cocktail party. We might also look for a pair of pants to go with the pink shirt we have to find."

"We're going to be shopping all night!" Sherri tried to sound mortified. But a night with her friend was just what she needed. "Can we stop at Piccolo's first?"

Piccolo's was the best Italian place in town. Whether you wanted to order in, or wanted a place to impress, Piccolo's was it.

But Annette knew her ploy. "No. If we pick a few things up quickly, maybe we can go later. We're on a mission. We leave in just a few days. It's now or never, my friend. Let's go."

"Okay, but I'm driving."

"What, you don't like *the beast*?"

"Not when there's a sports car to drive."

Three hours later, the women filled the car with boxes and bags. Even Annette had found a new dress on the clearance rack she was sure would be perfect for the cocktail party. It had been months since she'd purchased something new, something as frivolous as a cocktail dress, that she knew she probably wouldn't wear again. But she had a great pair of shoes sitting at home that would look perfect with it. And she'd found a deal on airfare, less than a couple hundred round trip. So she splurged.

As they fell into a booth at Piccolo's, Sherri laid a hand on her friends. "In all seriousness, thank you. We're going to look fabulous."

Annette smiled. "We are, aren't we?"

Sherri continued, "And I want dinner to be my treat. For all the help you've given me." Deep inside, she knew Annette was counting every penny this trip was costing her. And since she had a healthy bank account from the inheritance she'd received when her parents died four years before, she loved to pick up the tab when she could.

"No, you don't have to ..."

"You're right. I don't have to. But I *want* to. There's the difference."

They exchanged a look, before Annette finally conceded. "Okay."

After ordering glasses of chardonnay and an appetizer to share, they returned to their favorite topic since they'd signed up for the conference.

"Have you selected which tracks you're going to attend?"

The two had talked about each of them. They'd decided that they didn't want to do the same; they'd meet up for the keynotes and the party and compare notes.

Annette knew exactly which tracks she was taking. For the most part, it was a given. Because only one track in each session made sense. "I really want to take that writing and blogging course. I'm so intrigued."

"I figured you'd be at that one."

"I looked at the three women who are paneling it. Have you looked at their websites?" *Looked* probably wasn't the right word for what she'd done. *Obsessed* might be closer to reality. Annette had spent the last few days pouring over their sites. She'd read more blog posts, watched more videos then she'd ever done in her life.

"Maybe. I know most of the panelists are active in the group. When they post, they usually link to stuff they've written on their own sites. So I've probably clicked through."

"I'm just amazed by these women. And a little awed by them. How did they figure all of this out? I mean, I know it's the way of the world. But I wouldn't even know where to begin."

Sherri took a sip, then dove into the appetizers the waiter placed on the table. "That's why we're going. I'm sure they'll cover a lot of the details. And I'm sure you can ask. These ladies are all very candid and approachable. If you have a question, just ask."

The two women worked their way through entrees and another round of drinks as they made their final class selections. Though in reality, it didn't take much thought at all.

Self care? Of course, Sherri wanted to learn more about simplification. She'd been purging things all the time since she'd moved her parents' stuff into her home. She still had a storage shed full she'd give anything to make her way through. Annette had been cooking more at home, and was intrigued by the track on food and eating better.

"And I'm assuming you're doing the track on doin' it with your honey." Sherri bumped her friend's shoulder as they made their way back to her car.

Annette was nonchalant, even though it was definitely the course for her. "What makes you say that? There are other tracks ..."

"Like the *sex for the single lady* course? Um, no. I don't think you qualify."

"Maybe I'd learn something."

Sherri just eyed her over the car as she opened her door.

"Just think, you can find out about all the things you can do together, while I'll be taking notes on what I can do to myself." Sherri cackled.

"That's not necessarily true," Annette paused and looked at her friend as she climbed into her seat. When the doors were shut, she grinned at her friend, "There's always Ryan."

5

"You packed the shoes, right?" Annette peered into the backseat as her friend buckled her seatbelt.

Sherri looked up and made a face. "Yes, mom, I packed my shoes. And my new dresses. And the pink shirt. Everything. If I didn't, I have this feeling you'd take me shopping the moment we land. And I'm not going through that again."

Curt stifled a laugh as he pulled out into traffic.

"You're not helping matters. You know how she is." Annette shot him a look.

"Hey, I'm staying out of this."

"Wise man," Sherri piped up from the back. "Can you believe she made me shop for things I'll never wear again?"

Curt peered at her through the review mirror. "You're saying that to a guy who had to buy a new button-down shirt in a *pretty color* to wear to a play we attended last year. I've never worn that shirt again."

"Hey!" Annette playfully punched him. "That's a great shirt. You really should wear it more. I love it on you." She wiggled her eyebrows.

"All right already. Stop it you two. It's not right."

The three of them bantered all the way to the airport.

Curt slowed at the appropriate drop off door, put the car into park. He flipped the switch for the trunk, and moved to get both suitcases out.

"Bye. Thanks for the ride." Sherri gave him a hug, then moved her suitcase onto the sidewalk and put her bag on top.

"Sure. Anytime."

"Hey." Annette slipped her arms around his neck. "I'll see you on Monday."

She pressed her lips to his, lingered.

Curt tightened his grip around her waist, hugging her close. "I'll miss you."

"Me too."

"Have fun. Learn lots. And don't worry about me. I've got more invites then I'll ever be able to use."

"I know. Why don't they do that for me? Maybe I need to be taken care of

…"

He stopped her with a kiss. "Because you're the best. Everyone knows that, and they're just trying to keep me safe. For you."

"Oh. Your brownie points just went up. You might get a reward when I get home." She kissed him, laughing while he was wiggling his eyebrows at her.

"Come on, you too. You're sickening, you know that?" Sherri tapped her foot impatiently.

"Bye." Annette kissed him one last time, moved her own luggage up to the sidewalk and started towards the door.

"Love you. Have a great time." Curt waved over the roof of his car, watching her as she slid through the automatic doors.

They trudged along with the masses, standing in line for security, then making their way to the gate.

They settled into their seats, happy to have an entire row to themselves.

When the flight had reached cruising altitude, Sherri pulled out her bag.

"So, I've been thinking. Conferences are always great. But in most cases, you get home, get busy, and never complete one task. I don't want that to happen."

She pulled out a handful of papers and two pink journals. "I bought you a gift. I was in the bookstore a few days ago looking for a few new books for my free-reading shelf at school, and I saw these. These are better than paper and pencils. Look," Sherri flipped to one of the pages she'd been working on. "They're goal journals. Every section offers a different way of tracking your goals. You can date it. You can add steps. You can track your performance. There are spaces for notes. Even a folder in the back of each section for you to keep things safe."

Annette flipped through hers, stopping to read the titles of each question.

"I'm thinking we use this for this trip. We have four sections coming up this weekend. We'll each take four classes, outside of the keynotes, based on each of the four tracks. I'm thinking at the end of each class, we each choose one task. One goal we hope to accomplish once we return home."

Annette nodded. "That's a good idea."

"We can hold each other accountable. Put finish dates on them and check in to make sure we're both working to get things done."

"And provide help along the way too."

"Yes." Sherri turned to the first section. "I've already written in mine; I didn't do yours because I want you to do it your way. But I labeled the first section self, the second career, the third love, and the fourth dreams. I even wrote the title of the class I'm going to attend here in the notes. There are several pages of blank lines, which should be more than enough to take notes from the class."

Sherri closed the book and placed it on her lap. She turned, pulling her leg under her, moving closer to her friend. "I want this to work. I'm tired of it all. I just really want to make changes, and I want them now."

Annette reached over for Sherri's hand. "I know you do. Me too."

"Did you get the memo yesterday on the retirement plan?"

"You mean the one that said we'll be getting a two percent raise come January first, but all of it must go into our retirement fund because of shortfalls? Yeah. I got it." Annette reached up and turned the air so it was blowing on her. *Was it getting warmer or was it just her?*

Yes, she'd gotten it. She'd spoken to Curt about it at length the night before. She was fifty … fifty! She had years before she could retire. And if the retirement fund was already having shortfalls, where did that leave her when she needed it?

Sherri huffed out her breath. "Doesn't that just scare the hell out of you?"

Annette pinched the bridge of her nose, trying to remain calm. "More than you know. Curt and I both are relying on state funded retirement programs. How do we know anything will be there by the time we get there? And then there's the second mortgage we took out after all the medical bills. We're still paying some college loans for the kids. It really is too much."

"Sometimes you have to ask if all this is worth it."

"I know. I say that all the time now. At least Curt likes what he does. It's never paid the best, but he loves it. I'm not sure I can say that anymore. I don't even feel like I'm teaching; not the way I used to. It's more glorified babysitting and ensuring the kids do well on tests." She let her head fall back to the seat. When had it all changed? *Why* had it all changed? And who the hell thought this new way of *teaching* was great?

Sherri interrupted her thoughts. "What are we going to do?"

They've had this conversation a million times. And the answer was always the same. *Neither of them had a solid idea.*

She shook her head, and turned and looked at her friend once again. "Did you hear Jeff had a heart attack?"

"No. When?"

"Two nights ago. He's okay. Curt thought he'd be home sometime this weekend. He's planning on going over on Saturday."

"That's the second in our little group this year. Makes you wonder what's next."

"I know. We've already had our cancer scare, thank you very much. I just keep thinking: what if it had been real instead of a scare? What if the tumor hadn't been benign? What if? What if? I swear, I'm driving myself crazy with all of these *what if's* lately."

They stopped long enough to place their drink orders with the flight attendants. With a cup of coffee to warm her hands, Sherri looked back at her friend. "Isn't that the definition of a midlife crisis? Asking the questions and not getting the answers?"

Annette snorted. "Or maybe we just don't like the answers that are there."

"True. But maybe we just need to reinvent the answers. Maybe we shouldn't accept the answers they're telling us should be there."

"Who's the *they* you are referring to? The system? Our school? Life? Sherri, I'm just tired. Why does all this have to be so damn hard? I feel like

I'm swimming upstream. There's just so much. I have no idea what to do next."

"What about your writing?"

If she could fall deeper into her seat, she would. Annette sometimes cursed the fact she'd made such a big deal out of her writing.

She'd had good intentions. But somewhere along the way it all got shoved to the wayside.

"I've been busy." No excuses. No defense. Annette really had no idea what else to say.

She reached up and dotted her fingers under her eyes, wiping away the tears.

"Hey." Sherri put her hand on her friend's arm. She gave her a look of encouragement.

"Remember how we were convinced we were going to change the world when we first started teaching?"

Sherri laughed. "God, we were naive, weren't we?"

Annette couldn't have agreed more. They'd been so excited to get started on a career they were passionate about. They honestly did think they could change the world, one kid at a time. *Where did it all go wrong?*

As if Sherri could read her mind, she started listing the problems. "Laws. No Child Left Behind. Parents. Expectations. Gun control. Safety."

"I get it. I get it." Annette jumped in. She shifted, coming up to her full height. "Why do we keep talking about this? Why don't we *do* something about this?"

Sherri smiled. "We are. Right now. Here. We're going to this conference. We have our goal journals. And we're not going to let up until we're doing what we want to do."

"So let's make a pact. A midlife pact."

"A midlife pact?"

Annette let her enthusiasms swallow her. "Yes, exactly. Let's use our goal journals to not only stick to our goals, but to also change our lives."

"Okay."

"Like get-out-of-our-jobs kind of change."

"Okay."

"I want to make a go of my writing."

"You've said that. I think you should do it."

"You too. You hate this job anymore just like I do."

Sherri nodded. That was true. "I love teaching. But the red tape is just too much. Yet at least you have an idea. I have no freaking idea what I want to do."

"But you have more flexibility than me. It's just you. You're not married. You don't have medical bills. You don't even have a mortgage anymore."

"True."

"Your goal is to find what you want to do next. They even have a class on that."

Annette grabbed the stack between them. She flipped until she found the pages she was looking for.

"Right here. You were going to take the career class on being happier in your career, right?"

"Yes. I really don't have any other career goals. Not like you do, anyway."

"But what if you did? Come with me to the entrepreneur track. I know we said we were going to do different classes and share notes. But maybe it'd do you better to think outside the box."

"I've never wanted to start a business. Or write. Or anything like that."

"I'm not saying you have to." Annette was excited about what this could do for her, for them. "But what if this class changes you and gets you going in a new direction?"

"And what if it doesn't? I'm not really ready to start up a business."

Annette gave her a stern look. "I'm going to this convention because of you. I've expanded my viewpoint because you told me I should. Now it's your turn. Let's shake on it. Let's create that midlife pact. Let's go in and change our lives all the way around. What's the worst that could happen?"

Sherri took a deep breath. *Be careful what you wish for.* The adage rolled around in her mind.

She was the one who wanted something drastic in her life. She was the one who'd convinced herself, and then Annette, to head to the conference. Shouldn't she also be the one ready to be more spontaneous and to jump at something new?

"Okay." Sherri picked up her planner, the one she'd already filled in the names of the classes she'd thought she'd attend. She lined out the title with a pen, then wrote in the new class.

It's not like she couldn't change her mind again. She could.

But as she looked at the satisfied grin on her friend's face, she knew she wouldn't. She'd go. She'd attend this entrepreneur class, and see what ideas she could come up with.

6

Annette and Sherri inched towards the sign-in table. All around them, women chatted like they'd found their long-lost friends.

Sherri's eyes glowed in anticipation. Annette was on edge.

Sherri hip bumped her friend. "Stop worrying. You're going to have fun."

"It's just a lot of people. You know I don't do well in large crowds."

"Yeah, but this is going to an exceptional experience. We're going to have so much fun!"

Annette laughed. It was difficult not to smile at her friend's infectious attitude.

They stepped up to the table.

"Welcome!"

"Hi," the two said at the same time.

"If I can have both of your names, I'll get you everything you need to get started."

A quick check had them both confirmed. The host started filling up two bags.

"These are your swag bags. There are all kinds of things in there, including coupons for a lot of the products and services you'll hear about this weekend, plus a few for places right around this conference center. If you want coffee, we don't want you paying full price!" She winked.

"Can't have that now, can we?" Sherri played right along.

The woman continued as if the two were her best friends. "Here's the schedule for the weekend. Have you both determined which tracks to attend?"

Annette nodded. "Yep, we were talking about that on the plane."

"Perfect. I will tell you they fill up. Or at least they did last year. But the rooms are bigger this year, so that shouldn't be a problem. If you want a great seat, I suggest getting there early."

"Any suggestions? What's your favorite class?" Sherri had a habit of asking for referrals all the time. She liked to hear what others recommended.

"Honestly, they're all good. I don't know everyone this year, but they all sound great. I will tell you to head in now and grab a seat. You're going to love the first keynote." She leaned over the table to get a little closer. "And they're going to give out some pretty spectacular prizes. It's better if you sit up close."

They finished gathering their materials and found the keynote conference room. After leaving their jackets and bags on chairs, they made their way outside to take advantage of the coupons for coffee.

Everywhere they looked, women huddled in groups, chatting feverishly about expectations.

What do you do? Where are you from? Why are you here? The questions echoed as they walked along the hallway.

"I love conferences." Sherri nodded and said hello as they made their way back to the room.

"I hate conferences." Annette said under her breath at almost the same time.

Sherri linked her arm through her friend's and pulled her back to their seats. "Oh, come on. We're going to have fun. And we're going to change; that's what's most fun of all!"

The program didn't start for several minutes, so they introduced themselves to the women sitting near them. They settled into their seats when the lights were lowered.

After a few minutes of introducing the key players and providing general housekeeping announcements, the keynote speaker began speaking.

Beverly Stillman, an expert on reinvention, also told vivid stories with seemingly little effort. In just a few moments, both Sherri and Annette were swept up in her storytelling.

Beverly had spent over twenty years in corporate America. Then when she'd reached the proverbial glass ceiling, midlife set in. She stopped caring. She questioned everything. And slowly she found her new calling.

"I remember one day, walking with my husband. My world literally came crashing down around me." Beverly walked slowly across the stage, taking the time to make eye contact with as many women as she could. "I discovered I really liked holding his hand. I'd missed that. In that moment, I had reached out and twined my fingers with his. I didn't know what made me do it. But even he seemed to notice; he stopped for just a moment and looked at our connection."

She paused, put her finger to her lip. Then put her hands together in front of her, palms together. "I loved this man. With all my heart. We'd been together for twenty-five years. We had three kids together. We'd built a life. And yet life had happened, and we'd lost touch of who we really were, together. Do you know what I mean?"

She looked out over the crowd.

Annette's head bobbed up and down. She got that. She'd had that feeling. She'd even contemplated leaving Curt when the kids were younger. They'd fought for months about the long hours he worked trying to further his career. She grew weary of being the only parent in their home, taking charge of helping both kids with high school issues and getting into college. She'd given him many ultimatums until he finally relented and found a less stressful job. Then his cancer scare had scared them back together. Solid. For that, she was grateful.

Beverly turned, moved to the other side of the stage. "I knew right then and there that something had to change. I didn't tell him. I didn't talk about work. But I made a conscious decision that I was going to change. I wanted *us* to be important again. I wanted to have the time to devote to my relationship. Not just work, work, work. I flew one-hundred-and-seventy-five days that final year. I have my travel statement hanging on my wall to prove it - it's my reminder when I start to get too busy."

The audience chuckled. Working too hard seemed to be a universal complaint.

"I used everything I'd learned moving up the chain of command and put it towards my new career of helping women through midlife. In three years, I've authored five books. I speak to crowds around the globe, and most importantly, I have fun doing it. My husband retired recently so he can travel with me. He's here in the hotel somewhere. I'll meet up with him later today."

She moved back to center stage. "Before I do anything these days, I always ask myself two questions. Number one, does this help me with my career? Will it help me grow? Will it help me reach a more well-defined audience?"

She paused again. "And number two, I ask if this helps me in my relationship. If I take a speaking job outside of the country, for instance, can Robert travel along? If I agree to write another book, will it take time away that would be better spent with him?"

The audience seemed to grow quieter. Beverly's voice seemed to change, or at least Annette heard it differently. She felt a chill roll down her back.

"As I grow older, I seem to have a better sense of what's most important. I don't want to waste any moment of the day. I ask myself all the time if this is what I want to do, if this is where I want to be.

"Isn't that something we all do all the time? We're constantly working jobs we hate, doing chores we don't want to do, being with people we really don't like, all for the perception of keeping peace in our lives.

"Yet I'll tell you right now at midlife, I'm finding that most frustrating of all. Last year, I let go of a relationship with a friend I've had for more than twenty years. Neither of us were growing; in fact, we were holding each other back. We sat down and talked about it. We wished each other luck and realized this was for the best.

"Is it hard? You bet. But so is the alternative. Why spend an hour having coffee with someone I'll make small talk with, when I could be having lunch with my husband? Why do a job I really don't like, when I could be writing a book? Why spend hours with emails that don't matter, when I'd rather make love to my husband? Do you see how this works?"

Sherri and Annette exchanged a look. Oh yeah, they both got it. This was the very thing they'd talked about hundreds of times.

For Annette, it was as if Beverly was talking one on one, with her. It's the one thing she couldn't seem to get past. She spent hours of her life each day hating what she was doing. Why? She wanted everything Beverly was talking about.

She wanted to make every decision because it was hers to make. She wanted to wake up happy, not miserable because she had to face another day of misery. She wanted to do things on *her* terms.

This woman standing on the stage gave her hope like she hadn't had in a very long time. If she could do it, Annette could too.

"This works in all facets of your life. Your job. Your spouse. Your relationships. Where you live. Your hobbies. Your health. Everything."

Beverly picked up a bottle of water and took a sip. "In your swag bags, you'll find a small binder filled with handouts from every section. In there, you'll find a worksheet from me." She picked one up from the table and thumbed through finding the appropriate page. "It's on page twenty-three. It looks like this." She held it up for everyone to see. "I'm going to give you a few moments now to work through it. At the top, I have four lines. One for self, one for career, one for love, and one for dreams."

"Just like the theme of this conference," shouted someone from the audience.

"Exactly!" Beverly pointed out towards her. "You guys are smart!"

Rustling and a low chuckle filled the room.

As the noise died down, Beverly continued. "I want each of you to write one thing you want more than anything for each of these four items. And most important of all, I want you to write it as if you already have it. They can be big or small. Don't think much about the logistics at this point. Just write them as if you have them. Let me give you an example.

"On the way here, I filled out my goals." Beverly pointed to the top of the page, then turned her notebook so she could read. "For self, I have written down that I attend a dance class once a week. For career, I have two new books published. For love, I have a weekend getaway scheduled with my husband every month. For dreams, I moved into my new home." Beverly dropped the notebook on the table, then turned to move back to the front of the stage. "These are personal to me. Each of these things I'm working on and striving for this year. I've written them in such a way as if they are in my life. It makes them more believable. It also pushes me to the next step, which I'll explain in a moment. For now, I'll give you ten minutes to write your own four goals. And once you get them completed, turn to your neighbor and share. Go!"

Both Sherri and Annette started writing.

Annette had thought about this millions of times. Yet writing it turned out to be more difficult then she thought. Writing it as if she'd completed it turned her thoughts around. But in some ways, it also made her feel stronger in her endeavor. Was this what she'd been missing? Believability?

"Do you have yours?" Sherri dropped her pen on her paper.

Annette nodded. "I think I do."

"Okay, you go first." Sherri shut her book with her pen as a bookmark, giving Annette her attention.

Annette looked down. "Self - I am healthy. Career - I published my first book. Love - I do one thing to make Curt smile every day. Dreams - My finances have allowed me to quit teaching without any consequences."

She looked up. "Do you think those are good? They're kind of vague."

"No, I think they're great. I get them. Maybe you can give a little bit more for self. What do you mean?"

Annette picked up her pen, chewed on the end. "I guess I'm just always nervous since Curt had that problem. And now Jeff had the heart attack. And then there's my parents. And ..."

"It's midlife. We're gonna have that happen all around us. But how can you be more specific? How about working out?"

"Ugh, that's just so difficult. With work, and ..."

"That's what this is all about. What can you do to make change stick?"

"I hate the gym."

"I know. Me too. Hey, what if we went to that barre place up in the Centerwood shopping center? You know, the new place that went into that old hamburger joint a few months ago?"

"Oh yeah. I looked in the windows when I ran to the pizza place last week. It looks kind of fun."

"I'm sure they have classes right after work. And if we both go, we'll have each other to push when we don't feel like it."

"Yeah, but this is my list, not yours."

Sherri shook her head. "Nope. It's on mine too. See?" She held up her worksheet. "Self - lose ten pounds. This would be the perfect way for me to work off the pastries I eat every morning."

"Or you could just say no to the pastries."

"Are you kidding me? I'll never pass up a beignet. They're heavenly."

Annette just rolled her eyes. "So enough about me. What about you?"

Sherri tapped her pen on the side of the paper as she read. "Self - I've lost ten pounds. Career - I teach in a more satisfying way. Love - I've built a stronger relationship with my son. Dream - I have art back in my life."

"You can't use your son as your love goal."

"Why not?"

"Because you need love for you."

"Who says? Beverly never specified it had to be romantic love."

"But it was implied."

"Nope. Not buying it." Sherri sat back in her chair and smiled a satisfied grin. "I don't need a man in my life."

"I get that. But you've been the one who's been trying to find a guy for years."

"And how well has that worked out? I'm still single."

"Maybe you haven't kissed enough frogs."

"Or maybe there aren't any frogs left to kiss."

Annette was once again glad she still had Curt. Looking seemed so much more difficult at their age. "Maybe you need to go into the city more. Try a meetup there."

Sherri hissed. "I'll add that to my list."

"And what about your teaching goal? What did that mean?"

Sherri sat back once again, rolling her bottom lip with her fingers. "You know I love teaching."

"Yes."

"I also hate the way we have to teach."

"Yep, we talk about that all the time."

"I just think maybe I can find another way to use my skills. To still teach but avoid the stress of working in the school system."

"Like in a private school?"

"No, I don't know. Maybe."

"What about one of the colleges? Have you ever thought of working there?"

Sherri's eyebrows scrunched together as she thought about it. "No. It's always been about the kids."

"Well, if you moved over to the college, you could still teach. It wouldn't eliminate all the stressors. But some of them."

"True. But I think that's just trading one problem for another."

Annette leaned forward. "You know what I think? I think you're scared"

Sherri tipped her head, staring at her friend. "What do you mean?"

"You're too comfortable. You say you want something different, but you're at peace with where you are. And that means you'll never change. What if you didn't have a choice? What if everything changed tomorrow? What if you were fired from the school? What if you lost your house? What if you were forced to move to another state, and leave everything behind? What would you do?"

Sherri shook her head, trying to picture what Annette had just said. She'd never looked at her life like that before.

Was that why she hadn't moved? Or dated more?

Did she like her life just enough to not challenge herself to do something else?

Did she have just enough money to stay comfortable with where she was?

Is that why she talked change all the time, yet had never done much about it?

The more she thought about it, the more other questions popped up.

Beverly moved back to center stage. "How'd you all do?"

Sherri watched the animated conversations women all around her were having. But deep inside, she felt a part of her breaking apart. She'd put up so many blocks, and she hadn't even realized it.

Maybe this weekend was going to do her more good than she'd realized.

7

"How is everyone today?" The host of the conference stood at the front, chatting with the women seated in the first few rows.

Excitement bubbled in the air.

Annette had only been to a few conferences in her life. Mostly for teaching. She'd especially enjoyed going to them the first few years after she'd started her career. Back in the days when she still thought she could change the world.

Then when the shit hit the proverbial fan, so to speak, and the job began losing some of its appeal, conferences just became a way to escape the drudge of trying to keep up with the rules and regulations while monitoring an overstuffed classroom filled with minds that weren't all that excited to learn.

She hated the politics. She hated the requirements. She hated trying to deal with half a class of students who were on some type of medication. She'd grown weary of those glassy stares. She wanted to break through; she wanted her kids to be kids, filled with wonder, ready to take on the world.

She'd wanted so much. And look how all that was turning out.

"Are you ready for another exciting lesson?" The host cut through her thoughts, jarred her back to reality.

When had she gotten so cynical?

It's like all she ever thought about these days was what was wrong with the world. Her job. The economy. Politics. On and on it went. She knew she wasn't alone. Nobody lived without the stress.

She was tired of it. She wanted something new.

She moved, straightened so she could have a better view of the panel currently taking their seats.

Each of the four panelists gave a brief introduction about who they were and how they'd started and grown their businesses.

This was the part Annette had really wanted to hear.

Four women. Each had blogs that earned them tens of thousands each year.

One had a blog on Pilates; she provided guidance on home practice. She sold videos to help perfect each of the moves and had amassed a million dollar business in just three years.

Another blogged about country living. Her entertainment ideas had turned into several books. She had just been licensed through Target to carry a line of linens.

The third was a foodie, writing about her vegan lifestyle. She recently signed a deal with the Home channel, to host a show on vegan restaurants.

The final had a site on wealth building, geared specifically for women in midlife. She'd left the financial industry when she'd reached the glass ceiling, and found she wasn't satisfied playing in a man's world. She wanted to blaze her own path and found creating her own blog had given her the right tools. Now she had a following of more than a million women, and had just released her fifth book to rave reviews.

The crowd clapped and the conversation elevated as the moderator moved into position, ready to ask her questions.

"They're brilliant, aren't they?" Annette leaned into Sherri, whispering above the crowd. "I told you you'd like this session. The summary left me almost breathless. We're going to learn some great stuff here."

Annette settled into her seat as the roar of the crowd died down. She poised her pen to her paper, ready and waiting for every word.

The questions started easy: *Why did you start blogging?* And overwhelmingly, the answers were the same: As a creative outlet. They'd all had jobs they didn't like, careers that were going nowhere, and they wanted to do something different. They'd all found blogging in their quest for something more.

They'd each started up their blogs as a hobby, and eventually turned them into side gigs, earning them each small amounts of money. As they gained confidence and followers, opportunities opened up, and the income streams grew.

They got more in-depth as the session went on.

When did you first discover you could make money at this?

When did you realize this was a business?

How quickly did it turn from a hobby to a full time income?

How has this changed your life?

Annette sat there, mesmerized.

She'd thought about writing for years. But for her, writing was always more old school. She thought about writing for magazines. Maybe eventually a book.

Why hadn't she ever considered blogging before? She followed a dozen blogs and read their weekly newsletters with fervor.

Yet here she was, almost two years after she'd declared her future as a writer, and she hadn't done anything to move forward. Could this be the solution?

Annette scribbled notes as fast as her hand could write. She added stars next to the steps she wanted to take as soon as she returned home.

The host looked at her watch, and announced, "We have just a little bit of time left. I'd like to leave the audience with some action tips." She looked at the panelists. "Could you give one or two tips on what you would do right now, today, if you were thinking of starting up a blog for the very first time?"

Yes, great question. Annette sat up a little taller. It all sounded good; but what did she need to know to move forward?

The first, the foodie, took the microphone. "A lot of people think you have to have writing talent to create a great site. That's not true. The only thing you must have is patience to let it grow. If I was starting over from scratch today, I'd make a commitment to myself to create one blog post every day.

"Since I write about food, I can write about so many things. When I first started, I did posts on restaurants I like, I added my favorite recipes, I wrote about cookbooks I enjoyed. I attended a vegetarian conference - I did reviews of the classes, and snapped some pictures of the booths. I wrote about everything.

"It's difficult to come up with ideas at first. But that's part of the challenge. If you just make a promise to yourself that whatever you do, you'll create one post a day - or a week - or whatever you have time for - and you'll stick with it, I guarantee you really will start to see things happen in a short period of time."

She passed it to the next panelist, the Pilates guru. "I agree. I had no idea what my blog would look like when I first started it. I honestly had no idea I'd be making money at it. I'd completed my Pilates certification and was trying to drum up clients at the local gym. I started up the blog because I thought it would be fun to record my journey. And before long, it became the journey.

"You know, it was months before I even thought about using it to make money. I had a client who was moving to another state, but she loved my personalized training. She told me on her last day that she wished she could bottle me up and take me with her. She told me she'd do anything to be able to continue training with me, because I'd helped her improve her life so much. The bells went off when she said that to me. I went home that night and started searching online. I searched to find a way that I could stay connected to her."

The other panelists nodded their heads in agreement.

"I remember I found a personal training website started by a man just a few miles from me. I could tell from his site he was doing very well. I emailed him on a whim, just to see what advice he'd give me. And he's become one of my mentors. I guess my advice is not to live in a bubble. Do your research. Find people similar to you who you can mimic. Not copy, but emulate. Get your ideas from everywhere, reach out to those that are doing it to, and do it yourself. You'll be surprised at the results."

A round of applause rolled through the audience. A dull roar started escalating. The moderator toned it down before moving to the next panelist.

"Are you guys loving this?" She eyed the audience. "Even I'm picking up tips here and I've been doing this for a while."

The other panelists nodded in agreement. "I want to actually speak to those of you who are sitting here wondering what in the hell you'll blog about.

You're out there, aren't you?"

Laughter shook the walls.

"Exactly," Sherri eyed her friend wistfully. "Great ideas. But I have no clue."

"This is for you. I want to give you an exercise you can do tonight, tomorrow, or when you get home. I want you to start making lists of the things you enjoy. Write down ten things everyday that you like. That's it. Do it for a week or two. Then when you're done, start comparing your lists. What do you see popping up again and again?

"When I first started blogging, I lived way out in the country. I grew bored because it was too difficult to get into town. I had small kids. I thought I was going mad some days. I started my blog out of boredom and frustration for wanting more. And eventually, I started having followers that would say *Me Too*. They understood me. Even if they lived in a big city, they liked my tips. I started focusing on simple things because that was easy for me to write about.

"I gave tips on creating a simple meal to enjoy at home. Or simple tips for creating a romantic evening with your husband. Or simple ways of making your kids a little less stressed. Really, just all kinds of ideas. And slowly it morphed into Simple Pleasures, which was the name of my first book.

"I agree, if you just keep writing, things have a way of finding you. You discover what others like because they tell you. And you do more of it because it works. I wrote my first post out of boredom. And now I'm creating a home furnishings line in collaboration with Target. If you had told me that a few years ago, I would have laughed in your face. But this world is always looking for new approaches. You have no idea what your potential is; just start doing it.

"Write those lists every day. Find out what you think you're good at. And then just do it. The rest works itself out."

The moderator took the microphone for a couple of last-minute housekeeping items before turning it over to the last speaker. "Okay everyone, I know we're running out of time. But we have one more, and I want to make sure you get all you can." She passed it down to the wealth advisor.

"I love how so many people have turned their ideas into a business just by writing about a little of everything. Where else can you do that, right? Today's technology is fabulous."

A round of applause told her the audience agreed with her.

"Here's the thing. I knew what I wanted. I knew exactly what I wanted to do. I tried desperately to reach out to women and help them become savvier with the way they invested their money. We live longer than men. And we have more of a chance of living alone into old age. Yet we don't earn as much, and we traditionally have allowed men to be the financiers of the family. And that's just always pissed me off."

All heads in the audience were nodding.

"And the guys I worked for didn't get it, of course. They all looked at me like I was crazy when I wanted to focus my business on women. *But they don't have as much money to invest*, they said. I set out to prove them wrong.

"When I was in San Francisco, my target client was in the Bay Area. But I knew there were hundreds, thousands of women that fit my ideal profile. I knew they existed throughout the world, ready to learn all they could about taking care of themselves financially for the rest of their lives.

"Blogging was the way I could do that. I found others doing similar things in different industries, and took what I liked best from each of them to create my own business and website.

"That's my tip for you. If you know what you want, *when* you know what you want, get ideas from everywhere. Don't stop at finding people doing what you want to do. Think of your business as a giant jigsaw puzzle. You can get ideas from everywhere. Always be on the lookout for great ideas, and find ways to put them together, to find your approach to creating the perfect blog, and the perfect business. Don't give up until you have a clear picture, until your puzzle is finished."

Wow. Annette sat for a moment, scribbling as fast as she could to finish her notes.

The audience stood for a standing ovation. The thunderous applause was deafening. Women mobbed the stage, ready to talk with the panelists and ask their questions.

"I'm full." Sherri dropped back into her chair to place her notebook and pen into her bag.

Annette tucked her bag over her shoulder before glancing at her friend. She was happy to see her smiling since she all but pulled her into the training. "I know. Me too. Wasn't that amazing?" She was starving. "You ready for lunch?"

"Yeah." Sherri stood slowly.

"You okay?" It wasn't like Sherri to be quiet.

"I am. Just a lot to think about. Thanks for convincing me to come. This really was a great session."

"I know, right?" She linked her arm with her friends, pulling her out the door. "Where should we eat lunch?"

8

Annette tucked her credit card back in her wallet and dropped it into her purse. She picked up her glass and order number, before turning and looking out at the tables.

She nudged Sherri, "There's one in the corner, I'll go grab it."

Annette dropped her bag into the booth, then put her number on the edge of the table. She went back to the drink station and filled up her glass, grabbing napkins and silverware.

At the table, she pushed her drink next to the wall. Finally, she pulled her journal back out and opened it to the notes she'd just made.

"Okay, you were right. I loved that more than I thought I would. I'm glad I went." Sherri leaned in and dropped her bag, before mimicking her friend with an open planner and a pen in hand. "I never thought about blogging before. They made it seem so easy."

Annette snorted. "Yeah, well don't go giving up your day job. They make it seem easy, but they've also been doing it for years. Don't forget that."

"Oh, I know. But at least you've thought about writing before. I've never given any of this a thought." Sherri sipped her iced tea. "I spoke with a lady in the restroom right before this last session. She was at last years' conference and started up a blog right after. A lifestyle blog, I think she called it. I kind of let her story go in one ear and out the other. But I got her card. I'm a little more intrigued now."

As Sherri rummaged through her bag, looking for the card, their meals were dropped off.

"Here it is. Her name is Caitlyn." She handed the card to Annette.

"Nice card."

"She told me she was hoping to turn it into a full-time venture this year. She already has several companies advertising on her site."

"Really?" Annette jotted Caitlyn's website down on her notes. She'd look her up when she got back home.

"Yeah. I think that was what amazed me most. These women just started writing and now they're making money in all kinds of ways. I honestly had no idea."

Annette tapped her pencil. "I didn't either. In my mind, I thought I'd have to write a book or get a paid writing gig with a magazine or newspaper. I never thought about doing my own thing *and* making money in different ways."

Annette dipped her fork into her noodle bowl. She received dozens of electronic newsletters in her email. She read blogs all the time. But she'd never thought much about creating one herself. Until now.

Suddenly, Annette went into planning mode. If they could do this, she could too. Maybe a blog was just what she needed.

"I chatted with the lady next to me before the last session started. She designs websites."

"I heard that."

"She was the one that designed the Pilates speaker's site."

"I heard that too."

"After lunch, I want to go back and see if I can catch up with her. She told me she's worked with several writers. She said she'd show me some examples."

"I could see you with a blog. I can see you doing what those women had talked about."

Funny thing was, Annette could too. She chewed slowly, wondering how much a website would cost her. And how she could justify it to Curt.

Not that she needed to. They'd always had an unwritten rule: they could spend money on whatever they deemed important. If it didn't break the bank.

But she wanted him to buy into this too. Not fixate on how much it would cost. Hell, she didn't want to fixate on the cost. If it were only cheap enough to not feel the pressure.

Sherri finished and moved her bowl to the side. "Do you think I could do this?"

Annette shook her head, focused in on her friend. "You want to start a site?"

Sherri nodded. "Maybe. I don't know if anything will ever come from it. But I liked the idea of just writing about anything. I could write about my garden. And craft projects. Maybe even school. And painting." She said it quietly, almost to herself.

"I forgot about that. You haven't painted in years."

Sherri nodded. "I've been thinking a lot about it lately."

"When was the last time you picked up a brush?"

Sherri bit her lip. "Too long."

"You always loved that. Why did you give it up?"

"Oh, you know. The divorce. The move. Work. My parents."

"Life."

"Exactly."

Annette leaned over and tapped her pen on Sherri's planner. "Make that your *self* goal. Get back into painting. Buy some supplies. Take a class. Do it."

Sherri bit her lip. She hadn't seen Annette this motivated in a very long time. She liked her bossy side. "Yes, ma'am."

Annette closed her planner and dropped it into her bag. "Come on, I want to get back early so I can chat with a few people. And then I can drop my stuff on a chair close up."

As they made their way to the trash, Sherri grinned. "Look at you, miss motivator. And to think you fought me to come to this conference."

Annette linked arms as they walked back to the meeting rooms. "I know. Thanks for making me."

"Any time."

Annette stood in a loose circle with three other women talking to the web designer. She listened as the others spoke casually about their projects.

As one shuffled away, Annette reached out a hand and gave her name. "Hi, I'm Annette. I sat next to you at the last session. I really liked your work."

"Thanks, I'm Mickie. Wasn't that great? I think that was the best session so far."

"I agree. I'm learning a lot. I'm kind of on overload."

Mickie chuckled. "Then our work here is done."

Annette smiled. "I'm taking a lot of notes. You really captured my attention. Or should I say, the panelists did. I know we spoke in generalities earlier. I don't have a business yet, not really. But I do have an idea, and I'm thinking this could help me. Money is obviously an issue. How do you work? What do you charge?"

Mickie reached for a flyer in her bag. "I keep my rates affordable as most of my clients are startups like yourself." She opened her brochure, pointed to her various packages, and explained how they worked.

"A lot of people start with a basic site. Then as you move forward, you can upgrade as necessary. This right here also gives you a training class on Wordpress. All my sites are designed on Wordpress, and it gives you access to add your own posts and pages. It's as easy as creating a word document, so you can do a lot of design work yourself. Then I can help modify things as you need. It's really quite simple. It's how the two panelists I work with started. And now I'm on retainer for both of them and give them several hours a week of maintenance work."

Annette's mind started racing. She could do this. The basic package wouldn't set them too far back. She could put it on her credit card. More credit, yes. But this was for her business. She needed this.

"If I signed up with you today, how fast could I have everything in place?"

"In general, it takes a couple of weeks. But I do need things from you, like your logo, photographs, content, simple things like that. I can help you with some of it or refer you to places where you can get photos and logos and things. Once I have all that in place, it goes fairly quickly."

"And I can change things as we go?"

"Yes. That's the best thing about today's sites. You don't have to rely on a web designer for the basics. You can create content yourself. Do you have a business card?"

Annette shook her head. "I haven't started any of this up yet. I'm piecing this all together after the last session."

"Don't worry." Mickie reached into her bag and pulled out a notebook. "Write your name and email address here. I'll send you a link to a video I have that gives you all the details. It'll teach you more about Wordpress and give you more ideas too."

Annette wrote down her info then returned it to Mickie. "Thank you. I've enjoyed speaking with you. I'm excited about this. I've thought about making this my career for a couple of years. Suddenly, I can see how I can do that with this idea."

"What do you do? Now, I mean?" Mickie slid her notebook into her bag, before focusing her attention in again on Annette.

"I'm a teacher. I've taught fifth grade for years. But it's not as much fun anymore. I've wanted to change careers, but I never quite knew how. This last session really gave me some great ideas."

"That's what we're here for. I'm glad I got to speak to you. I'll get that video over to you, and then maybe we can chat next week."

"Perfect. Thanks."

"Enjoy the next session."

Oh, she would.

Annette would never have guessed how much she would enjoy herself. But she truly was having the time of her life.

Annette saw Sherri ending a conversation with another woman. She hurried up beside her. "Hi. I just spoke with Mickie, the web designer. Look at this!"

Annette held up the brochure, and started reading. " Can you believe this price? I can do this!" She felt a little breathless as she said it.

For the first time, she didn't even have any regrets for wanting it as bad as she did. She really could see how this could make a difference in the way she approached her business.

"Really? That's all she charges?"

Annette flipped the brochure over. "It's a basic package. She says as I grow, I can add on other options. But she said that's where most clients start."

"That's totally doable."

Annette could see the wheels turning in Sherri's mind too. "You could do it too."

Sherri nodded.

Annette continued, "Mickie said she'd send over more information. I can forward it to you too."

More nodding. Then Sherrie looked up. "We're doing this, aren't we?"

Annette laughed. "You're the one who dragged me here. I'm just pulling you with me.”

Sherri rolled her eyes. Then smiled. “All part of that midlife pact.”

“Yep.”

The commotion around her, women running into meeting rooms, and attendants shutting the doors had Annette turning to head back to her room. “I’ll see you after this session. How about we meet here?” She pointed to the pillar they’d been standing by.

“Okay. Enjoy!” Sherri hustled in as the door closed behind her as Annette squeezed in to her own room as the announcements were beginning.

She rushed to her site, smiling at the women next to her. She dropped her bag to the floor and opened her notebook to the next open page.

She glanced up and sat at attention, waiting for the next ideas to hit her full on.

9

"How many of you nurture the romance in your life as much as you did when you first met the love of your life?"

Annette didn't have to look around. Just like herself, she knew very few in the room raised their hands. She squirmed a bit in her seat, the conversation hitting a little too close to home.

She flipped to the notes provided by the speaker.

Nan Ferraro referred to herself as a marital sex advisor.

Annette had chuckled to herself when she read the summary of the class back at home.

Are things just a little too boring in the bedroom? Do you feel like you've done everything you can with your man? Oh, have you a lot to learn ...

That had done it. Annette knew Nan's class was the one for her. In fact, she'd even talked to Curt a bit about it before she left.

He'd assumed because they had sex every Saturday night that things were okay. She wasn't quite as sure.

Was it wrong to want more? Was she unusual in wanting to spice things up a bit? She'd been a little nervous adding this class to her list. But one look around at all the smiling faces at full attention told her she was among friends.

Friends that *got* her. She wasn't alone.

The laughter from the women around her brought her attention back into the room. Her eyes roamed back up to the front of the room.

"When was the last time you dressed for dinner?"

The audience was quiet.

"When was the last time you flirted with your husband?"

You could have heard a pin drop.

"Now I'm not talking about, *Hey, honey, tonight's the night.* I mean actually flirted with him, made him wonder what the heck you're up to. That's an art form in itself."

Why flirt when it's always the Saturday night special?

"Everyone complains today that there isn't enough time for anything. But I would counter that with we give too many mundane things too much of our attention. We're busy-busy when we really don't have to be. We pay attention to people and things that really don't matter. But what about the guy you love?"

What about when you were both too exhausted to do anything else?

"I can hear you. You're exhausted. You both work long hours. Then there's the house. The kids. Family commitments. Friends. The minor emergencies that delicately weave into our lives. When the hell is there time for flirting?"

Exactly!

"I'll counter that with: How can you not?"

"Once upon a time, our society didn't have all of this busyness. We didn't have Tinder to find a date. We didn't work our asses off only to come home and work that much more. We didn't overcommit and run around twenty hours a day. Because we couldn't. That form of living didn't exist.

"We didn't dive right into sex. Instead, we flirted. We took the time to get to know one another. We teased. We promised - and delivered, all in due time. Let me ask you something; do you treat your *rendezvous'* like you *have* to or because you *want* to?"

Lately, they'd all been because she wanted to. Sort of. Of course, the Saturday night expectations were always there. But she enjoyed them.

"When was the last time you had sex more than on your expected night of the week? Or month?"

Annette ran her fingers through her hair. *Yep, way too close to home.*

"I see you squirming out there. I've been in your shoes. It's time to get a new pair."

Then Nan did something totally unexpected. She kicked off her trusty black pumps, reached into her bag, and pulled out stilettos with lots of bling. She slid them on and moved back to center stage, eyeing every woman in the first few rows.

"What do you think my husband did the first time I met him at the door wearing these?"

"Laughed?" Someone yelled from the audience.

It took a few minutes for the chatter and roar to tone down. But Annette kept her eye on Nan. She watched as she took it all in. And all the while, a wonderful idea was brewing in her mind. That's what had been missing. Herself. She'd been holding back from doing what she really wanted to do.

"We all say we want more. But when was the last time you gave?"

"Romance is a two-way street. You must give to get. You must set the stage in order to receive. If you want change, you must *be* the change. And trust me, your man is going to meet you more than half way. Once you kick it up a notch, he'll jump in with both feet. I've met more women who make subtle changes, and their husbands quickly move to entirely new levels. Flowers. Chocolates. Weekends away."

The money ...

"And it doesn't have to cost a lot of money. In fact, you can do a lot of this for free. How about a picnic in the park? Grow your own roses so you can have a fresh bouquet on your table several times per year? Dinner by candlelight instead of leftovers thrown on the table? Or even just baking him his favorite dessert and presenting it on a fancy plate. The ideas are endless once you start putting different ideas together."

Maybe it was time to turn Saturday night into an all-day thing ...

"But this is more than what you give to him. This is also about taking what you need. When was the last time you had a really good mind-blowing orgasm?"

And the giggles erupted. Annette smiled - it was like she was back with her fifth graders. Mention anything around sex, and it was nothing but a fit of giggles.

"When was the last time you gave yourself a self-induced mind-blowing orgasm?"

Not as many chuckles. Annette bit her lip. As if. She was a good girl. That had always been Curt's job. She'd read about such things, but she'd never exactly done ... *that.* In all her fifty years.

"All of you here are fifty-ish. I know from experience that a lot of you were taught to be a *good girl.* And that meant not participating in such things as self-pleasure. But if you don't know what pleases you, how is anyone else supposed to know? It's okay to say what you like and don't like. It's okay to find out what you like and don't. And I have a few ideas for you."

Annette could feel herself blushing. It's not that she hadn't read things. Or done things. She'd read Fifty Shades. But reading and doing were two different things entirely. She'd never had the guts to buy anything. Or talk about it with Curt. So life carried on in good girl fashion.

"My heels," Nan pointed to her shoes. "They're for him, right? Or are they for me?"

Nan strutted her stuff across the stage, from one corner to the other. "When you find the right shoes, they make you look different, feel different. And that's the goal. There's more."

"Lingerie; we assume that it's a visual for men. But what about the way silk and satin and lace makes you feel? As it touches your skin, glides next to you as you go about your day. It makes you feel a bit sexier."

"Or what about a spritz of your favorite scent? I feel every woman should have a signature scent. Something that lingers on your man's mind long after he's with you. If he gets a hint of it, he thinks of you. You can spritz a card and leave it for him to find in his wallet. Or sneak to put a card into his desk. Little things to capture his imagination."

Like tucking a card into his work bag, Annette frowned. *Was that even possible when your husband played with dirt all day?*

Annette jotted down each idea in her book, adding a few notes of her own. She loved the picnic idea; they'd done that in college all the time. It could be a wonderful way of bringing back old memories. She liked the weekend getaways too. They'd been talking about getting into the city more. Maybe she could find a few cheaper hotels.

"And don't forget about toys." Nan pulled up another bag and placed it on the table. Then she proceeded to show off several things Annette had never seen before. Fifty shades, indeed. Vibrators, cock rings, and handcuffs, oh my! Annette chewed on her lip, feeling her nerves bubble to the surface.

She couldn't, could she?

Why not?

"I know a lot of you have never tried any of these things before. Get over your fear. Fear is simply the unknown. And if you have more confidence in who you are, what you want, I guarantee your man will find this entire process *very* sexy." Nan pulled up one toy at a time, showed how it worked, how to incorporate it into the bedroom alone and with a partner, before moving on to the next one.

"Whether you, your man, or both of you are new to toys, there's something for everyone. You can start simple. Grow as your comfort level changes. No pun intended!"

Every toy looked intriguing. Annette wondered where the hell she'd start.

"And I know what a lot of you are thinking right now. Where do you start? What's your first step? I'm glad you asked. Head back to the handouts I provided in your workbooks."

Sure enough, Nan had a list of how to prioritize toys.

Annette scanned her list, read through the suggestions for how to introduce the concept to your man. And then she found something else that caught her eye. At the bottom, one paragraph spoke of Nan's membership program. A monthly box to help jumpstart play. A box filled with goodies to motivate a couple in more ways than one.

Annette brought her finger up to her mouth, chewed on the nail. She imagined opening a box with Curt.

How shocked would he be?

They didn't really discuss sex. They just did. Action. And assumptions.

They'd been so young when they met, married. They'd experimented and felt their way to what they were today.

They didn't talk about it. They just did. And she'd never really thought much about it before.

Maybe it was time to expand and explore.

It's not that she was unhappy. Annette just wanted to up the experience.

Maybe she hadn't had a mind-blowing orgasm. How did she know? She'd never given herself one.

Maybe it was time.

She envisioned Curt's surprise as she met him at the door with nothing but a skimpy bikini and a pair of high heels. She imagined his surprise as she handcuffed him to the bed and pulled out a few other surprises.

She put her hand up to her mouth, hiding her smile.

She could do this.

Handcuffs. Yeah, wouldn't Curt be surprised?

Actually, she imagined her own surprise at being able to handcuff him to the bed. She could do this. Soon.

With a little *help* from Nan.

10

Sherri and Annette dropped their bags and fell to their chairs. They found a little nook away from the hustle and bustle of the terminal. With two hours to kill before their flight, they settled in with sandwiches from the deli.

Annette pulled out napkins she'd tucked into her bag, handing one to Sherri. Then sat back and devoured her grilled veggie delight.

After they deposited their trash and cleaned up their space, they pulled out their planners and started comparing notes.

"So, was it worth it?" Sherri grinned at her friend.

Annette just grinned. She couldn't wipe the smile off her face. It had been plastered there since the beginning.

Or maybe since she'd purchased a box from Nan. A three-month subscription plan would find Curt grinning as big as she for the next several months.

"What's our first steps?" Annette opened her planner to the first goal on her list. She made a few notes, writing down some ideas that had been stewing since the night before. "Do you feel like the ideas just keep popping up?"

Sherri nodded. "I've written a dozen things this morning alone. I feel like I have all these ideas, and I don't want to forget anything. I just want to take action when I get home, and I'm afraid if I don't get everything down, I'll just fall back into my old routine."

"I know. Me too. That's why we gotta be there for one another. I know we see each other all the time, but what if we hold special meetings just for staying on track? Maybe Thursday after school, we could grab a coffee and check in like that last keynote speaker told us to do."

"Okay. Thursdays are perfect. How about if I create a worksheet we can use for the process? That way we make sure we cover everything and hold ourselves accountable."

"Perfect."

Sherri settled into her chair, reading through her notes.

She was feeling a bit surreal.

She'd taken her fiftieth birthday hard. She'd never really told anyone just how hard it had been. Not even Annette.

In her twenties, she was a dreamer. Not just a dreamer, a doer. Whatever she'd set her eyes on, she'd stuck with it until she achieved it.

She'd signed up for a goals course through the career office on her college campus her last semester. The guidance counselor had given her worksheets for building her future with one-year, five-year, even ten-year goals. She'd kept those worksheets in her nightstand and looked at them for years as she was checking things off. She still had them in one of her first journals.

She'd wanted so much out of life. Not just a job, but a career. Not just an average relationship; she'd wanted the ideal.

Maybe that's why she'd taken her divorce so hard.

They hadn't wanted the same things out of life anymore. And the harder she'd tried to find something in common, the more he walked away. It was hard to keep a marriage together when only one person was willing to work at it.

He'd filed the divorce papers. And after many nights of soul searching, her father had been the one to convince her it was for the best. *Let him go.*

So she did. And somehow felt like she'd failed.

She'd had so many goals. She kept telling herself *someday*. And then - wham - fifty hit like a punch.

She'd wallowed. Probably longer than she cared to admit.

But she wasn't the wallowing kind. Eventually, she picked herself up, dusted herself off, and found a fifties group online that spoke to her heart.

She used that as her starting point. As her guidance to creating a new life. Because now it was time to do something. Anything. It was time to move on.

She turned the pages, reading through her goals.

Somehow they felt … shitty.

She wanted to lose a few pounds. Like that hadn't been on her to-do list for years.

Or paint. She'd loved her art classes in college. She'd dreamt of being a famous artist since she knew what that meant. Did *paint* as a goal really motivate her to do more than she'd already done the past couple of decades?

Or her relationship goal. Date. What the hell did that even mean? She was happy. Dating was nice. But it's not like she'd ever found someone who she was remotely interested in doing anything long term with. She doubted if she was capable of that anymore. She was just a single for life. Not good or bad, it's just what she was. And she was okay with that.

But dating. Dating could be good. God knows, the mind-blowing orgasms the singles class instructor talked about sounded heavenly. And she hadn't had a man in her life to give her one in a very long time. And there really was something different between one and two playing that game.

And then there was her dream goal …

"What?"

Sherri looked over at Annette, her eyebrow raised. She gave her a quizzical look.

"You just sighed like the world was coming to an end. What's up?"

Sherri moved in her seat, tucked a leg underneath and turned to face her friend. "I know I was the one that really wanted this trip. But somehow I feel like I'm further behind then when I got here."

"What do you mean?"

"Have you looked at my goals?"

"Last night. I told you they were a bit vague. We talked about how you can fix them."

"That's the thing. I've done nothing but think about that, and I'm still trying to figure it all out. I feel like a lot of the stuff has been on my list for years. I need to change it up a bit. But when I think that, I have no idea what I want next. I feel like I'm on a hamster wheel and I can't get off." Sherri grabbed a curl beside her cheek and started twirling. "I feel like your goals are great. You've really shined here. I can already see you making headway. And I feel like I'm back where I began."

Annette put her hand gently on her friends and squeezed. "I don't feel that way at all. I feel just as mixed up about this as you. Maybe I've written things out clearer, but I'm nowhere near feeling good about everything."

"Yeah, but you have solid goals. Like the website you're going to build. That's solid."

"Didn't you put down to start up your art again? You even said you wanted a website too."

"Yes, but those are both vague. I've had painting on my resolution list for years. And a website? It just sounds like fun. I don't really have direction."

"Then change it up a bit. Be specific. We still have a few days off with no school. Make a list. Go buy paints. Invest in a new easel. Find a class to take to help you improve. There are a lot of things you can do in the next few days to make it real. And I'll forward you Mickie's email when I get it. We can get together and plan our sites out. We can talk even more with Mickie; I know she's going to be willing to help us out."

Sherri nodded. "I guess you're right."

"Hey, if I can bring home a vibrator, you can go buy paints."

Sherri's eyes got big. "What?" She grabbed Annette's bag and started digging into it. "You didn't? Why didn't you tell me?"

Annette pulled her bag back. "We didn't talk much last night. Not without a group around, anyway. And it just didn't come up. I mean, *Yeah, I bought a vibrator today* just isn't something you say to everyone." She grinned.

"But a vibrator? How could you *not* tell me that? What? Why?" Sherri bit back the laughter.

"I got caught up in the relationship class. And she talked about orgasms and pleasure. And she sells these monthly romance kits to spur action. And I bought one." Annette sucked in her breath, biting back a panic attack. Quietly, she added, "And now all I can think is: what the hell did I do? What the hell is Curt going to say?"

"I don't think telling him has anything to do with it. Showing him ..."

Annette swatted at her friend. "God, what did I do?" Her head fell to her hands. "It's not even the vibrator. Okay, it is. But the money. Why did I sign up for something delivered monthly?"

"Hey, it can't be that much, can it?" Sherri knew her friend struggled with the extras. She tried to sneak in dinners and extras now and then. She knew the medical bills were still weighing on their minds.

"No. Yes. Oh, I don't know. I just get so guilty buying something that isn't a necessity, you know? We count every penny, trying to pay off that damn hospital bill. And then I go and do this."

"Annette, stop. Screw the hospital bills. You both have your health now. You both deserve a little happiness too. I'm glad you did something, just for you. And Curt will be happy too."

Annette looked up to see her teasing eyes. She burst into giggles. "You know, the speaker went on and on about adding spice back into a relationship. And I swear to you, I'd mentioned something like that to Curt just a couple of weeks ago. Not that I don't love what we have. But I wondered out loud if we had become too ... predictable. And Curt was all over it, saying no way, he loved what we have. But I still wonder, you know?"

Sherri watched as Annette babbled on, justifying what she'd done in her own mind.

She let her ramble, knowing she needed it. "Feel better?"

"Yeah."

"So you handed over your credit card with the best intentions."

"Yes."

"And you want to do something exciting, just for you and Curt."

"Yes."

"Then why feel bad about it? Consider this your date night and be done with it." Sherri grabbed her friend's hand. "You deserve fun too."

"Yeah, but not when I'm about to tell him I invested in a website too. What was I thinking? I shouldn't have spent this much."

"You said you put it on a card you've kept for you. For emergencies."

"Yes."

"Well that's what this is. You have to invest a little in your business if you want your writing to be successful. Think of it that way. This is your starting point. Your launching pad. The two purchases are separate entities. One's for business; the other pleasure."

Annette grinned. "Since when did you get so smart?"

"If I could only listen to my own advice."

"Exactly!"

"That's why we need each other! To keep us both in check."

"Point taken." Annette flipped to the back of her book. She grabbed Sherri's and turned to the same page, before handing it back. "Write down what you're going to accomplish before our next meeting. Next Thursday." She clicked her pen and started writing.

Sherri pulled a pen out of her bag and wrote. Buy supplies. Sign up for a class. Yep, it felt good to write it down and actually mean it.

Because something inside her told her this was different. It was more meaningful.

This time she'd change once and for all.

She had her friend to help her.

11

Annette dumped her suitcase in her bedroom, unzipped it and emptied it on to the floor. In minutes, she had everything put away, and stowed her suitcase in the closet.

She dropped a load of laundry into the washing machine and made her way back into the kitchen.

She knew she had a couple of hours before Curt returned home. She wanted everything to be perfect. She had so much to tell him.

She peered into the refrigerator, contemplating dinner.

What did you make when you talked about changing your life forever?

Here, enjoy the pasta. And by the way, I bought a website. And I'd like to have more sex too. Please pass the salt.

She slammed the door shut.

She really had to think of a better way to say all of that.

Her phone buzzed on the counter.

Hey, you back?

Yep, just a few minutes ago.

Did you have fun?

She started typing, then backspaced. She started up again.

How did she say everything in a text? Yes? It was so inadequate for what she was feeling. She hadn't really wanted to go, was nervous as hell about being around so many people. But somewhere in the middle of it all, she'd found that she really hadn't been living. Not LIVING living, the kind where she was excited about who she was and what she was doing. Not the way she'd been living when she'd first met Curt, when they married, when she'd gotten her job at the elementary school. Not the way she'd felt when she could take on the world and do something to change it.

How could YES possible cover all of that?

Or the fact that she might just know what it was she wanted. And it was going to totally, completely, blow his freaking mind. Sure, he'd bought her a chair. He'd been happy, even rah-rah'd around her when she'd started up her writing again. But deep down, she knew he'd assumed that was just her little "pet project." They were sensible, after all. There were bills to be paid. And no matter what, teaching paid the bills. No matter how crappy the insurance currently was, no matter how badly the policies had become in the past few years, it was still insurance. And they were fifty, with potential health problems that fifty-year-olds can get. She couldn't just leave it; it was far better than his crappy plan.

Yes? Yes, I had fun. Yes, it changed me. Yes, I can't do this shit anymore. I want to change everything.

Yes didn't cut it!

But she simply typed:

Yes

She sat there, staring at the screen. Maybe through osmosis, he'd get what she meant.

Cool. Glad you're home. What do you want to do for dinner?

Ugh!

Annette picked up the phone, ready to hurl it at the closest wall.

She put it down and chose to jump up and down instead. Just for a moment.

She dropped to the floor, crisscross applesauce, and put her head in her hands.

On Monday, she had to get up and go to work, as if nothing had changed. And yet everything had. She had a plan, dammit, and she wasn't going to let anything get in her way.

Now if she could just find a way to put all of *that* into words. If she could just find a way to get through to Curt, and have him understand.

They say a way to a man's heart is through his stomach. Annette knew for Curt, that was true. Because he worked outside every day, he usually came home ravenous. She'd often teased him when their kids were still home, she had two teenage boys instead of one. The two of them often had tried to out-eat one another. And Curt had often won.

That was also another reason to *hate* him. No matter what he ate, he didn't look much different than when she'd married him. He worked it all off in his gardens. Not that she minded. She'd caught more than one woman checking him out. And she was always happy to pull him in, knowing he was hers.

But tonight, she had a different strategy. She decided to make him his favorite meal, make him comfy and full before telling him about her plans.

She ran to the market for the ingredients, which was no easy task when she knew half the town. Settling on eggplant parmesan, she moved as rapidly as she could through the aisles, picking up a little of this and that. She grabbed a loaf of fresh bread, planning on baking it with garlic to add to the meal.

She returned home. She chopped. She sliced. She diced. She simmered. She sautéed. And finally, she had everything right where she wanted it, and waited to finish the rest when he got home.

As she hung up the last of the laundry in her closet, she changed into something nicer. Her good pair of jeans. The pink satin shirt she'd purchased for the trip. She even added her newest pair of silk panties, with the pink bra to match. If everything went right … maybe. She did have a box, after all. And at the last minute, she dug to the back of her closet and found the shoes. Not stilettos, really. But three-inch heels felt like stilettos to her.

She moved back to the kitchen just as Curt came in through the door.

"Hi," he hugged her tight and kissed her. "I missed you."

"Hi, I missed you too." His hugs were always so good. Warm. Comfortable. And just a bit …earthy. She pulled several blades of grass from behind his ear. "Are you saving these for later?"

He chuckled, grabbed them, and threw them in the trash. "We might've got a little crazy with the trimmers today. We're changing out a big section in the park. We're going to replant it with plants instead of grass."

He washed his hands and took a peek into the oven. "The good stuff?"

She chuckled. "Yes, your favorite. I know we haven't had it in a while, and I had the time."

He was on her like glue. Picked her up off the floor in a bear hug and planted a firm kiss on her lips. "I'm really glad you're home."

"Oh, shut up," she teased. "You're just saying that cause you like my food."

He nuzzled her neck. "I like you, too." As he set her down, he homed in on her shirt. "Is this new?"

"Sort of. I brought it for California. You like?"

He rubbed his hand down her arm, taking in the texture. His eyes returned to hers, "I do." He planted his lips on her one more time.

He went to the pantry and grabbed a bottle of red. "I got this from Jeff. Wanna try it?"

"Sure," she reached into the drawer and withdrew the cork screw. She took two wine glasses out from the cupboard. "How is Jeff?"

"Good, actually. I went over last night, brought a pizza for Karin and the kids."

"You brought a pizza? He had a heart attack."

He grinned. "I brought salad too. The kids wolfed it down. Jeff picked at it. Karin didn't eat much."

"I know the feeling. She's probably worried sick. They still have two in high school. That's a shock to the system."

"Yeah. She was pretty quiet too."

"I'll call her this week."

"She said to tell you hi. She was envious of your little trip."

Annette flinched. Her *little* trip.

She knew he didn't mean it like he said it. Still. It bugged her.

"How was it?"

He'd poured the wine and settled in at the bar, watching her the way he always did. He was good at giving his undivided attention. That's what had made them so good all these years.

She took her glass and settled in beside him. She turned just enough to meet him eye to eye.

"It was good. Great."

She took a sip. Took a deep breath and knew she couldn't hold it in any longer.

"It was actually better than great. It was unbelievable. Curt, I've never been to anything like that before. Everything else has always been about work. And this was about me. I really didn't expect very much. But from the first presentation, I felt like I was in a place that *got* me. That I was with others who felt what I'm feeling. We all had this emptiness inside. We all were there searching, for something, and each session built on that. It started from the very first one. And it never let up."

He sipped his wine, watching her. She loved him like that. Watching her. She continued.

"The first speaker was amazing. You know, she quit a twenty-year corporate career in order to start up a business on her own? She writes books. And speaks to audiences around the globe. She was brilliant." She absentmindedly tapped her fingers on her wine glass.

"She started the entire program off by having us really think about what we want, right now, where we are at this age. And I don't know if I'd ever really thought about it in those terms. Life's always been about reacting. We just take it all as it comes. But she made us see we should choose. Just like she did. She chose what she wanted to do for a job, and it works. Sherri and I talked about that; we want that too. I want that. Because you know I can't do this teaching thing much longer."

Curt nodded. Took a sip. "I know. We talk about that a lot."

"And then, ohmigod, I went to this section on business, on writing. I never knew. It was a panel, and all of these women are making hundreds of thousands of dollars a year by blogging."

"Blogging? What the hell is blogging?"

She snorted. "Really? You have to pay attention a little more."

He simply raised an eyebrow. He'd never get technology. She was the one who changed the settings on his phone.

"Web logging. See? Blogging. It's an easy way to design a website and fill it with information. One of the panelists has a site on food, another on Pilates, another is a financial consultant. I have so many ideas. In fact, it's even made my writing ideas that much stronger."

"That was good? You can use that to give your writing a go?"

She nodded. "Yes. I'd like to show you some of these sites. Get some ideas from you."

"Okay. You know I don't get that stuff much."

"I know. But I have some ideas. I'd like to bounce them off you. Maybe this weekend we can sit down at my computer."

"Sure." He reached for the bottle and filled up both of their glasses. Then settled back down, ready to listen.

She took a sip for courage. She bit her nail, trying to put together the right words.

"And then I went to this class. It was … eye-opening. She talked about things I'd never heard of. And everyone around me seemed to get it. And I didn't. I mean, I do. I'm fifty, for God's sake. I read. I listen. But I really didn't get it. I don't think I do anyway. I mean, how would I know? There's only ever been me and you. And maybe I have. In which case, it's great. But what if I'm missing something? What if I - we - could make it better? Shouldn't we try for that? Shouldn't we reach for that? Cause I'm young. And I really want …"

Curt leaned forward and put his hands on her arms. He squeezed gently. "What the hell are you talking about?"

"I want a mind-blowing orgasm."

That stopped him. He fell back to his chair.

She watched as a million things crossed over his face. Questioning. Wonderment. Then a crestfallen look.

She moved forward and settled her hands on his shoulders. "No. No, no, no."

He blurted over her words, "You mean you haven't … You've never …" He looked her in the eyes, hurt. "You've faked it?"

"No. That's not what I mean. Not at all." She blew out her breath, choosing her words carefully. "It's just, we're sitting there, and the speaker starts talking about *things*. And she mentions mind-blowing orgasms. And talks about *toys*. And *things*. And this a-ha settles over the crowd, like they're all in on this secret. And, I don't know, it just left me wondering. I mean, it's good. I love you. I love being with you. But …"

She chewed on her lip. How did she proceed without pissing him off? How did she say what she was feeling without making him feel like a total shmuck?

Before she could figure it out, he began.

"So you're saying I'm your one and only. And the women in the audience had worldly views. And you're wondering what you've missed?"

She eyed him carefully. "Sort of?" She judged his demeanor before proceeding.

He moved, leaning into the table. He had both his hands around his glass, watching the liquid twirl round and round. "And did these worldly women talk about how they go about getting mind blowing orgasms?"

She bit back a smile. "Maybe?"

His head snapped up. "Maybe?"

She moved, mirroring his posture. She made sure her leg was touching his. With both hands on her glass, she leaned in, her arm nestled into his.

"This isn't about you or what we have. I love us. But we're … routine. I've only ever been with you. And I don't want anybody or anything else. Ever. I wouldn't trust anybody but you with this."

She paused. Then continued. "I just listened to all of these wonderful women who have traveled the world and experienced … everything! I've led this sheltered little life right here. Same job, same house, same everything. And while I don't want *everything*, why not spice up what we have? What I have with a wonderful man like you? Whom I trust with everything."

She turned, grabbed his chin, and shot him one of her looks. "I want a fucking mind-blowing orgasm."

She didn't kiss him, didn't move. Her eyes held his, calculating his next moves.

He snickered. He roared. He reached for her, wrapped a hand around her neck and pulled her in for a kiss. "Okay. And how do we go about giving you this thing you ask for?"

Her eyes twinkled. "I have a box."

12

"So, I bought a box." She focused on her wedding ring, turning it around and around.

"Just a box? Hopefully you didn't pay much for it. I could have brought one from work."

She stopped, looked up, to see his teasing eyes. She took a deep breath and smiled.

"This must be some box."

"It was an impulse purchase. I got wrapped up in this class. And, I don't know, it just sounded amazing."

"Obviously."

"You know, I've only been with you … I mean, there's never been anyone else. It's always you."

"Are you having regrets?"

His eyes looked so concerned.

"God, no. No. Not at all. You're it. You're my everything. I have no regrets. But …"

Curt turned his chair, so he was in front of her. He moved a little closer. His knees bumped up against hers. He leaned forward, elbows on his legs, staring at her. "But …"

"We were so young, you know? And we just did everything by figuring it out on our own."

"Uh huh."

"And I love us. I love everything about who we are."

"Uh huh."

"And we've always been good together. Great. And I can't imagine anyone else. I mean, you're wonderful. And I love …"

He linked his fingers with hers. "You're talking in circles. Just spit it out. It's me. You can't say anything that's going to piss me off. Well, unless you've had an affair."

She looked up, shocked, one more time. Saw his teasing face, rolled her eyes, and relaxed. She'd never thought about losing herself in another man, ever. And she trusted him heart and soul too.

"It's just, I sat there while this woman was talking about things I'd honestly never heard of before. Not really. I mean, I read romance novels. But experienced some of these things? Never. And I felt so naive, so vanilla. And I just thought that maybe I - we - could have more. Because if I'm getting *more*," she looked at him to make sure he knew what she was insinuating.

He smiled. "And by *more*, I'm taking it you mean that mind-blowing orgasm you were referring to a moment ago?"

She nodded. "I mean, obviously, I've had orgasms. But it was just this feeling with everyone shaking their heads around me. The way they talked about *toys* ..."

She dropped her head, put her hands on his shoulders, and tapped her forehead against his a couple of times for good measure. "I'm losing it. You've got to be sorry I went to that conference. I'm sorry."

He moved so fast, she caught her breath. His hands were on her face, tipping it just so. He dove in and presented her with a kiss she hadn't had in a very long time. Deep. Hot. It made her ... horny.

When they came up for air, he kept his hands along her jaw, searching her eyes, trying to see deep within her soul. "I love you. You, you're my everything. No, I don't think you're losing it. And I'm not sorry you're exploring who you are. We've had a rough few years. But we're far from being old. We're *far* from gliding into old age and just *being* because we give up. If this is what you're feeling, that's okay. If this is what you want, let's explore."

"Really?" She laughed at her own squeaky voice.

"Really."

"And you don't think I'm being ..."

He kissed her hard. "You know, I think I'm going to come out ahead in all this too. I mean, I'm a guy. My wife wants more sex. She wants to make our love life better. Like I'm really going to argue."

She chuckled. "When you put it like that."

"Exactly."

She just stared.

What had she done in her life to deserve him, this? How had they found all this, so good, when others didn't or couldn't? She asked herself that all the time. "I love you."

"I love you too." He stood, pulled her up alongside of him. "So, about this box ..."

"It's a little more than a box." She pulled it out of the closet, where she'd stuck it, mixed in with her shoes. She hadn't even popped the seal, a little embarrassed about what might be inside.

He watched as she dropped a pink cardboard box onto the bed. "That looks like a box. Am I missing something?"

"I actually bought into a three-month subscription service. We'll get new boxes for the next three months."

He laughed. Not just a chuckle, a very large, very loud belly laugh.

It wasn't what she'd been expecting. She felt relieved. She couldn't help but laugh too.

"Not only did you decide you wanted the best orgasm of your life, but you wanted to ensure you could have as many as possible for the next three months?"

"Well," she looked at him, bit her lip. She might be a little shy and naive on some levels. But she could be saucy when she wanted to be. "I figured after three months of *training*, we wouldn't need a box anymore."

Yeah, that got his attention. She watched his eyes turn the smoky gray-blue she loved more than anything. "Open the box."

Inside, nestled in pink and red tissue paper, were five separate boxes. One at a time, Annette pulled them out and started reading.

"Strawberry warming massage lotion. Completely edible, glide this on your lover for all-over pleasure. That sounds simple enough." She handed it to Curt, then reached in and grabbed the next product.

"Green tea massage candle. Made from natural soy, it will not burn the skin. Set the mood and discover a delicious smell that pleases the senses. In minutes, it liquifies and turns into a massage oil that enhances every loving touch."

Curt took it and turned it so he could read the back. "We pour it on each other?"

"Um hmm. I guess so. It says it melts into massage oil, and it won't burn your skin."

"Okay." He set it on the night stand.

Annette pulled out the next box, the largest of the five. She gasped and covered her mouth with her hand. "It's a finger fun vibrator."

"Finger fun vibrator?"

"Yep." She turned the box over and continued reading. "Don't let this small size fool you. Big fun often comes in small packages. This micro bullet vibrator lets you dial up three separate settings for the perfect amount of pleasure. Simply stretch it onto your finger and it'll stay in place to be the perfect addition any time, any place. Turn your bath, shower, or bed into perfect pleasure, every time."

Curt grabbed it out of her hands, and slid it out of the box. With a quick twist, it was on his finger and he turned the button on. They both giggled as the sound intensified as he tried each setting. He wiggled his finger at her as she fell to the bed. "This might just do the trick."

He pounced on her, grabbing the hem of her shirt and pulling it over her head.

She was grateful she'd chosen to wear her sexiest bra and panties. Not that Curt ever seemed to care. He had anything she wore off in seconds for their Saturday night trysts. But something seemed different. He looked at her hungrily. And if she wasn't mistaken, he felt … hard, really hard. Like they wouldn't have to spend a little extra time getting him ready.

She palmed him and moaned at what she felt. "You're so hard."

His shirt joined hers on the floor.

She reached for his button, but he jumped back.

"I'll be back."

What the hell? She watched as he disappeared out of the room. She ran a finger through her hair, wondering what just happened. How could he even run in his condition?

But before she could think any further, he skipped back into their room, stepping on his pants trying to remove them. One hand was pushing his underwear to the floor, while the other held the lighter they used to light the fire pit.

She giggled as she kicked off her shoes, undid her jeans and pushed them to the floor. She left her panties in place; he'd have to remove them himself. She scooted to the middle of the bed.

He threw all the products onto the bed, then stopped.

Her eyes wandered from top to bottom, settling on his massive erection. She'd made love to him hundreds - thousands - of times. Yet she still was hungry for him every time she saw him standing at attention.

"You're beautiful."

Her eyes returned to his. She swallowed.

Massive orgasm or not, she was happy. Deliriously so. She was loved. She knew it, could see it in his face. Whatever other women experienced in no way compared to what she had right here, right now, with this man who loved her heart and soul. What else did she need?

She looked at the box he held in his hands. Oil. Definitely oil. "Would you light it already?"

"I can't get it open." He struggled with trying to get the top off the candle container.

She sat up, took it from him. Then broke the seal that was holding the lid in place. She lifted and threw it on the bedside table. "Voila." She handed it back to him, then flipped over and made herself comfortable on the pillow.

He just shook his head as he lit the wick. He threw the lighter on the table, then watched as the candle melted. A clean, woodsy scent filled the room.

He held it up, closer, to his face. "Wow. I like this."

She eyed him with a sideways glance, with amusement.

He tipped the container to and fro, watching as it liquified. He dipped his finger in, rubbing it on his hand, testing it out. Then went back in for more.

"Is this a party for one or can I play?" She grinned as his eyes met hers.

"Just testing. I don't want to burn your delicious skin." He straddled her legs, careful not to put his full weight on her. He ran his palm over her back, lightly tracing the lines of her bra and panties with his finger.

She let her eyes flutter closed.

He blew out the flame, then tipped it slightly, dripping oil into his hands.

His warmed hands slid confidently over her body. The heat was perfect; not too hot. He released the back closure, sat up while she removed it, and threw her bra on the floor. She felt his hands play, rubbing teasing, just the way she liked it.

Only better. The heat somehow made it better. And when he leaned down and scraped her with his teeth, she jumped. His eyes glanced up, "You okay?"

Her eyes floated shut once more. "Yep. Perfect."

Seconds turned to minutes. She turned, letting him work his magical fingers on her back.

She moaned. Who needed an orgasm when a massage could do the trick? She hadn't realized she had so many kinks.

She was lost to his touch. His hands roamed every inch of her. He rubbed his way down, then slowly made his way back up, stopping to add more oil as needed.

Maybe it was the excitement of being home, ready for a change. Or maybe it was the anticipation of what was to come. Either way, she felt every nerve standing on end.

His hands stopped on her ass, massaging, kneading. Then he slipped his fingers underneath her panties, teasing.

He tugged, sliding the fabric down her legs. Then flipped her over and started his descent once again. Every swipe of oil he followed with his tongue.

She tingled. She ached.

And as he moved farther down, she felt the heat deep in her core continue to build.

She grabbed his hair, nudging him where she needed him to be.

His voice was music to her ears. "You taste so good." "I love you." "You're my everything."

She felt her breaths come in tiny shockwaves, responding to his touch. And as much as she loved what he was doing, she still wanted more.

She sat up, pushed, until he fell to his back. "My turn."

With what was left of the massage oil, she worked her own magic. Caressing. Stroking. Enjoying every moment of his body, and how he responded to her touch.

When she took him in her mouth, he let out a deep moan. "Baby, more. More."

She knew him well. Knew every movement he made. She brought him right there, right to the edge, before sitting back up once again.

A sly, sexy smile had him pouncing on her once again.

"You're not playing fair."

"I'm not?" She batted her eyelashes. "I'm sure you'll get everything you want."

He raised an eyebrow and gave her a wicked grin. "Then I guess I better get back to it."

She watched as he reached for the vibrator, fiddling with the buttons.

The vibrator was small and discreet. Barely larger than his thumb, he pulled it until it fit comfortably on his index finger. He turned it on, adjusted the speed, getting comfortable with each setting.

Then his sultry smile returned once again. He fell down beside her, propped himself up on his elbow. Flipped the switch and lightly touched her tummy, right below her belly button.

"Oh!" She squealed. They'd never played with a vibrator before. They'd never even talked about incorporating toys into their play.

He chuckled. "Feels weird?"

"Yeah. Like a shock almost. In a good way."

He moved down. Touching her, letting her adjust to the feeling.

He touched. He watched her eyes. He pressed down.

"Ohmigod." She arched her back, tipping her head back. He nibbled at her throat as he kept applying pressure. "Curt …"

"You okay?"

"Yes …"

She felt it build. Slow. Strengthening. An aching pressure creeping up from the very depth of her being.

Until … lights, stars, pure magic.

"Holy. Fucking. Shit." She felt herself sink into the bed.

He laughed. "I take it that was good?"

She reached a hand around his neck, pulling him in for a deep kiss. In between tongue swipes, she murmured, "You have no idea."

"Guess you can check off mind-blowing orgasm," he leaned down and nipped at her breast.

She playfully pushed him until he fell to his back.

She straddled him, guided him home. Then leaned down and whispered, "I don't know. I think we're going to have to do it again."

13

When had she fallen out of love with herself? When had she started thinking her personal life was anything but worthy?

Sherri uncorked a bottle of her favorite chardonnay and poured herself a hefty glass.

She'd expected a lot of revelations to come out of the seminar. She'd expected to come home after the weekend feeling many things. A low sense of self-worth wasn't one of them.

She dropped to her favorite couch, looked out of her window at her spectacular view. Her home sat on the edge of a forest; a wide valley resided just off in the distance. She'd sat here and watched everything from deer frolicking to hawks diving for their dinner, amazed at the wonders of it all.

This had been why she'd settled on renting this place. One look out the window and she'd fallen hook, line, and sinker. Even now, years later, she wouldn't think of anyplace else she'd rather live. It inspired her.

"Shit."

How did she even know what that meant anymore? Inspired? It inspired her to hide her true feelings, obviously.

She grabbed the journal she'd been writing in throughout the conference. She gazed at her notes, the ones from the speaker who'd uncovered her *problem.*

You know it's time to work on you if you work hard at being successful and do everything you can to feel worthy in your job. You identify as your position, and introduce yourself as your career, but have trouble adding anything more. The only way you feel successful is if it's tied to your job.

Yes, yes, and yes.

She was the one who volunteered for all the extra committees started at the school. She was the one who often volunteered ideas in order to stay more active at work. She'd been the liaison for the parent and teacher's association for the past several years. She organized teacher parties throughout the year.

Outside of work field trips? She'd taken charge and planned plays and restaurant visits more times than she could count.

But all of that had been fun. That wasn't work. Was it?

The more she'd listened in the class, the more unsure she had become.

Because deep down inside, she knew it wasn't because she wanted to do it all. Or that she even enjoyed most of the company. If Annette or several other of her friends didn't attend, she often contemplated how to back out.

She did it because … Because it filled a hole. That's what the speaker had said. Was it true?

Did she have a hole that needed filling?

Did she do more than her fair share, simply to cover up a more deep-seated problem?

"Fuck." She sipped.

Well, she'd just have to think about this some other time, thank you very much. She didn't know what the problem was, but she was willing to bet somehow, some way, a bunch of it came back Burt.

He was always the problem.

She ran a hand through her hair, set her glass down, and picked up her iPad.

She flipped it on, then pulled up a browser window.

Her ex could piss her off like no other. He'd drained her, frustrated her, irritated her. He'd done it for years, long before he'd filed for divorce.

He'd said she was too clingy. That she'd tried too hard to make it work. What the fuck were you supposed to do when you were married? Weren't you supposed to put all your energy into the relationship? Weren't you supposed to try things to make it succeed?

And then there was his relationship with his son. What was up with that? He claimed to want to build a legacy for Tanner, and yet he rarely spent any time with him.

Why did Burt drive her so crazy? Why did she *let* him drive her this crazy?

She had to stop. She had nothing to feel guilty about. She'd done all she could.

She'd tried til the end. And when it hadn't worked, she put her time elsewhere. She'd started saying yes at work for something to do.

And now, she was over him. Or at least she should be.

Of course, when he crawled back into her life every other year or so asking for money, she'd discovered old wounds were hard to heal. She just needed to learn to say no.

Maybe she had to have a reason to say no.

She shook her head, wondering where that came from.

A reason. Right. Like she needed someone else in her life. Like she had such good luck with the few dates she'd been on since the divorce.

Like she had a chance of finding someone who could be her reason in this small town.

She shook her head again, wiping the image out of her mind.

She knew what she needed. Something to break her habits. And something to do with her nights that didn't involve work.

Something she wanted to do. Just her. A secret. Something that gave her chills.

Painting.

That thought had been there so long, she'd almost forgotten about it.

She loved art.

She'd spent hours on her artwork at school. Had even minored in it in college.

And yes, it had been one of her "volunteer" activities at school, for the kids. When they'd shut down much of the art department thanks to budget cuts.

But that was for work, for the kids.

What she was talking about was painting, just for her.

Adult painting. A way to pick up a brush and create magic.

On a whim, she typed in *adult painting*. Why not? That's what she wanted.

Sip and paint parties. Yeah, right. She'd organized three for the teachers.

Nope. Not what she wanted. Uh uh, no how.

Next.

She kept clicking, reading, diving down. Until …

Intuitive painting. *What?*

Come ready to work. Leave your inner fears and insecurities behind. Whether you're trying to release your inner artist for the first time or are bringing the creative you back to the surface, this course will leave you breathless with excitement, more charged up about life then you've been in a very long time.

Yes, please!

Sherri felt a shiver run down her spine.

She kept reading.

I believe that creativity comes from your inner soul. Your artistry is deep inside waiting to burst free. This is painting on an entirely different level, I promise you you've never experienced anything like this before. No matter how you come in for your first class, you'll leave a changed person.

Sherri took a deep breath, released slowly.

She clicked. She read. She lost all track of time.

Everything about the site appealed to her.

Including the instructor.

She clicked over to the About Us and started reading. He'd graduated with a degree in fine arts. He'd traveled all over the world. His work hung in galleries and private collections in forty-two countries.

She scrolled and read. His paintings were breathtaking. She'd gladly have any of his pieces hanging on her own walls. She got his style. She even had a few pieces that blended with his look.

After a few moments, she found she was looking as much at him as she was his work, his class.

He … intrigued her. And that startled her.

She couldn't put her finger on it. Infatuation? Maybe. He was a good-looking guy. Tall, dark, and handsome; yep, he had classic, rugged good looks.

But it was more. Like he reminded her of someone or something. Like she'd known him at some point in her life.

Looking at all he'd done, she knew it wasn't possible. But still. The feeling wouldn't go away.

Was that a sign this was something she should do?

She leaned over and picked up her planner, the one she'd brought back with her from California. She flipped to the last page.

There in her own careful handwriting were her goals. Buy paints. Set up a new easel. Sign up for a class. She ran her finger over the ink, remembering the moment she'd written it.

Annette had made her. Sherri wrote the words feeling motivated yet uncertain. Annette had seemed so gung-ho and had such specific dreams; she'd wanted that too.

She wrote her goals down because in the back of her mind, she'd always wanted to return to her art.

But somehow over the years she'd lost what painting meant to her. She'd forgot that fire that used to sit deep in her gut, the one that begged her to do something with it.

She'd lost it when she married, had a child. As one year turned into ten, then twenty, and now almost thirty.

When did all that happen? How had she quit dreaming?

How had she quit living?

She looked down at her iPad once again. A tear dripped onto the screen. Right below were the words: What will it take to find the natural gifts and talents you know you were born with?

Sherri thought back to her favorite class in college. Professor Gilbert had taken her under her wing, stood beside her many hours late in the evening, when she'd return to the studio while other kids were out partying. She'd play with color, shadow, depth. And Professor Gilbert would show her how to go just a little further, dive in a little deeper.

And it had worked.

That's what she loved most about it.

That feeling. That hunger.

Where had that hunger gone?

Sherri tapped the screen. It was right here.

She searched the calendar and found the next class. It started in two weeks.

Another click and she was on the reservation page. Six Saturdays. She could do that. She *would* do that.

She grabbed her credit card from her purse, filled out the form, added her information, and hit the purchase button.

A few seconds later, she was reading through the welcome page.

She heard the familiar ding of her email, letter her know she'd received her email, with instructions on how to get there and what to bring.

She was ready. She was going to do this. And she found herself more excited then she'd been about anything in a very long time.

Maybe her motivation to attend the retreat in California had been spot on. Maybe it had done her more good then she'd given it credit for. She'd had her concerns, that last morning when all she felt was confusion and terror.

She knew she didn't want her old life.

She knew her best friend was about to change and leave her behind - move away from teaching and into what she wanted, writing.

Sherri wanted that too. Desperately.

She loved teaching, just not the bullshit.

She loved staying active, but she could do that in many ways.

She wanted to feel alive again.

With a click she was looking at the instructor's face once again.

Wesley Kotkin.

Just a few years younger than herself. He looked tall. At least he was always the tallest one in his photographs. She imagined her head falling just beneath his chin.

His shock of black hair was gently greying at the temples. He had that sexy two-day beard the guys were all sporting nowadays. She didn't think it always worked. On him, it did.

And his eyes. Dark pools of … hot.

She'd just booked a class with something she didn't quite understand.

And the more she thought about it, the more excited she became. Yep, she couldn't wait to find out what it all meant.

14

"Hey, you. Whatcha doing?" Annette was sitting at her desk, staring at her computer. Her nails were click, clicking on the wood, as she pondered what to do next.

"I'm just cleaning up a bit. I thought I'd give the house a good cleaning, since I have a couple of days before spring break is over." Sherri held her phone up to her ear with her shoulder while she tucked the clean, folded sheets back into the linen closet, then shut the door. "What's up?"

"It's Thursday."

"So it is."

"We're going to do Thursday meetings. To stay on track."

Sherry grinned. "I figured we'd start next week. Since we said we'd go out for coffee after work. Would you like to meet today?"

"Could we?" Annette knew how her voice sounded. She could hear it. Just a hint of desperation. She'd been sitting at her desk with her finger poised over the purchase button for the website she'd wanted built for thirty minutes. She just couldn't settle her fears down.

"Peet's?"

"Could you come over here? I'll put a new pot on."

"Be over in ten."

Annette made her way to the kitchen and tidied up. Not that it was ever a mess. But she wanted to stay busy until her friend got there.

She started the coffee, grabbed two mugs from the cupboard. She'd baked muffins earlier and put two out on plates.

The coffee maker chimed its familiar bells as Sherri opened the back door and let herself in. "Hi. Smells good in here."

She kicked her shoes off and hung her jacket in the mudroom. She dropped her bag in a chair before sitting down at the counter.

Annette pulled the pot out and filled both mugs. "Hi. How's the cleaning going?"

"Good, actually. I got this sudden burst of energy yesterday and decided to freshen up the place. I finally put the flannel sheets away. It's been nice enough for the last couple of weeks I think I'll be fine with the cotton."

"I did that last week. I think I only leave the flannels on two months anymore. I get so hot at night."

"With that hot husband of yours, it's no wonder." Sherri batted her eyelashes at her friend, teasing her.

Annette blushed. She turned, dropped a spoon. "Um, a muffin? Would you like one?" She busied herself with the napkins, taking several seconds to peel two from the stack. She turned back to see Sherri eyeing her inquisitively.

"Are you okay?"

"Yeah. Why?"

"You look … nervous. Is everything alright? I didn't mean anything …. I always tease you about Curt …"

Annette shook her head. "No. It's nothing. Not really." She dropped to the chair next to Sherri and busied herself cutting into her muffin. "It's just," her voice dropped to a whisper. "We had a good time."

Sherri cackled. "You showed him the box."

Annette felt her face flush again. She covered it with her hands. She couldn't say a word, so she simply bobbed her head.

Sherri shoulder bumped her. "Good for you. No questions. No details." She dove her fork into her muffin and savored the bite. "Mmm. Muffins. Moist. Delectable."

"Ohmigod! Shut up!" Annette jumped up and brought her plate to the sink. She turned around, grinning at her friend. "Yes. The box was good."

Annette came back to the island and leaned over it. Moving closer to Sherri, she whispered, "Holy shit. I had no idea."

Sherri sat back, bringing her mug to her lips. She sipped, "So you're no longer questioning your purchase?"

"No. Not at all. I can't believe we've never done anything like that before."

"That's what long term marriage does to a couple. You get stuck in your ways."

"I know. We were young and naive. Then we had kids. Life just had a way of zooming by. I guess I never paid attention." Annette refilled her mug, then returned to her chair. "I can't believe I never thought of making what we had better. Not with toys, anyway. I mean, I've read Fifty Shades. I blushed sitting in the same room as Curt while I read it. I've never even thought about bringing *that* into our lives."

A sly smile lit up Annette's face. "Trust me, even though my box wasn't even close to Fifty Shades level, I'm rethinking everything."

Sherri snorted. "Okay, okay. Give this single girl a break."

"Maybe you should find someone to give you a *boost*." Annette winked. She felt like she was finally throwing her *good girl* away. And getting just a little saucy.

Sherri just gave her the standard "no way" look she always did when the subject of men came up. So Annette changed course.

"Have you done anything with your goal list? I know we've only been back a couple of days. Did you start in on your goals?"

Sherri stopped for a moment. Then nodded. "I signed up for a class."

"Wait, what? You did? Tell me more."

"I was sitting in my living room last night and I got this wild idea to start searching for a class. And before I knew it, I found the perfect one. It's called intuitive painting. It's six weeks long, and it sounds perfect for me. Every page spoke to me. I couldn't help but sign up. It's like it was calling to me, and I didn't have a choice. It starts in two weeks."

"Seriously? Wow, I'm impressed. I thought I might have to nudge you a bit." Annette knew her friend had second guessed her decisions, she could tell it when they'd spoken at the airport. "So tell me about it."

"I can do one better." She reached beside her and pulled out her iPad. With a click, she was at the website and maneuvered through to a couple of pages that talked about the class.

Annette moved the tablet in front of her and read.

Intuitive painting is about finding your inner spirit. It's like meditating with a paintbrush in your hand. You'll discover your hidden talents. You'll explore your inner voice. You'll learn to connect to the inner you, and answer questions you haven't been able to answer before.

"Wow. I can see why you signed up. This sounds enticing. Too bad I don't have more artistic talent." And money. But she left that part off.

Sherri tapped, moving to different pages on the site. "I've never done anything like this before. But it ticks all my boxes. I think it'll bring back the part of my life that's missing, my creative side. And it may help answer the *what's next* question that won't stop circulating in my brain."

She tapped the courses page and pointed. "The instructor has several different tracks. He has classes for people who have never picked up a paintbrush before. I liked this one because he talks about getting back into your art and finding your love for it once again."

"Wow. Some of these people have serious talent. I love the colors. Look at what some of his clients have done before." Annette scrolled down the page, pointing to women standing near their finished paintings. She pushed the tablet closer to Sherri again, "Look at this one. That's gorgeous. I'd love to have something like that hanging in my office."

Sherri sat a little straighter. "I'll paint you an S.E. original here soon. Then you can say *you knew me when*."

Annette shook her head and smiled as she grabbed her mug and sat back in her chair. "I like seeing you like this. I'm glad you found this class so easily."

Sherri nodded. "You know, I am too. I sat down yesterday and did a search on a whim. I didn't really think I'd find anything. It was just more of a split-second a-ha moment. This site came up and I think I spent more than half an hour on it. I came back to the class page several times. I finally just clicked, paid, and that was that. No buyer's remorse either. I got another email from the instructor today, and I'm more excited than ever. He has most of the materials in his studio, but he did make a few recommendations for things to bring, and a few ideas to stock our home studios. I'm thinking of running into the city tomorrow and picking up a few of the things."

"Wow. I am impressed."

"Well, we promised each other we'd do things. So there you go. This is me, taking action."

Annette couldn't help but smile. If she'd doubted the conference before they'd attended, she'd never admit it now. "I think this is going to be our year. I think we're both going to do wonderful things."

"Me too. This course will bring me though the rest of the school year. I'll see how I feel then, but I'm thinking I'll have even more time to paint in the summer. And if I love it and am doing well, maybe I'll see if this instructor has something else to see me through the summer. Or if he can recommend something. I don't know, I'm just feeling … energized by all of this. I know I didn't really have a clear picture when we left L.A., and I still don't, not really. But I do feel good about getting back to my artistic side. And I guess that's half the battle, right?"

"Exactly. That's what we learned. Baby steps, my friend. One step at a time. And I think you made a very big step here. Good job. It looks good on you."

"I could say the same for you. You seem to glow. Must be that box." Sherri winked at her friend.

Annette just rolled her eyes. And grinned. "Not complaining. Not at all." She hopped up and put her mug in the sink. She leaned over the counter once again. "I called you because I need you to talk to me. I'm nervous about paying for the website. I should do this, right?"

"Yes. You should. What's your hold up?"

Annette bit her lip. *Money. It was always money.*

"It's still the money?"

Annette eyed her friend, grateful she could read between the lines. She nodded. "It's always the money."

"I thought you were okay with investing in this? We talked about it back in California."

"I know. But that was then, this is now. I just have trouble, you know?"

"Is there something else?"

Annette stopped. Money, yes. But what else?

She'd started down this path two years ago. And every time she sat down and even thought about her writing, something came up. The kids needed something. The family needed her. The cancer scare. An unexpected task at work. She'd always found some way to push her writing to the back burner.

What if she invested this money and pushed it all to the back burner again?

What if she wasn't the successful writer she wanted to be? What if she never got her big break?

What if she failed … miserably?

Sherri interrupted her thoughts. "Look, you said this would help you start to build your portfolio."

"Yes."

"And this could very well give you what you need to pull in a few jobs."

"Yes."

"It's not that much. Not really."

"No." Annette had labored over the brochure, staring at the price since she received it back in L.A. "Not really."

"Okay, then, end of discussion." Sherri jumped up and started walking to her friend's office.

"Where are you going?"

"To your desk. I'm going to watch while you buy."

Annette breathed deep while she followed, feeling like a child. "Yes, mom," she said under her breath.

"I heard that." Sherri glanced over her shoulder with a cheesy grin. "If I can buy into a class on a whim, the least you can do is invest in a website you've been planning for the past several days."

Sure enough, Sherri fingered several pieces of scratch paper strewn across the desk. They had drawings, copy, arrows, and notes - the basic ideas of a website already in the formation stages.

Annette just shook her head as she fell into her chair, avoiding her friend's eyes.

She clicked to awaken her computer. And there was the buy button, staring up at her from the screen.

"Click the button."

She did. Annette clicked, and started filling in the blanks. Name. Address. Credit card information. A few answers to basic questions.

In five minutes, she'd finished. And she had an email waiting for her telling her Mickie would be in touch to start the design process within the next couple of days.

"See how easy that was?"

Annette nodded as she printed off the details, gathered it all up and put it into a file folder she'd created for the project. "I did it." She took a deep breath. "I did it," as if she needed to convince herself it was okay.

But deep inside, she was. Maybe this is what she'd needed all along.

Something to tell the world her intentions. Not just keep it to herself, her husband, and her best friend.

Once a website was together, she couldn't hide it anymore. She'd be ready to go.

Now all she had to do is figure out what she was going to write.

15

Sherri made a wrong turn. Then another. How did one even do that with Siri directing your every move? She mumbled in frustration. She'd obviously found the weak point.

She pulled into a small parking lot that was filled with other cars. She glanced at the clock on her dash before she turned the key and dropped it in her purse. *Not really late. One minute didn't count, right?*

She walked quickly to the front door. Only as she felt herself enter did she allow herself to take a deep breath and start relaxing.

The building was just as described on the website. A perfect artist's retreat. Nothing more than four walls, it was all in the ambiance. The ceiling soared easily twenty feet above her, angled to meet at a point in the middle, with exposed wooden beams that crisscrossed from side to side.

From the front entry, you could see everything. A small kitchen to the side - just a discreet space with a small refrigerator, a few cupboards, a microwave, and counter space. A perfect place to grab a cup of tea before picking up a paint brush and getting to work.

The main area was nothing short of spectacular. The wall in back was floor to ceiling glass. Beyond was a spectacular view of the valley - something she was sure the owner had wanted to highlight when the building was constructed.

Scattered around the floor plan was several different work stations. Tables were set up at each with a wide variety of paints, brushes, and more. Each had a small sink for rinsing and cleaning. And instead of an easel, each had a wall with the largest canvas Sherri had ever seen.

"Come in!"

She looked to the side to find the host greeting her with a smile and a friendly wave.

His intense good looks made her falter.

She'd noticed Wesley Kotkin on his site, but nothing had prepared her for how striking he'd be in person.

Tall, she looked up into his dark eyes as he stopped in front of her, shook her hand, and led her to her place. He was several inches taller than her, but that didn't stop her from studying him. His dark hair pulled back into a short ponytail. His well-trimmed beard that added to his austere. The cleft in his chin, visible when he smiled. And the dimple, no, she couldn't ignore that.

But it was more than his looks; it was his presence. Somehow, she felt as if she knew him. Like they'd crossed paths before.

"I'm glad you made it."

"I apologize for being late. Siri had me turn too early. Then I got mixed up."

He grinned. "I hate technology. It's always doing that. For some reason, it gets confused between Scotts Place and Scotts Road. It's always directing people to the wrong place."

Was he staring a little too long? Or was she imagining it? She couldn't remember the last time someone had made her feel as flustered.

"Well, you're here. And we're glad to have you." He turned, moved back into the middle of the six stations. "In fact, we were just getting started. We're going to be together for six weeks, so we were introducing ourselves."

He turned, eyeing each of the attendees, before returning his gaze to Sherri. "Luckily, I was just introducing myself, so you didn't miss anyone. I'm Wesley, but then I think you already know that."

He circled around to the six attendees - all women - and continued flirting with them all.

Sherri didn't know whether to be appalled or turned on.

Charismatic; she'd give him that. He knew how to work a room.

He was also possibly the most gorgeous man she'd seen in a very long time. At least by her standards.

She always did like a tall, dark, and handsome. And that damn dimple; he knew how to use it.

She was sharing six sessions with these women, so she paid attention as they each introduced themselves.

Jean, a grandmother with thirteen grandchildren trying to find something new in her life. She'd recently lost her husband of forty-two years.

Nancy, a single mom raising three teenage boys.

Kris, married with two kids in college.

Brit, grandmother to four, great-grandmother to two, she announced to the class she was just getting started at life.

Bo, a free spirit, she'd traveled the world over, only recently settled in the area to care for her aging mom.

Sherri guessed they ranged from fifty to seventy.

All looking for something more in their lives; all in the class for about the same reason. They'd loved art in the past and were looking for a way to bring it back into their lives.

"Ah, you've all come to the right place. I'm going to make you love this process more than you ever have before."

Sherri had no doubt of that.

"Is everyone ready to get started?" Wesley circled, looking at them all as they nodded their heads. "Then come on in here into the circle."

"We're going to begin every session with a deep immersion into your own creative process. We're going to talk about who you are and what you wish to portray to the world. Each of you is more creative than you could ever imagine. You've just forgotten how to use it."

"But what if I'm not creative? What if we make mistakes? Can we go back and correct things as we learn more?" Jean had a nervous look on her face. "I haven't painted in years."

"I assure you, there is no such thing as a mistake. This is a safe place. You are each here to learn about who you are as a person as much as you are to discover your hidden talents as a painter. What you will experience here in the next six weeks is about the magic that lives deep within your soul. I say this is a safe place because we won't judge. The seven of us are on this journey together. We're here as a family; to learn from one another and to grow together."

They all nodded, falling a little deeper under his spell.

"When you get here, we'll spend the first thirty minutes doing a little meditation, a little learning about what our souls are here on this earth to accomplish, and what your strengths are as a person. We're going to share stories, talk out problems, and lay the groundwork for the work we'll be doing throughout the day. So, if I can have each of you either select a chair or a cushion if you prefer to be closer to the ground, and we'll get started."

Sherri dropped to the ground. She crossed her legs, put her hands on her knees, and took a few deep breaths. While the rest of the class settled in, she couldn't help but notice the beauty in front of her. The floor to ceiling windows were truly the best part about the studio. She could feel herself relaxing, just from looking out. Trees. Forest. Blue sky. The wind rustling through the colorful branches of leaves, turning with just a hint of the spring air in their buds. She found herself longing for future Saturdays, when she knew this spot was going to be breathtaking.

Wesley guided them through a short meditation, then followed it with a primer in how to use the supplies.

Each work station had a variety of brushes, rags, paints, and other tools to allow them to create with perfection. While he had each stocked with every color in the rainbow, he was happy to help create different colors if the need arose.

"You'll also notice there isn't an easel at your workstation. Instead, I have a free-standing wall with a canvas sheet attached from the top. That's because I don't want you to limit your creativity. I want you to think large. I want you to color outside of the box, so to speak. I want you to experiment with expressing yourself in big, wide strokes. Get used to this, this will be our normal practice. Even when I bring out canvases, I put several together to make you think beyond the norm. *Think different* is officially our motto in this class." Wesley had examples he shared on the television screen located off to the the side. He breezed through them quickly, not wanting anyone to have a preconceived notion going into the project of their own choosing.

"Now, everybody up. We're going to do our first lesson. And to get you started, I want each of you to choose one of these colorful scarves. Then we're going to dance."

Sherri grabbed a blue one, her favorite color, but stopped when she heard his final words. "Dance?"

He came over to her, took the scarf from her hands, and wrapped it around her as if it were a shawl. She grabbed the ends, then followed his motions as he moved across the floor.

"Yes, dance. Breathe in, breathe out. Twirl. Let your spirit soar. Feel who you are. Then we'll continue with the music while you each get set up."

Sherri was nervous. She wasn't a dancer. She'd always felt self-conscious about letting her body go.

She moved, just a little, watching some of the others. She smiled as she picked up on who were the free spirits of the group. They wooped and hollered, clearly enjoying themselves.

As she watched, she also noticed Wesley watching her. He smiled. Raised his arms to the sky, then back down.

She could tell the dance had rhythmic tones to it. Tai chi movement, back and forth. Not that she was much into that either. But she'd organized enough events in her school to know what it was. She was a planner, not a doer. And she'd always grown bored with those events before.

But today, she was enjoying herself. She caught herself wondering if this could be what she'd been missing.

16

It was late in the day. Sherri couldn't believe how fast time had flown by. It seemed like she'd just entered the studio space, and it was already time to clean up.

Sherri rearranged her station, put the caps on the paints and the brushes in the bin to soak.

Wesley had gone over the house rules before they'd started painting, had a list taped to each work station. She'd smiled when she saw it; it reminded her of the way she ran her own classroom. She even chuckled when she saw the pictures he'd drawn next to each rule. A true artist, heart and soul.

She finished cleaning up, grabbed her bag, and made her way out to the parking lot following the other women. She'd made some great friends today. She'd had fun. She couldn't wait to come back next weekend.

As she approached her car, she dug in her bag, looking for her keys. They weren't in the pocket she normally placed them in. She took a few things out, dug a little deeper. No keys.

She glanced in the car to make sure she hadn't left them in there, then started retracing her steps. She'd been in such a hurry, she could have dropped them anywhere.

She approached her workstation and found them where she had placed her purse. Picking them up, she turned, ready to head back out to her car, and ran straight into Wesley.

"Oh, my, I'm sorry." She felt equally bad as he jumped back, splashing tea on both of their shirts. "Wesley, I'm sorry." She looked around for paper towels.

"Not a big deal." He moved to a sink, reached underneath and took out two towels, handing one to Sherri. "I didn't know you were still in here, you surprised me. I shouldn't have snuck up on you like that."

"I couldn't find my keys. They'd fallen out." She held them up, as if that explained everything.

"Well, as long as you're here, would you like some tea? I was about to sit down for a little downtime. I've got a bright, sunny spot down in the corner of my studio. A couch and a couple of chairs. A wall of glass with a great view. I call it my sunroom for obvious reasons." He tipped his head towards the *sunroom*. "I'd love for you to join me if you have the time."

Sherri bit her lip. Of course, she had the time. It was just her and an empty house when she got home. She'd dedicated her entire Saturday to this class. She hadn't dared book anything else. She'd wanted to spend the day fully immersed in her new class and have the entire evening to think about what she'd learned.

A few more minutes could help her reflect even more.

Plus she'd been eyeing his *sunroom* all day.

He chuckled. "Come on, I can see you eyeing my corner."

Her brow furrowed, "You're sure?"

He nodded. "Of course. I wouldn't have asked if I hadn't meant it. The sunroom is the best room in this place. Don't get me wrong, I bought this property because it's the perfect space for painting. And the windows. I knew it adds a bit of magic to my classes. But the sunroom? That's just for me. I don't use it for classes. I use it to meditate. I use it to read. I use it to plan. I can sit there and drink tea, watching the world go by, and be perfectly happy."

"It does look inviting." Her eyes took in every detail.

"Go on. I'll just grab some more tea and throw the towels into the laundry." His eyes twinkled as she guiltily apologized once again with a blink.

She walked down two steps into the corner room. It felt warmer than the main studio space. She attributed that to the three walls of glass and the sunlight still streaming in.

The room had a small love seat on one side, a table and two chairs on the other. Several small tables were scattered around the room, holding artwork and books.

She stopped in front of an easel and took in the brilliance of the blues and greens. She could tell it was one of Wesley's, abstract, yet something about it told a story.

"What does it say to you?"

She turned and glanced at him as he approached, accepted the mug of tea before turning back to the painting. She sipped as she contemplated. "I would say it's sky fading into water. Rough seas. The calm before the storm. Or maybe the calm after a storm. The way color returns when the sun is trying to peek through the skies after all of that turbulence."

She glanced at him. He motioned towards a chair near where she was standing, before taking a seat near her. "Am I right?"

He smiled. His eyes studied her as he sipped, meeting hers over the rim of his cup.

She felt a little unnerved by the entire experience, wondering why she'd said yes. She hadn't even thought about it when he'd asked. She loved it here and had been dying to spend time in this very room.

But the way he watched her, it did something to her. Unease. An uncomfortable feeling, but in an entirely good way.

"It's called *Storm*."

It surprised her. It jolted her back to where she was, talking about a painting. Not what she was feeling.

"How did you get started painting?" She'd read some online. But now that they were here, snuggled down into their chairs, she wanted to keep him talking. The tea was good. The comfort of the room was outstanding. And she found she really wanted to know more about this man.

He chuckled, leaned back and moved deeper into the pillows. "Honestly, I can't remember a time when I didn't have a paintbrush in my hands. My mother was an artist, she taught at the local high school. She sold some of her work on the side, but never very successfully. She was always more of a trainer than a seller. She preferred to show others how to find their unique talents."

"Is that where you get it from? Your love of teaching?"

He rolled his head, pondering. "Maybe. I suppose so. I remember from the time I was six or seven years old, I'd come home from school and find my mother in her studio. She held afternoon classes quite often with adult students. I'd grab a snack and plop down beside her desk. Then I'd draw and paint while she'd walk around directing her students. She never really told me how to paint. I just picked up on all the lectures she'd give her students. And somehow it worked out."

"Did you major in it in college?"

"Actually, I majored in math."

She studied him once again. She could see that. He had a look that easily crossed between technology geek and successful artist. "You did?"

"My dad always told me I'd be better off going into engineering. Or maybe going to medical school. So I followed my love of math all the way through school. But I'd sneak into the art room during my off time. I took a couple of classes as electives, so the instructors knew who I was. They'd let me come in and play around because I was always quiet, kept to myself. One instructor thought I had real talent, tried to talk me into taking more classes."

He raised an eyebrow. "You know how that goes. If you could only go back and shake yourself, knock some sense into your brain before you get started on the wrong track."

"I take it you followed the math path for a bit?"

"I actually started medical school. That lasted for six months before the school and I came to an agreement I should choose another path." His face said it all.

"And you've been painting ever since?"

"Um," he huffed out a breath. "More or less. I can't say it was great for the first few years. My dad always had the *I told you so voice* when I saw him. I couch-surfed among my friends for a bit. But eventually I figured it all out."

"And now you're here."

"Yup. This is me."

"I read about you online. I know your artwork hangs all over the world. I was impressed; I guess that's why I'm here."

"You're here because you want to paint."

Sherri took a sip, tipped her head back and looked out the window. There was a flock of birds flying by. She loved watching them soar, staying together in pattern, depending on each other for survival. "I am. And to learn more about me."

"Ah. The intuitive part resonated with you too. More than the painting, or was it the combination?"

"A little bit of both? It was just something about what you said online that intrigued me. I've been wanting something more and had no idea what. I knew I wanted to get back to my roots, back to doing something creative. And when I found your site, it just jumped out and said *pick me*."

"What do you do? For a living, I mean?" Wesley crossed his legs and leaned forward, his leg creeping closer to hers. He gave her his full attention.

That movement left her unsettled once again. He had a way of making her feel like she was the most important person in the room. She wasn't used to someone so focused on what she had to say. Not a man.

"Um, I teach." She set down her mug, crossed her legs, and pulled a finger up to chew on the nail. A nasty habit, but it was the only thing she could do since she felt like she was on display.

"What do you teach?"

"Third grade."

His eyes lit up at the same time he swallowed. The tea went down the wrong way. He coughed, then recovered. "Wow. That surprises me."

"It does? Why?"

He rubbed a hand over his face before playing with his beard once again. "I don't know. You look … creative. I just don't see you as a school teacher. At least not elementary. I see you more in the arts. Maybe music."

"I do play the piano. I used to play with a band, many, many years ago."

"What kind of music? Jazz?"

She startled again. "Yes …" How did he keep doing that? It was as if he could read her.

"I teach intuitive painting. I'm somewhat *intuitive*. I just have this way of seeing into people, looking at who they really are."

Sherri found herself relaxing, more than she had in a long while.

How had she found this place?

Maybe it was meant to be.

Good conversation. A great instructor. A place to find her love and passion for the arts all over again.

The more she talked about it with Wesley, the less fear she had about her future.

Maybe Annette had been right. Maybe she had been afraid to let herself go.

If that was the case, this might just be the solution.

Wesley's class had woken things she hadn't remembered about herself. After just one day, she felt more alive than she'd felt in years.

Annette had her writing. And Sherri knew if all went well, Annette

wouldn't return as a teacher in just a few short months.
Maybe she could have something new too.
A new path. A new zest for life.
And Wesley might be the solution.
As she finally said goodnight and drove home, she smiled.
It felt good to be alive.

17

"Ohmigod, just kill me now." Annette fell into the coffee shop chair, nearly spilling her drink as she dropped it to the table. She'd agreed to meet Sherri at the coffee shop for their Thursday meeting a little late, after her impromptu meeting with the other fifth grade teachers.

"What was that all about? It looked very intense when I walked in." Sherri brushed a napkin over the few drops of liquid scattered over the table. Then wadded it up and moved it towards the side of the table.

"You're not going to believe this. We're going to finish out the school year with a safety course. We just got the books today. The school board decided that all fifth graders needed this before they move to middle school next year. This book is crazy." Annette pulled it out of her bag.

"Look at this. There are lectures on gun safety, inappropriate touching, online porn. I kid you not, the stuff in each chapter of this book could take hours, weeks on its own. And we're expected to teach this to fifth graders thirty minutes for each chapter in the next few weeks. Some of my kids are still innocent enough not to have a clue about this. They won't even have sex ed until next year. And yet we have to shatter their worlds and teach them the ins and outs of this stuff at record speed. Give me a break."

"Seriously?" Sherry picked up the book and thumbed through it. "I'm glad I teach third grade."

"Stay there. Trust me."

"I'd heard rumors. Marcie was talking about it the other day."

"I know. I've heard the chatter too. I knew it was coming. I guess I thought it would be next year. I figured they'd put together a solid plan and incorporate it slowly into the curriculum instead of springing it on us like this."

"Have they told the parents? This isn't going to go over well."

"They're sending a note home tomorrow. Parents have the weekend to decide if they want to opt out. We start teaching next week." Annette took a sip, then stared at the ceiling for a bit, biting back the tears. "I teach online porn next week. Granted, it's basic, all about appropriateness if they wander onto a site that *doesn't look right*. But I'm supposed to just dive into this?

Look at this chapter."

She flipped the pages of the book Sherri was holding back to the beginning. She pointed to a few of the finer details, the websites she could reference for ideas on verbiage, and the bullet points to stick to for class discussion. "There's a workbook that goes along with it. That's where I can copy the worksheets we'll use for class discussion. And for homework assignments. And get this, I have to foot the bill for copies. I'm way over budget already on my yearly allotment. That means I'll be paying for this garbage." Annette gathered up her hair in a ponytail and pulled the band she'd had on her wrist around to secure it.

"What did the others say?"

"What could we say? I didn't really stick around long to get into the details. I wanted to meet you. I'm sure we'll chat in the morning before the kids come in. We'll all have time to think."

Annette breathed deep, trying to push the ugliness of the last hour away. She picked up the book and dropped it back into her bag. Just one more cause for her to make her writing work once and for all. She pulled out her journal and read through her weekly goal list. She grabbed her iPad and laid it on the table, pushed her thumb on the button and found a new browser window.

She closed her eyes for a second. She breathed deep. She smiled. "Look at this."

On the screen was a mockup of Annette's website. Though it still needed the finishing touches, she was starting to feel pretty good about it.

It was clean and simple; just what she'd ordered. She'd settled on a simple logo, one that Mickie had helped her create.

She scrolled up and down, clicked and moved to several different pages. There wasn't a lot of content; Mickie had assured her she could fill it in over time.

"I've started watching the videos that come with the package. I never knew blogging could be so easy. I've even started writing a few articles; samples I can put online once we make it live. I've had several things in process since I started this. But I've actually finished a couple of them and I'm going to post them once Mickie gives me the okay."

"What's your URL going to be? So I can follow you, and say *I knew you when*," Sherri teased.

"AnnetteHinton.com. I figured my name was the best way to go since I really don't know what I'll be doing for a while. I can write on anything that way. And change it if I ever get my act together and finish a book. Even if I add services down the road, it'll still work well for me. Mickie said a lot of her clients use their names; it's an easy way to link it to my social accounts too. I'm adding my writer information to LinkedIn and Facebook too."

"Wow, I'm impressed. You've done a lot since last week."

"Yeah. It's funny, all I needed was permission to buy the site. That flipped a switch inside. I feel like I have to make this successful now. I've been working on it every night since we met."

"What does Curt say?"

"You know, it's funny, he's taken an active role in this too. He pulled out his iPad a couple nights ago and found this site for me." With a couple of clicks, Annette pulled up a freelance site with the title: Hundreds Of Resources Perfect For The Freelance Writer.

"This page has eight hundred magazines, and provides the link to the writers guidelines with just a click. Not all magazines pay, but a lot of them do. I found a parenting magazine that pays over one thousand dollars for a featured article. I haven't done a lot with it yet, but I have pulled the guidelines for several magazines I think I'm a good fit for. I've read through their notes and am starting to put together submission ideas. I know I probably won't get a job the first email out. But I have to start somewhere. Maybe if I can even get a free article or two, it'll give me something for my portfolio."

Sherri held her cup up in the middle of the table, tapping it gently with Annette's. "You go, girl. I'm impressed. You've really done a lot in a week."

"Thank you." Annette grinned. "I'm taking our midlife pact very seriously."

"Good for you. I'm proud." Sherri took a sip. "I've done a lot too."

"Do tell." Annette closed her book and sat back, giving Sherri her undivided attention.

"I'm a little obsessed with painting. I finally got my easel set up in the spare bedroom two nights ago, and I painted until eleven last night. I'm going to grab something from the market on my way home and spend another night painting tonight. Wesley shared so many ideas. I've kind of gone into overdrive. Look." On her own iPad, Sherri pulled up her photos and scrolled through several, sharing some of what she'd learned.

"I really can't believe I let this go all of these years. I have no idea where this will go. But already I'm feeling different. Relaxed. And I'm super excited about this weekend."

"Tell me about the instructor. You said he's good?"

"He's great. I felt a pull towards his class when I read it. I told you that. But it was even more stark when I walked into his studio. I felt … at peace. I know it's corny. But I really felt different by being there.

"Oh, I didn't tell you, I lost my keys when I was leaving. They'd fallen out of my purse at my workstation. And when I went back in looking for them, I got to talking with Wesley again. He invited me to stay for tea. I wish I would have taken a picture; he has this sunroom that sits just off to the side of the workstations. It's by the glass that overlooks the valley. We sat there for another thirty minutes or so talking. He's just so … personable. That's really not the word either. I don't know. I just really enjoy him. I'm going to like this class. I've already been back on his site, thinking about what's next."

Annette reached over and squeezed her friend's hand. "I'm glad to see you so excited about something. For you."

"You know, me too." Sherri started chuckling. "During recess today, Kate came up to me and asked if I'd take charge of planning the end of school picnic. I think she thought it would be an easy yes, since I always do it. I told her no."

"You did? That must have shocked the hell out of her. What did she say?"

"She actually laughed at first. She didn't think I was serious. I told her about my class, and that it was taking all of my time, and I just couldn't do the planning this year. It took her a minute before she mumbled and walked away. I think she was going to see if Emma would do it."

"Emma? Oh God, are we in trouble."

"I know. I figured she said that just to rub me the wrong way. It didn't work. If Emma does do it, we'll just suffer through whatever she plans."

"Ha! Oh, I love it. Their *yes person* is now saying no. Sherri, I'm proud of you. I think we've both done a lot in the last couple of weeks. I think we're going to have great success this year."

"I think you're right. Aren't you glad I made you go with me to California?"

Annette sucked in her lip and thought about all the things she'd done.

For as much as she worried and complained about going, it was the best thing she'd done in a very long time.

For the first time, she was excited about the future, not dreading the next bill that landed in the mailbox or the next phone message when she arrived home.

Sure, that was all still there. But she had motivation. She had other things to think about.

Yep, it was going to be a very good year.

18

Annette was tired and restless. She hadn't slept right the night before. She had too much weighing on her mind.

She dropped her bag and her keys at her desk before hanging up her coat. She ran her lunch to the kitchen down the hall.

Her room felt colder than normal, so she turned up the heat. Then she sat down to pull everything together for her daily routine.

"Hey." Sherri popped her head around the corner. "A bunch of us are thinking of going out for drinks tonight, are you in?"

Annette thought for a moment. She'd planned something easy for dinner. She always had an hour or two alone before Curt came home. "Sure, why not. Where?"

"We'll figure it out after school."

"Sounds good."

The bell rang and the kids started filing in, taking their seats.

She looked at their faces. She could pinpoint what each of them was thinking.

She could see the tired expressions on several, the ones who had a troubled home life.

She knew which hadn't had breakfast. She knew which wouldn't have completed their homework. She knew which would raise their hands and have all the answers.

She had each child pegged in just days of meeting them. She'd dealt with so many issues over the years, she was finding it even easier to do.

She made her way through math. She was just getting the kids into reading when she first heard the noise. Just a random *pop, pop*.

Then a voice over the announcement system, "Active shooter. This is not a drill! Shelter in place."

She froze. She felt the blood drain from head to toe. She felt surreal - this couldn't be happening!

And then her training kicked into gear.

She turned out the lights and locked the door. She ordered the kids to do as they'd rehearsed.

Tables for protection.

Random objects from the class box to potentially use as weapons.

"Quiet. Quiet." She heard herself saying it repeatedly.

Resting a hand on one child trying to keep her calm.

Assuring another child who was sobbing.

She sat on the floor, staying hidden from view. Waiting. Listening.

Her actions were right there, doing everything she could to keep her kids safe. They were kids! Who … Why?

She swallowed her fear, trying to keep her mind right here where it needed to be.

But part of her escaped.

Why was she still here?

Why did she stay?

They weren't paying her enough for this shit. She just couldn't do this anymore.

"Ms Hinton?"

She felt the tap on her shoulder, and turned, grabbing the child, and bringing her down. "Wynn, you need to stay down. You need to be quiet. Do as we've rehearsed."

"But …"

Annette could see Wynn's lip trembling. She could feel her hands shaking as she buried them in her own.

Beautiful Wynn. She'd always thought of her that way, though she'd never admit it out loud.

Her long black hair gave her an angelic look. Her eyes were the color of dark chocolate. And her dimples … they'd have the boys on fire in the not too distant future.

Yet she'd also seen her rambunctious wild side. She knew somewhere deep within her, she was the one in her class most likely to succeed. She aced every assignment. She'd do it without any trouble and come back for more, surprising her once again.

As she held her on her lap, Annette smoothed a hand over her hair, trying to comfort her. She leaned in close, whispered into her ear, "I need you to go back to your spot and do as we rehearsed."

Wynn nodded. "I'm scared."

It was barely above a squeak. But she'd watched as several others around her nodded their heads in agreement.

"I know." Annette whispered, hoping it wasn't too loud. "I need you all to be brave."

She felt the panic creep up. She swallowed, swallowed again. *Push it down. Push it down.*

Her mind drifted to all the reports she'd read on other schools, other teachers, right here in this very situation.

She'd often wondered how they coped, how they survived.

She saw them now, in her mind. Saw them in their own classrooms, with their own classes, hiding behind tables, wondering what the fuck their lives would be like *after*.

How did you sit here and not go crazy? How did you look at all these wonderful children, and not think about what might happen? What the aftermath might look like?

She scratched her forehead, trying to cope. Trying to keep it all together.

She heard a buzz. Her phone.

She crawled over to her desk, and very quietly opened the drawer. She pulled her phone out, and the stapler for good measure.

She almost laughed holding it in her hands. Stapler versus semi-automatic; there'd be a very clear winner.

Are you there?
  Are you okay?
  Are you all right?

Over and over, Curt had texted her. She had texts from her kids, Clara and CJ, in much the same fashion.

She typed, backspaced.

What the hell did she say? *Hi. I'm here. But I might die soon?*

She saw Sherri's name pop onto her screen.

Shit fuck shit fuck

She bit her lip to keep from giggling. Giggling! At a time like this! Yep, she couldn't have said it better herself.

Would that be her last communication? Would that be what people found?

Would that be what she went down with? What a perfect way to describe what she was feeling.

Annette ignored everyone else's texts, and responded to Sherri's with

Agree

One simple word. She knew Sherri was okay. And now Sherri knew the same.

For the moment.

She crawled down to where two boys were starting to tussle. "Hey!" She whispered as loud as she dared.

"But he took my book."

"No, I had it first."

She sat down, gently put her hand over both of their mouths, and pulled them into her lap, into a hug. Between them, she whispered, "We'll be alright. We will." She rocked.

This wasn't supposed to happen. This shouldn't happen in elementary school, in the fifth grade. It shouldn't happen at all.

She'd threaten to quit when she'd gone through her first training.

Then Curt's cancer scare.

And some part of her had shut down. School was comfortable. Teaching was what she knew, what she did. How could she even think of leaving it?

It wouldn't happen to her.

Not to *her*.

It happened in other schools.

And now, here she was.

She thought of Clara's twelfth birthday party. Clara had begged the two of them to have a sleepover. And in the end, they'd relented. She'd been fighting with her best friend for weeks; Clara had been so sure it would bring them back together.

Anette thought of her daughter's tears when her BFF hadn't shown. None of the other girls mattered, she was simply inconsolable.

It had been one of the most painful lessons in her young girl's life.

Of course, they'd moved on. She'd eventually made up with her BFF. They even lived together a year in college.

But that night. That night had been pure torture.

And CJ. CJ had been such a cranky baby. He'd been the one who cried early in the morning, every morning, for almost the first full year. Every morning, one of the two of them rose at four just to hold him, rock him. It became a pattern. It had been one way to keep him quiet, a way to get him to sleep for a little while longer.

She remembered whining with Curt about how tired they were.

She also remembered whining about how much they missed it, when one day, a few weeks after he'd stopped, they finally realized he'd moved on.

She kept rocking, holding these two small boys, who had curled up into her.

Annette heard rustling at the other end of her line.

She pulled the two boys close once again. "I need you both to be good and do as we rehearsed, okay?"

They both gave a tiny nod.

She pushed them down, back towards the table. She pulled away, watched them both settle in before she scooted back down to the other end.

More cuddles.

More back rubs for just a second of assurance.

More coaching.

More words of encouragement.

She found herself humming, almost silently, just enough for those closest to her to hear. The song they were learning for the school musical at the end of the year.

Annette strained to listen. She tried to distinguish good sounds from bad. She could hear sirens outside. She could hear banging and yelling from just beyond the windows.

She could hear rustling in the hall.

And just like that, it was over.

After minutes - hours - crouched behind tables, hugging Purell bottles and crayon boxes to their chests, a SWAT team member entered their classrooms and led them out.

Single file, just as they had rehearsed several times in the past few years.

Walking in a line.

No talking.

Hands in the air.

No, you can't get your backpack.

No, you can't hold Jackson's hand.

They marched, out the door, down the hall, outside, into the cool, spring air.

Into the drizzle that matched her mood.

Single file, through a never-ending field of police, looking on.

All she saw were guns resting in their arms.

A battlefield.

A war zone.

A fucking elementary school.

How were they supposed to learn like this?

How the fuck was she supposed to teach like this?

They marched into the holding zone, just as she was taught.

She checked them all out. Made sure everyone was accounted for.

Held hands and gave hugs as she worked to match each child with their waiting families.

And he was there. Curt.

She looked through him, into their past, their future.

She saw his young face, the day they'd met.

She heard his voice, the way he'd teased, flirted.

She saw his lust, the first time they'd held each other close.

She saw him declare his undivided love.

She saw him on their wedding day. The day she'd given birth to each of their kids.

He'd been her rock, always, even when she didn't know she needed his strength.

And now, all she saw was his fear.

He reached her, wrapped an arm around her shoulders, another around her waist.

He pulled her in, hard.

His head tucked into the crook of her neck.

A sob.

"Annette," he breathed into her. "I love you." Over and over again.

She had her hands wrapped around him, squeezing, pressed into his back.

He separated just enough, just to look into her eyes. "Are you okay?"

She heard him. She tried to answer. But nothing would come out.

She just held on. Pushed back into him. She just breathed - let him breathe for her.

One breath at a time. Trying to come back down to a safe place. Trying to get her legs under her. Trying to live.

Sherri was there. They brought her into their circle.

Annette felt the tears. Tasted the salt.

And wondered what the hell happened next.

19

Annette raced back into the house, barely making it to the bathroom before she threw up her breakfast. A few minutes later, after changing her shirt and brushing her teeth for the second time that morning, she inched her way out of the garage, down the driveway, and out into the street.

Slowly, taking every side road in the neighborhood, she pulled into the parking lot of her school.

It had been two weeks since Annette had stepped through the doors of her school.

It had been two weeks moving from bed to living room chair, and back again.

It had been two weeks of eating pint after pint of ice cream.

It had been two weeks of checking every lock in the house, only to check them once again.

It had been two weeks of saying there was no way in hell she was returning to the school. And yet, here she was.

Sitting here pondering why she was going back to a life she no longer wanted to live.

It was a teacher work day. They'd decided to bring back the staff for a day, to work together to create new plans. The kids would return the following week and undergo training from what the school system decided.

If she'd hated her job before, she didn't even have words for what she felt now.

She sat there staring at the front doors, wondering how she was going to survive.

She fished a cracker out of the package she'd pulled from the cupboard on the way out the door. She bit, chewed, and gagged it down. A little water confirmed she'd quit while she was ahead. She tucked all of it away into her bag. She'd just have to ignore that little growl until lunch.

She'd been dreading this moment for days. But now that she was here, sitting in the parking lot, trying to work up the courage to march back into her classroom, her fears hit her square in her chest. She absently rubbed her skin in the v-neck of her shirt.

She couldn't do this. She just couldn't. It's the only thing that raced through her mind.

She'd been thinking a lot about quitting since returning from the convention. She'd been very quiet since the *event*, as she now called it, turning all her thoughts inward trying to piece together what to do.

But sitting here, looking at her past, something clicked.

This place honestly did feel like her past.

After everything she'd been through, after dreaming bigger dreams, falling hard after the shooting shook her world, and now getting herself back here, she knew she'd had enough.

She knew what she had to do.

She didn't think.

She grabbed her purse but left everything else in her car.

She used her key card to buzz herself into the school.

Teachers were everywhere, huddled together, talking. Trying to pull themselves back to normal.

She passed them all with just a nod, barely a hello. She marched into the front office with only one purpose in mind.

She grabbed a piece of paper from the supply table, took a pen out of her purse, and wrote *I Quit* in big letters. She signed it and moved past the other teachers standing around talking, moved into the head of school's office, and placed it on Principal Robert Neil's desk.

And even as she nestled her paper front and center so he wouldn't miss it, she couldn't help but build up courage as she looked around. A book titled *Surviving a Shooting* was placed on top of several other books with equally disturbing names. Several news articles from local and national news sources were scattered around.

She marched by him on her way out, just as he turned to make his way back into his office. He'd been talking with several men in suits. She recognized one of them from the school board.

Annette kept walking, with only the thought of escape on her mind. She needed out.

"Annette. Annette." He ran after her as she went down the steps outside the front of the building.

She heard him. She knew she had to talk with him. In a different capacity, she actually liked Robert.

He'd been the principal for five years. He'd come from a big city back east, returning home to his roots. He'd grown up in Oregon, and had chosen to raise his family here. He'd been a great fit for the community.

Annette liked his wife. She'd had lunch with her several times. But right now, none of that mattered.

Right now, she only felt like he was the enemy.

She stopped without turning around. "I can't do it, Robert. I can't do this anymore."

He stopped a few feet from her. "I know it's tough. But we've got each other here. We'll work through this. We can't let him win."

Him being the infamous asshole who had destroyed their little world.

Of course, there'd been a reason. In this case, it had been a child custody battle. Lorraine Kirkland, one of the first grade teachers, had been battling with her husband over their kids for more than two years. She'd complained about it multiple times in the teacher's lounge. Everyone knew he'd been a volatile mess the last few months. But no one had ever suspected him capable of doing this.

Nobody was shot. Nobody was hurt. Yet Lorraine was taking the rest of the year off, dealing with the situation. Robert was currently sitting in jail. And their two kids would have to deal with the aftermath for the rest of their lives.

"I know he had a target, Robert. I know he wanted one person. But what about the next time? What happens when the next one enters our school?" She whipped around and met his stare. She dared him to look away.

He held firm. "All I can say is I hope there isn't a next time." His voice was quiet, shaking.

"See, that's the thing. You can't make a promise. You can't really do a thing. All we can do is put in another lock on the door."

"We can do other things ..."

"Like arm our students with hand sanitizer? Do you know Missy Tooney armed herself with the Purell dispenser sitting on the corner of my desk? She was seriously going to whip that at someone if they came through the door. Purell bottle versus semiautomatic. I'll tell you which would win."

His chin dropped towards his chest. His hands reached up, combing through his hair. "I don't know what to say, Annette."

"I know you don't. You honestly have nothing to do with this. I totally respect you and what you have to do here. I get it. I do."

And the funny thing was she did. Life had to go on, or the bad guys won.

But in her world, she'd concluded that the bad guys had simply woken her up.

"I just can't do this anymore. After Curt's cancer scare, after all of *this*, I'm done. This may be stupid; I know it's something I really can't afford to do. But dammit Robert, I'm fifty years old. You can't pay me enough to put up with this anymore. I have to do something else.

"And it's not even just this anymore. It's babysitting the kids who have a crappy home life, trying to get them to care enough to do their homework, being their social worker. It's about trying to get the kids on ADHD medicine to try and pay attention. It's about trying to follow the guidelines of No Child Left Behind. It's about teaching to the test instead of making kids want to learn. And yeah, it's also about wondering every single day I walk through those doors if this will be the day. Here it was. This was my warning sign. The next time could be that much more tragic. And I just don't get paid enough for all of this. Not anymore. I. Just. Can't."

Robert nodded. They stood watching each other, as if they weren't sure what to say. "I'll tell you what. I'm going to hold this for a couple of days.

We're nearing the end of the school year anyway. Take some time." He motioned to her signed note he held in his hands.

"I'm not going to change my mind. I just can't." Something clicked inside her brain. She blurted out, "I've never been more sure of anything in my life."

He nodded again. "I know. But still. I'll have it. Call if you need to. Talk with Curt. Think." He took a step back.

She knew he had other things to do that day. She knew he was being more than kind and fair. "Thanks."

He went back into the school. And she drove home. Ready to start the next chapter.

Annette banged around in her kitchen. She slammed her coffee pot back into its holder, spilling coffee all around. *Shit.*

After she cleaned it up, she threw the rag into her laundry room, missing the basket with a plop a few inches away. A big brown stain spread in all directions, with tiny dark droplets filtering further. *Shit!*

She wasn't sorry for what she'd done. No, not at all. The fact that she'd made it this far said something.

She'd hated her job, like, forever. Everybody knew it. Her parents. Her sister. Her kids. Her friends.

But those people didn't matter. Of course, they'd look at her a little funny. *Are you sure*, they'd say? But in the end, they'd simply nod their heads in agreement, tell her the things she wanted to hear, and ask her what was next?

But Curt. Dammit. Curt was going to have more to say.

He'd start in with the logical stuff. Like how they needed the money. How she'd acted irrationally by quitting on the spot. He'd say all kinds of logical stuff.

Ugh!

She was always the logical one. Always. That's what he'd say.

Like the time she'd questioned his decision to take the job with the bigger landscaping company that serviced the state. It paid more than his current position. He'd focused in on the raise. But very quickly they'd discovered what that "promotion" really meant.

The job worked him fifty or sixty hours a week. The job took an hour or more commuting to each day. The job had almost cost them their marriage.

She'd carefully laid out a plan and presented it to him one night when he'd arrived home late as usual. She put supper on the table in front of him, with her pro and con list right next to it. She'd given him an ultimatum. And within a month, he'd had a different job, the one he currently enjoyed.

She grabbed a piece of paper. A pro and con chart. Perfect!

Pros to quitting:

The job sucked.

She had to look at the terror on little kids faces who were wondering why she had to arm them with pencils and tape dispensers against bad guys with guns. Why would anyone do that as a part of their job description? Definitely a pro to quitting.

And she had to exist year after year without a raise - *budget cuts, you know*. Who would keep doing this job without compensation?

Parents; fielding questions and accusations about how she wasn't treating their little geniuses up to their high expectations had reached a new level of loathing. She'd had a dad transfer his son out of her class earlier in the year because she wouldn't change a C into an A.

And the rules! Every year, having to meet new quotas and figures. One screw up and it could cost her everything. How could you survive with that much stress? No other job had that much stress! Yes, that was definitely a pro for quitting.

Cons to quitting:

The freaking, no good, way too low, salary that no matter how crappy it was, it still paid the bills.

And after she'd lectured him about reducing his income with the other job just a few short years ago, how would he take that they no longer even had her crappy income? That she hadn't consulted him first? That they didn't make this decision together, like the two rational people they were?

Shit.

She got up and paced. Think. Think.

I hated this job. I did.

And we don't have the kids anymore. Not really.

Sure, they still were paying some of the student loans. They'd agreed to that with the kids.

And the medical - yeah, whatever. They'd have that the rest of their lives. Maybe she could negotiate once again and decrease the monthly payment. They'd done it once before.

Maybe she could explain she was out of a job. And they'd give her a break.

And she could pick up an odd job if she needed to. Like a barista at the coffee shop. Or maybe she could work at sales at her favorite store.

Ahh! She flopped down in her chair once again, pulled her feet up under her. *No, no, no.*

If she did that, it would take time away from what she *really* wanted to do. Write.

Remember that. I'm going to be a writer. I AM a writer.

She grabbed her pros list one more time.

This will give me eight solid hours every day to write.

I will find freelance work that pays me for my writing.

I'll get freelance jobs writing while I'm working on my book.

Annette dropped her list back on the table, drained her mug, and took a few deep breaths.

She looked up at the image of the two of them that hung on their wall. Their wedding photo, looking picture-perfect.

She remembered that day like it was yesterday. Two naive kids thinking they could take on the world.

And yet, they'd been so happy. So in love.

Even now, looking at his beautiful face, she felt a tingle deep within. He'd done that to her the moment they'd met.

She'd been working in the coffee shop on campus. And when everyone else had always mumbled or grumbled as they picked up their order, he'd smiled at her and said thanks. Their hands had lingered, touching, as she pushed his takeout cup towards him, and he'd reached out to grab it. They'd stood like that for a minute - or an hour - until her boss had barked a "*get busy*" in her ear.

He'd been there, waiting on the park bench outside the restaurant, when she'd walked out later in the day.

She'd looked at him quizzically, wondering why he was there.

And he'd just popped up in front of her and said, "I found my destiny."

She'd laughed, telling him he was corny. But it had worked.

They'd never been apart since.

It truly was destiny. She couldn't imagine herself with anyone else.

All the good times they'd had, even the crappy times, they were always doable because it was them, together.

"I quit." Annette filled her wine glass with Riesling, then brushed past Curt into the living room. She dropped into her favorite chair and pulled her legs up under her.

"What do you mean, you quit?" Curt was in hot pursuit right behind her.

He sat on the edge of the coffee table, and leaned forward, resting his elbows on his knees, his hands under his chin.

She stared at him over the edge of her glass. She took a long sip, hoping it would push her fear down with it. She'd told herself over and over she wouldn't cry, wouldn't get emotional. Not when she knew how he would react. *I won't cry. I won't.*

She breathed deep, followed it with a heavy sigh. "I quit. I marched into the front office, wrote *I quit* on a piece of paper, signed it, and gave it to Robert. Then I came home."

She'd really done that. She still couldn't believe it. It had felt almost like a dream.

But when she walked through the front doors, she knew there was no way she'd ever be able to work there again.

She knew it was what she had to do. But she hated the look on Curt's face. She could tell he was desperately trying to hold it all together. To not go off like he really wanted to do. She'd seen that look before. He'd had it more than once in their marriage; the exasperated *what the fuck now* look.

He dropped his head further into his hands, scrubbed them over his face, as if trying to push his budding headache away. Or trying to figure out how to hold it all together before the wrong words flew out of his mouth.

Or maybe a little of both.

He leaned further, towards her, took her glass away and put it down on the table behind him. He grabbed both of her hands and held them in his own. "Okay."

That shocked her. "Okay?"

He nodded. "Okay." He said it with conviction.

And she burst into tears.

It wasn't a calm cry. No, she was done with that. After all the emotion of the day, of the past two weeks, she finally was ready to let go.

She sobbed.

She cried tears she didn't know she had.

Curt stepped away for a moment, just long enough to pull a tissue box from the bathroom before returning to her. He reached down and pulled her up. Then he fell into the chair, taking her with him. He just pulled her into him and let her go.

"It's all right." She pushed into his touch, the feel of his hand as he rubbed up and down her back.

If only she could believe that. She wanted to, with all her heart.

But she was fifty, somehow feeling like she was going on ninety. She was so tired of it all. Of the world. Of people fighting. Of the constant bickering and arguing over gun laws.

She was sick of it all.

That asshole had marched into her little world and changed it forever. He had purchased a gun days before, even with a restraining order on his record, filed by his wife months before.

It didn't make sense. None of it made sense.

And she was sick of trying to make it so.

The more she sobbed, the more she felt her strength, bubbling up inside, telling her that she was going to be alright.

She'd made the choice to live, to fight, to do what she wanted to do.

And with a little work, she'd be fine, they'd be fine.

She'd do what she needed to do. And she'd find a way to do it.

Because she no longer had a choice.

She'd quit. She'd have hours every day to do what needed to be done.

She'd show Curt. She'd show her kids. She'd show the world.

She was going to do this. She was.

She'd find a way to replace her income as quickly as possible. She'd write so well, the work would flow in.

And she'd start on that tomorrow.

Right after she melted into her husband for just a little longer.

20

"I'll get it." Annette knew who it would be. A quick peak through the window told her it was true.

"Hi." Sherri was on the other side of the storm door, looking … Annette couldn't quite put her finger on it. Pissed? Upset? Sad? "Are you mad at me?"

"Can I come in?" Sherri nodded to the door.

"Of course. I'm sorry." Annette unlocked the door and moved aside so she could enter.

Sherri dropped her coat and bag in the entryway, before moving into the kitchen and filling up a mug of coffee. She turned and leaned into the counter, eyeing Annette as she entered the room tentatively.

"You quit."

Annette nodded.

"We're you planning on telling me, or did you think me hearing it through the grapevine would be fine?"

Annette could hear the hurt in her voice. She rushed up to her and gave her a hug. "No. No! I would never do that to hurt you. You know that. It just kind of … happened. And then I rushed out. And I panicked a bit when I got home, trying to think how I was going to tell Curt. And you were still working. And I had to think about …"

Sherri pushed back, looking her in the eyes. "A spur of the moment thing?" She grinned.

Annette laughed, though it sounded more like a barking seal even to her own ears. She couldn't stop the tears that started trailing down her cheeks.

Sherri grabbed her in another fierce hug. "Hey, it'll be okay."

"I know. I have all these ideas. And Curt wasn't as freaked out as I thought he'd be. And I know I'll get something; I'll find work. I know this was meant to be." She blabbered on a few more seconds, enjoying the comfort of her friend's hug. She stopped, pulled away and slapped at Sherri's hands playfully. "And this is all your fault anyway. Getting my spirits up by taking me to that damn seminar."

Annette filled up her own mug with coffee, refilled Sherri's, then they took their favorite seats at the kitchen island.

"I couldn't believe it. I mean, we've talked about it for years. But I was shocked when Deb walked into the teachers' lounge and announced what you'd done. I think we all were. I had to ask her to repeat herself."

"I was wondering how everyone took it. I kind of surprised myself even. And Robert," Annette put her hand up to her mouth, trying to stifle her grin. "You should have seen his face. The more shocked he looked, the more he egged me on. I seriously think he added fuel to my fire. He kept looking at me as if I'd gone mad. And it made me *mad*. He even told me he'd hold my resignation for a few days in case I changed my mind."

"Would you? Change your mind?"

"No. No way. The hard part's done. I actually quit. And I'll tell you, I feel freer. A little petrified too." Annette bit back the terror that had had a grip on her since the day before. She picked up her mug and sipped. She hadn't slept a wink. Her brain wouldn't stop creating plans in her mind. She'd even gotten up twice to write her ideas down.

"Hey, how are you?" Curt walked into the kitchen, giving Sherri a hug. He grabbed a mug before leaning in beside his wife. "Can you believe what she did?"

He hip bumped Annette, put an arm around her and pulled her in with a kiss on the top of her head. They chatted for a few minutes, going through the process once again.

"I'll leave you two to talk." He looked at Annette. "I'm going to run to the store. Need anything?"

"No, I'm good."

They watched as he disappeared back into the house.

"He seems good with it."

Annette sighed. "He is. For the most part. He shocked me a bit. He didn't yell or lecture or anything. I'd built up this entire conversation in my head. And then when I carried on and started building my case, he just sat down in front of me, took my hands and said okay. I still can't believe it."

"Well, it's not like he had a choice. You had already put in your notice. Such as it was."

"True."

"But Curt's a good guy. After all you guys have been through, I can see how he'd be okay with it all. He's not the angry person some people are; more of a go-with-the-punches person."

"Yep, that's my Curt. Though I have to say, I really thought he'd push back a little harder. I thought I'd have to justify it a bit more, even if I have been talking about it for months."

"I saw his face that day. The way he was looking at you when I walked up. *After*. With that expression, I don't think he'd ever argue with you over quitting."

Annette just nodded. "I know. We never even spoke much about it. Still haven't. Others want to dive into the details. We don't. He just touches me, holds on. If I'm near, he won't let go of my hand. It's our new normal."

"That's not a bad thing. To have that kind of love at our age."

"I know. But I hate how we got here."

Sherri leaned forward. "It's called life. This is where we are. This kind of shit doesn't hold everyone together. It tears some people apart."

Annette thought for a moment. She nodded. Yeah, she knew that was true.

Over the past two weeks, she'd tried to put herself into Lorraine's position. What must she be going through? To have her world so completely ripped apart? To have a husband sitting in jail for completely losing it, for destroying their family, for shattering the tranquility of the community.

And what he'd done to their kids' lives ... they'd be impacted forever. They were small, still in grade school. But this kind of thing effects a person forever. They'd always be trying to outrun the ghosts of their father.

As bad as Annette felt, for as low as she'd gone, for the rollercoaster ride up and down, she'd never be as low as all that. Because deep down inside, she knew her highs and lows would never be that low. "I can't even imagine what Lorraine must be going through. Have you heard from her?"

"No. I guess Robert has spoken to her. She's with her kids at her mother's up in Washington. I don't think we're going to learn much more for a while. She's off for the rest of the year. Who knows if she'll return in the fall?"

Annette breathed in deep, blew out her breath. Yeah, at least she wasn't that low. She shook her head, coming back to her reality. "Part of me is so grateful right now I pushed through and had my website developed. I think it's helping me piece together what's next. I really have to focus on getting some gigs."

"Any ideas?"

"Yeah, actually. I'd been looking a lot anyway. You know, *before*. I've found a few freelance sites I'm going to try. I can always look at job boards; do you know they have boards specifically for work at home? I've found quite a few content jobs. So I'll play around with that too. I'm not going to be as picky right now. I'm going to spread out my options and apply for anything I can, just to get some money in. As things work out, I can be more selective."

Sherri nodded. "Sounds like you have a plan."

She did. Annette tried not to show it, not to Sherri, not yet, but part of her was more excited than she'd been in years. She had a chance to do something fabulous with her life. Screw all the crap she'd lived with for the past twenty-five years. This was her chance to come back to life.

"I know we haven't had our Thursday meetings in a couple of weeks. Maybe we should start those in once again."

Sherri smiled. "I'd like that." She bit her lip, and sniffed, holding back the tears.

"Hey," Annette reached over and laid a hand on Sherri's arm.

"It's just that I've missed you. I know I have everyone else at work. But it's been you and me for so long. What am I going to do without you?"

"You're going to figure out what's next in your life too. There are only a few weeks left before summer break anyway. You're going to do something fantastic this summer. Maybe a retreat. Did you go back to your painting class this past weekend? I never asked"

Sherri's head dropped. "No. I just couldn't."

"Why? I thought you loved the people? I thought you enjoyed the class?"

"I do. It's just …"

Annette sat back and watched a whirlwind of emotions cross Sherri's face. She waited, wanting to give her space to think. She knew she'd jumped quickly, but not everyone would go at her pace.

"It's just I've lost my spirit. I just don't know if I can paint."

"Oh, come on. Maybe it would be good for you. Let out some of the tension."

"That's what Wesley said. He called and left a message, told me everyone was thinking of me. He said I should come, and just do what I can do."

"Well there you go. I think you should do it. You enjoyed it so much. *Before.*"

"I did. But maybe now isn't the right time. I'm thinking I'm going to take it easy. Maybe put all this off until the fall. Tanner and I talked about going away for a week - can you believe it? My son said he'd do a trip with me this summer. Maybe that's what I need. A chance to do nothing. To just sit back and figure life out." She rambled on repeating many of the things she did every day. Things she'd done for years.

"Are you done yet?

Sherri looked confused. "What?"

"You've just talked about doing the same old shit you do every year. Weren't you the one who talked about change? Weren't you the one who found the Fabulous at Fifty conference and forced me to come along?"

"I wouldn't say *forced* …"

"Weren't you the one who had big dreams? Weren't you the one who said we should find a way out of the hostile school environment we were both growing weary of?"

"Well, somebody's gotta stay there."

"Really? A *shooting* didn't wake you up? Our worst fears came true, and you want to walk back into it?"

"Yes. No. I don't know."

"What kind of safety procedures are you going to have to go through now? An armed security guard? Or maybe they'll double up and give you two? Is there going to be a metal detector? Are you going to have to wear body armor? What? Tell me!" Annette whipped out of her chair, knocking it backwards to the floor. She slammed her coffee mug down into the sink, then turned back into Sherri, just a few inches from her face. "Are you really just going to go through with all of this as if nothing has changed? Are you going to throw away everything we've talked about?"

Sherri backed up, inched her way around the kitchen island, putting a few feet between them. "Look, I don't have to answer to you. And I don't have to make a decision. Not now. Not any time soon. I'm just not ready."

"So you're going to hide?"

"I'm not hiding. I'm not." But her voice trailed off, and Annette knew she had her thinking.

She slammed her fist to the counter. "Do something, dammit. Don't just fall back to your old routine. I liked who you were when you painted. I like who you were when you dragged me to that seminar. I like the fact that we've both woken up enough to want something more. And I don't want some asshole taking that all away from you."

"And you think I do? I'd give anything to go back in time. But I can't. I can only do the best I can do."

"Wake up, Sherri. Don't let him win. Live. Do something fun this summer. Make a plan. Anything - jeez, just do something!"

Annette bit her tongue and sucked in a big breath. She let it out slowly. She watched her friend, near tears. She should say something, she should. But she just couldn't. She really meant what she'd said.

Then Annette watched something that had never happened in their relationship before; Sherri walked out the door without a word.

She left. And never looked back.

Annette bit her lip, holding back the tears. She suddenly felt so alone. Like she'd lost everything. But she couldn't go after her, wouldn't. She truly believed Sherri had taken a giant step backwards.

And she wanted her to think about it.

Why had life turned so difficult?

21

Sherri sat in her car, looking at a place she'd fallen in love with, and was now scared to death to enter. She sat there watching the other artists - women who had become her friends - and yet felt jittery joining up with them.

The funny thing is she wasn't quite sure why she didn't want to go in. She loved the women. She loved painting and creating. She'd even had numerous conversations with herself on her budding friendship with Wesley.

But everywhere she'd gone since the event, people questioned her. She hated it.

How do you feel?

What was it like?

Were you scared?

She'd grown weary of saying what she was supposed to say. The things society dictated in order to remain with the people around you. I'm fine. Yes, it was scary.

Instead, she'd wanted to throw her hands in the air and scream and …

And what?

She let her forehead fall to her steering wheel. She was so tired of this internal conversation going round and round and round …

Knock, knock.

She jumped, bumping her head against the window.

Wesley was leaning down, looking at her with a concerned look. "I'm sorry. I didn't mean to scare you."

She eyed him, debated for half a second, before touching the button so the window could glide down. "Sorry. I was just … thinking."

He nodded. "Come on in and paint."

She sat there for a half of a second longer, and then took his advice. She rolled her window back up and grabbed her bag. Then locked her doors and double checked to make sure they were locked.

She stood for a moment, assessing what Wesley was going to say. Was he going to start in like so many others; nothing but questions and more questions? She bit her tongue, waiting for his action.

But then he surprised her. He took two steps, turned, waiting for her to fall in line. "I started getting out the blues and greens you love. Unless you want to add a different color today, you should be able to get right to it. You're also in for a real treat. I've put everyone's completed paintings up in the front hall - a mini art gallery today. I just love having everyone's work on display. We'll take a little time at break to walk through them, maybe comment a little on what they mean."

He opened the door, holding it for her to enter. "Wait till you see what Bo's been up to." He grinned.

Bo. The cackling eighty-year-old that surprised all of them every single week. She'd been the most boisterous with her expressionism. The big, bold colors she always chose. And when they shared stories on their breaks, she left all of them speechless. They'd all agreed; Bo was their role model. The person they all wanted to be when they hit their eightieth birthdays.

Sherri got to her station, dropped her purse on the shelf, and tied her apron around her. She kept her eye on the rest of the class, taking in their behavior.

None of them seemed focused on her. None of them rushed her, expressing their concern. And as the minutes ticked by, she found herself breathing a little easier.

She went to join the group, who were pulling out mats and blankets and getting ready for their meditation. Her spot was waiting for her in the middle, surrounded by the women she'd grown to love.

She could hardly believe their six weeks was almost up. She'd already talked to Wesley about continuing, maybe with the advanced class. She knew some of the others were considering it too.

And she really was excited to talk to him today. She'd grown fond of their time together.

With meditation about to begin, she walked to her place, past Bo's, and she stopped and stared. She bit back a smile. And then started laughing.

Bo hopped up from her spot on the floor, met Sherri at her station. "You like?"

Sherri giggled. "Ohmigod. Is it …"

Bo nodded. "I call it *Sex*."

And that was unquestionably what Sherri would call it too. It was abstract. But she clearly got the impression it was a male and female in the heat of the moment. It was bold and breathtaking. It made her feel as if she was peeking in on intimacy between two people who loved one another.

"Bo, you never cease to amaze me."

"Or anyone else. I may even keep this up and see if I can get a showing at a gallery. Wesley told me my work is very original, and he thought it could do well in some places."

Sherri looked over to Wesley, who was leaning against the windows, taking in the conversation, a grin from ear to ear.

Bo grabbed her hand and pulled. "Come on, I think teacher over there is going to get his panties in a wad if we don't take our seats." They both dropped to their cushions.

Sherri took a quick look at everyone. They all held her eyes for a moment, offering support. Yet they also told her this was a safe zone, and she wouldn't have to talk if she didn't want to.

A quick glance back at Wesley told her they'd all agreed they would support, not barrage her with questions. And once again, she breathed deep.

At least here, at least for now, she was safe.

Her old life might not be what it was, but she knew she had love and support around her in many different ways.

And for at least today, that meant she could do what she came here to do. She could paint.

Sherri stood back and looked at what she'd created. Her work had always been more subdued. Not today.

She'd even gone back to the paint station and selected a few reds and oranges.

Mixed with her standard blue and green hues she always preferred, the bright color popped from the canvas. And yet it spoke volumes, it said exactly what she was feeling.

"I love it." Bo was the first to step up and look at her work with her. "I especially like your brush strokes here." She motioned off to the right. Then she turned to her, pulled her in for a hug. "Tomorrow's another day, honey. Always remember there's good in everything. Everything's for a reason. You just have to find it."

She left Sherri a little shellshocked. She sucked in, fighting back tears. She watched as she walked out the door.

One by one, every woman in the classroom silently came up and hugged her, before they left for the day.

Not one word. Everyone seemed to understand that she just couldn't talk. They'd let her do what she needed to do. And for that she was grateful.

She took her time washing up her brushes and screwing the tops back on the paint. By the time she'd pulled her apron off and had her work station in order, Wesley had appeared with two mugs of tea. It had become somewhat of a ritual. She was glad to see he assumed they'd continue with it today.

He handed one to her, then made his way to the sunroom and plopped into his chair. She followed, selecting her favorite.

The sun was getting lower in the sky. The color in the trees was deeper, many of the leaves already in place.

She eyed a flock of geese making their way across the blue sky. Such an unusual color for this time of year in the Pacific Northwest. Normally it was nothing but rain. But this year the temperatures had spiked early, and the skies had remained clear. Somehow it seemed to make her mood just a little brighter, especially today.

As she sipped the last of her tea, she leaned forward and set it down on the table in front of her. Then she kicked off her shoes and pulled her legs up underneath. "You never really know how you'll react until it happens."

He didn't say a word, just turned and watched her.

"The stupidest thoughts went through my head. I had no idea what was happening, none of us did. We're sitting in a locked classroom with the lights off, barricaded in by the desk I'd pushed up against the door. The kids were crouched down behind tables, trying desperately to be quiet. All this training had me crawling on the floor, coaching my kids to remember what they were supposed to do. It was like I was another person, just going through the motions." She looked at him, studied his dark brown eyes.

He'd come to be such a good friend to her over the past few weeks. Their Saturday conversations had become the highlight of her week.

She'd never questioned if it was more. But she couldn't deny there was a pull between them.

As she watched him, she realized that since the shooting, this feeling was the only thing that kept her going.

She loved her life. She loved her friends. She loved her family. She even loved the house she was renting. She didn't hate her job. But she loved teaching. She loved the community. She loved being active. And she was only just starting to realize she could do that in different ways.

But Wesley, he was bringing something new to her life. And looking at him now, she'd wondered how she'd missed it before. Lust. Good old-fashioned lust.

She was fifty. And it had been so long since she'd had someone in her life. She'd told herself it didn't matter. But after the past couple of weeks, she knew that was no longer true.

Screw acting my age! Go big or go home!

Sherri moved over, sat near him on the loveseat he'd always preferred. She faced him, leaned on her arm that dug into the back of the couch. "Can I ask you something?"

"Of course."

"How many people do you invite here after class, to join you in your sunroom for tea?"

He studied her for just a moment. He reached out, touching the back of her hand that was lying between them. "Just you."

"And why is that?" She wanted to hear him say it. To have him say he felt whatever this was. That it wasn't just her.

"I find myself fascinated with the human spirit. Have you ever noticed that there are different people in your life; acquaintances, some who turn into friends. And then there are the others, your soul keepers."

She loved the way he spoke. His thick, rich tone. The way he rolled his r's, not really in a way that would say he was anywhere but from America. But there was a certain catch to his pronunciation. She'd always picked up on stuff like that; call that the teacher in her.

She leaned forward. "Define soul keeper."

He mirrored her movements. "It's a person you feel instantly connected to.

Like somehow you've known each other before. You feel it in your soul, from the time you first meet."

She wasn't quite sure about that. She'd never really thought about how she got to know the people in her life. But she found his definition filled her with wonder. "Do you have a lot of soul keepers in your life?"

He drained his cup, then put it down on the table in front of him. "I've only met three so far. I don't think it's possible to have a lot. You must have a deep relationship to be a soul keeper. But they sure pack a punch when you meet them."

Sherri watched his eyes as they held her own. Was that what this was? Is that what she was feeling? She'd noticed it from the moment she first met him. A familiar feeling, like he was an old friend.

She'd noticed it when she walked in. The smell, something familiar, yet she had no idea what it was. The way he kept his studio was similar to the order she placed in her own home. Even the sunroom, where they were sitting now, was a room she'd give anything to have.

"You feel it too."

She felt it now, sitting there with him. She'd known him for just a few weeks, as a friend. And yet somehow, it felt like more.

"Yes. I felt it immediately. The first time I walked up to you and introduced myself."

She looked down at his fingers, which were currently tracing along the back of her hand. She moved her hand, put her palm up next to his and interlaced their fingers. It fascinated her, the way their hands molded together.

Then her eyes caught his movement, as he came even closer.

Inches from her, his dark eyes smoldered. She got lost in the story they told her. And all she could think about was learning more.

He gave a quick nod of his head, asking permission.

She tipped her head slightly, moved for a better fit.

And just like that, she melted into him. Just a light kiss, touching, tasting. Warming up to something more.

22

Holy, freaking, shit. Every cell in Sherri's body suddenly jolted alive.

She'd felt a connection to Wesley from the moment she'd clicked on his site.

But not once had she ever envisioned kissing him.

Nor had she ever fantasized about how good it would feel.

The old her would never act in such a bold way.

The old her would have remained in her chair, never moved to the sofa next to him.

The old her would never have flirted in quite the way she just did.

And the old her would never - NEVER - have responded quite the way she was to this man's kiss.

And now all that was going through her mind was: *why the hell not?*

Sure, she'd talked about dating with her friends. She'd went out here and there, mostly with friends.

Somewhere in the back of her mind, she'd thought her love life was over.

But as he nipped at the corner of her mouth, she felt the blood rushing to places she'd almost forgotten she had.

It had been months since she'd even remotely been attracted to anyone. Outside of her puppy love infatuation with Mr Nevins. But that didn't count; most of the female staff had a crush on Mr Nevins. What wasn't there to love?

Sherri slid her fingers into his hair, playing with the curls at the nape of his neck. She'd noticed them week after week. But she'd never imagined *doing this*.

It was like she was waking up for the first time after a very long sleep.

Their fingers remained connected. She'd tried to pull away, to be able to wrap her other arm around him. But he'd held steadfastly attached. His thumb gently caressed up and down her finger. Slid lightly over her palm. Back up, over and over. It was tantalizing. It was beginning to make her ache.

Finally, he pulled his fingers free, reached up and framed her face with his hands. He took her lips, gently biting, teasing. Then he trailed down her neck.

It was as if he were taking notes. He moved, kissed, nuzzled, then moved forward. She whimpered when he'd touch her just the right way. He'd give her a little more attention, then continue on his journey.

Down and around, over and over again.

Where her other dates dove in quickly, Wesley didn't seem to be in a hurry. In fact, he seemed quite content to remaining where they were. He seemed to enjoy every tortuous moment.

And she discovered it was the biggest turn on she'd ever experienced.

It almost felt … naughty. Like they were two teenagers making out in the basement of their parents' home. Like all they wanted was each other yet were still a little too nervous to move beyond.

Wesley made his way from one side of her neck to the other, and back again, kissing her over and over. All she could do was brace herself, to stay sane, while his sweet torture made her shiver from her head to her toes.

She had so much whirling through her brain. She felt like one big lightbulb, with light flowing out in every direction. Every node was lit up. Every cell in her body was screaming, more, more!

Then slowly, a switch flipped. She was fifty.

What was this? What the hell was she doing?

Did she want love again? Did she want a new career? Did she want a life with someone? Did she want to move somewhere else in the world? Did she …

She sucked in a breath and pulled away. She breathed deep, trying to catch her breath. A feeling of panic, overwhelm, caught her off guard.

"You okay?" He anchored her by twining his fingers with her and pulling her in.

His eyes bounced back and forth, taking in her mood. Watching as emotion ran deep within her eyes.

"I don't know …"

"Tell me."

How did she explain this? "I just saw my life flash before my eyes." She gave a nervous laugh. "That sounds crazy, doesn't it," she half asked, half tried to convince herself.

He reached up, grabbed a strand of her hair and tucked it behind her ear. Every touch to her cheek started a new fire. She lit up with every connection he made.

She studied him, bouncing from eye to eye, almost trying to reach deep into his soul. *What is this?*

"I have no idea."

She shook her head. "Wait, what?" She hadn't thought she said that out loud.

He chuckled. "You didn't. Say that out loud, I mean. But I can see it in your eyes. You're wondering what the hell that was."

"Exactly." She pulled away, stood up, and walked over to the window. She watched the shadows play amongst the trees for just a second before turning back around. "Wesley, I have no idea how that just happened. Or how we got here. Or where this is going. Or …"

He was by her side before she could finish her sentence. With both hands alongside her face, he pulled her in and planted a kiss on her lips. "Let's sit, okay?"

She nodded and returned to her chair; a safe distance from where he sat on the loveseat.

Wesley sat back with his arms resting on his thighs. "Tell me what you're thinking."

Sherri debated where to begin.

She'd been caught up in the whirlwind of her life for the past two weeks. And no matter what she'd thought about Wesley, no matter where her fantasies had taken her, she'd never pictured what just happened just a minute ago.

She wasn't even sure she was thinking straight after all she'd been through. The last thing she wanted to do was bring someone else into the picture.

So she started there.

"I've been through hell and back this past couple of weeks. I never in a million years thought I would ever be one of *them*; the teachers who could add school shooting to their resume. I mean, we train for it. All the time. Technically we're prepared. But I never really thought it would happen to me. I guess all teachers say that until they join the *club*. But no matter how much I thought about it, I never really thought it would be me. Does that make sense?"

Wesley nodded. He cocked his head, just a bit, ready to listen even more.

"But then it did. And I can't even tell you everything that's gone through my mind. It's like at first, it was all about life and death. I imagined everyone around me dying. What I would do without the ones I love. What I'd do if something happened to my kids; my classroom kids. And then it transferred to my son, Tanner," a tiny sob escaped her. She gave a couple of short breaths to get back on track.

"Because no parent should ever go through that. No teacher should ever have to deal with that. I went through all of this mind-shit the past couple of weeks, trying to piece it all together. I spent a few days up at my son's place, just hanging. Doing nothing. We talked. That's about it. Then I came home. And sat. And did nothing. And thought. About nothing and everything. I can't really describe it in words. It's just I've had this life-changing experience and I pulled off the path for a bit. Like I've shut down and turned everything off."

"I get that. You've been through a hell of a shock."

"And then we went back in to the school for a day, just us teachers, to decide what to do next. Do we reopen the school? Do we continue where we left off? And right then and there, my best friend quit. She turned in her resignation, and that was that.

"And she'd been talking about it forever. I always knew someday she'd do it. But I didn't. She's been talking about it for months. And after going to that retreat in California a couple of months ago, she's really gotten serious with her writing. I'm proud of her. But somewhere in the back of my mind, I never thought she'd do it. At least not now, not this quick.

"But she did. And she's excited. And she'll do well. That only pushes me further into thinking about what I want. And I really have no idea, I don't. I love painting. The past few weeks have woken up a part of me I didn't even know existed anymore. It's shocked me into a new reality. It's made me think about things I haven't thought about in a long time. I guess I feel that's been my life lately. Eyes wide shut; eyes wide open. And nothing in between. All or nothing. What it's doing to my insides ..." She moved her hands up to her chest, taking a breath, feeling her heartbeat speed up.

What it was doing to her soul.

It reminded her of when she was first out of school, trying to figure out what to do with her life.

But that had all been about the future. About starting a career, getting married, having kids.

This, this was different. This was about her second act. It felt more personal. Like she could do anything in this great big world, and it would matter only to her. She no longer had parents. Her son was in a good place. She hadn't thought about a lover in a long time. She was financially set. She knew she could easily have thirty or even forty more good years. The world was literally her oyster, and she could do whatever she wanted.

And that's why it made everything such a mess!

She wasn't sure she had time for romance. She wasn't sure what she wanted next. So she changed direction altogether.

"I fought with Annette. My best friend."

"I'm sorry."

"It was horrible. I walked out on her."

"I'm sure she'll understand."

"I know she will. Eventually. But she said some mean things."

"Did it hit a little too close to home?"

She shook her head lightly, but she couldn't deny. "I know she was right. I was the one who dragged her to California. I was the one who kept saying we needed to change. And then she went up and did something about all of it, and I was upset. She left me."

A small sob escaped. She wrapped her arms around herself, and said in a quieter voice, "She left me."

"Okay," he kept his face neutral, not sure where she was going. "Tell me what all that means to you."

She thought for a moment. "I don't know. I'm not planning on quitting teaching, not like she did. I just can't. But that doesn't mean I don't want to do something different. I just have no idea what. And I do have options. I'll be off for the summer. I know I talked with you a bit about it last time, *before*. Is there some way I can continue here? Or maybe something else you could recommend? I have no idea what I should do. I just know I'll go mad if I stay here, like this, doing nothing."

She bit her lip, holding back, waiting for him to make the next move.

"I've got just the thing." Then he popped off the couch and disappeared, returning with a brochure in hand.

"It's a villa just outside of Rome. It belongs to a friend of my mine; she's great. She and her husband own a ranch in Italy and she offers summer retreats. You stay on site, and she offers both instruction and seclusion, helping you define what your artistry means to you." He held out the brochure and placed it into her awaiting fingers.

"Italy," she said half to herself, as she unfolded and read. And quickly fell in love.

"It's perfect." Because it was. She had the same feeling as when she'd found Wesley's class. "It's just what I need."

Wesley nodded. "You'll love it. And I think it will do you some good. To get away from all of *this* for a bit."

Yep, getting rid of *all of this* was just what she needed. Though staring at Wesley, she felt a tiny pang at the thought of leaving him.

"It's kind of late. Do you think she still has room?"

He reached over and took back the brochure. Then popped his phone out of his pocket. A few punches at the keyboard and he held it up to his ear. He paced near the window as he spoke in broken Italian interlaced with English. She could just make out what he was saying. Within seconds, she realized - she was going to Italy.

"It's all set. Francesca is expecting you. You just have to connect when you get home. Email her and it's yours. You're on your way."

Just like that, her summer plans were made.

She was going to Italy.

She was going to paint.

She was going to explore.

23

Annette slipped on her jeans. She stared at herself in the mirror.

Jeans. She was actually wearing something other than her yoga pants and comfy sweatshirt. How long had it been?

Day after day, she got up and did the same thing.

Get up. Kiss Curt goodbye and pretend she was going to have a productive day. Dawdle in the kitchen having breakfast and making tea. Read through job boards, send out a handful of resumes and proposals. Then sit back and surf.

Rinse. Repeat.

Her life was already feeling a bit hum-drum and way out of control. And it'd only been a few weeks since she'd quit.

But not today. Today, she was making a change.

She'd started reading self-help blogs and had several bookmarked about becoming a writer. Her favorite, a lifestyle blog, had made a suggestion about getting more done. *Get out of the house*, it declared. *Change up your normal routine.*

So that's what she intended to do. She'd decided to spend the morning working in her favorite coffee shop.

Today would be different. It would.

She parked, pulled up the hood on her raincoat, and ran through the drizzle to find the little shop buzzing with noise and excitement. Annette glanced around to the tables filled with people typing away, earbuds in place. At other tables, people were meeting, laughing, making deals.

She bit her lip to keep the grin from spreading across her face.

Just what I needed.

She breathed deep. *Ah ...* The smell of success. *Her* success.

This truly was what she needed. Maybe now she'd quit being sick of everything.

Of her house.

Her pajamas.

The bills that stared up at her from her kitchen counter.

Her office that was growing a little too confined by the day.

Her website that just sat there, blink-blink. Staring at her and trying to tell her she'd spent a lot of money. The least she could do is make enough to pay off her credit card bill.

She hated her email box, it always had more junk in it than anything else.

Why, oh why, couldn't it have just one piece of good news?

Just one thing that said: You've done it! You've found work!

Maybe today would be the day.

Because I deserve it ...

She ignored the two little back and forth voices in her head, ordered a bagel and a coffee - toasted with cream cheese, please. She knew it was a splurge, one she couldn't afford anymore. Not on a regular basis. But this was going to be her office for the morning. Her toasted bagel was rent.

There was just no way in hell she could sit at her desk, in her home, one more day without going absolutely insane.

She bit into the creamy goodness, turned on her computer, and waited for it to boot.

She pulled up her profile in Freelance, Upwork, and OnlineWriters just to see if she'd won any of her bids. No. And no.

With a deep sigh, she started hunting, typing, all over again.

She pulled up ads looking for writers. Answered a few queries. She perused Monster and LinkedIn until she thought she'd scream.

How the hell did those *I Made A Million In Thirty Days* articles make it seem so easy?

Maybe teaching wasn't such a bad thing ...

"Hi, Ms Hinton. Annette, right?"

Annette looked up to a smiling face hovering in front of her table, a guy she recognized from somewhere. "Yes."

"I thought that was you. Ben. Ben Mitchell. You had my daughter Clara in your class two years ago. Rachel's my wife."

"Ben, hi. Sorry, it's been awhile. I didn't know you without your wife." The game of *who are you* was getting more difficult with age. She always had parents coming up to her. Sometimes the kids too, after they'd grown up. It always took a minute to place the face.

"I get it. I travel a lot."

"How is Clara? Does she like middle school? I've seen Rachel a few times at meetings, but I never get to ask her how Clara is."

"Clara's great." A cloud fell over his face. "Does it ever get any easier?"

When he saw her puzzled look, he quickly went on, "The teenage years."

Annette laughed. "Ah, I see you've met your diva daughter."

"It's spooky. I never knew anyone could change like that. She really scared me this morning. The yelling. The crying."

"She transforms before your eyes."

"Yes!"

Annette had to hold a hand over her mouth to stop from giggling. Curt had been the same way when their daughter had hit puberty. "You had brothers, didn't you?"

He cocked his head. "That's what my wife says. You're telling me this is normal?"

"Yeah. That's why I taught elementary."

He laughed. "I totally get that."

He hung there, looking at her. She'd checked her email, and was almost done with her proposals. She decided a little distraction couldn't hurt. "Would you like to sit?"

"Um," he glanced at his watch. "Sure, just for a minute. I'm meeting someone here in ten minutes. But I can chat until he gets here." He dropped his notebook to the table and slipped his coat over the back of the chair.

"I heard about you quitting." He looked at her guiltily. "Sorry, small town. Rachel mentioned it after the last parent association meeting."

It's not like she was hiding it. Still, she wondered how many people talked about how she'd left. "I get it. I'm sure I was the talk of the district. I just couldn't do it anymore."

He shook his head. "No. Rightfully so, *the shooting* is the talk of the district. But Rachel said you are on a pedestal now. A lot of the teachers talk about how brave you were to quit like you did. Most wished they could. You did it. There's something to be said for that."

Annette swallowed, forcing down her emotions. She had no idea her old friends spoke of her like that. She figured they all thought she was crazy.

"I'd talked about it for years. And it got harder. *After.*"

He merely nodded.

After. The word that connected everyone in town. Nobody was left untouched.

Ben glanced at his watch, then quickly glanced at the door. "What are you doing now?"

"I'd always wanted to write a novel. I'm working on that. But I'm trying to pick up some writing jobs too. At least until I get my first book out."

There, she'd said it, just like all the training programs said.

Say it with force.

Say it as if you believe it.

Say it with intention.

Say it as if you're already there.

"Wow. That's always been on my resolution list too. Someday, I'd love to write a novel. But for now..." he shrugged his shoulders. "Gotta pay the bills. What are you writing?"

"It's a mystery, with a little spy and espionage built in. I developed the characters and plot over a year ago. Now I'm finally getting down to writing the chapters."

It was the truth. Sort of.

She really did have the characters and plot mapped out. Sure, there were holes in it. She didn't have a solid plan. But the basics, they were there.

"That's my favorite kind. I love James Patterson. Lee Child is good. And I love David Baldacci."

"I know. They're great, right?"

"Well, when you're published, I'll buy your book. I'll say I knew you when."

She felt a sudden warmth fill her, from a man she barely knew. She'd heard a similar phrase several times since she'd quit. She really did love her small community more than ever.

"Thank you."

"Sure. Are you publishing short stories for now?"

"Um, yeah, I'm trying. I'm also trying to pick up freelance work. A lot of companies are looking for writers. It'd help if I could get a few regular gigs."

"Like website work? Posting on Facebook and such? Or blog writing?"

She wasn't one to argue at this point. "Yes."

"Hmm." Ben picked up his phone. "I may have a connection for you. Our company works with an ad agency. And they work with all kinds of companies here in the Pacific Northwest. Just last week at a meeting, my account manager was talking about how difficult it was to find good writers who could write online copy. His packages include blog articles, and he said he wished he could find more people who could write. You being a teacher …" His grin was infectious.

"I can only imagine his pain. At least elementary kids have an excuse of youth. Some of the work the high school teachers talk about …" She shuddered at the thought. "Plus I've seen it in some of the sites I follow. A lot of the writing is flat out bad."

"And yet it's still up there, on reputable sites."

"Exactly. Sometimes I wonder what's going to happen in the future when nobody can spell or create a sentence with good grammar."

"Drives you crazy, right?"

"You have no idea." That really was one of her pet peeves.

He tapped his phone a few times. "Why don't you call Brian Phelps. He's with Phelps Digital Group. Just tell him I told you to call. Here's his number."

Ben gave her a few ideas on projects they'd worked on.

She soaked the information up like a sponge. Maybe this would lead to work!

Ben waved to a man entering the shop. "There's my meeting. It was great running into you. Good luck. And let me know if I can do anything else to help."

Annette jumped up and shook his hand. "Thank you. I really appreciate it."

She sat down and looked at the name and number in front of her.

This was the best lead she'd had since this whole thing started. For the first time, she felt like this could truly be a solution.

Maybe not a full-time answer, or one that would give her the salary of her now defunct job. But it could be a start.

She pulled up the website of Phelps Digital Group and carefully looked at all the services they provided. She dove into their blog and read through the content. Then she clicked on the about us page and read through Brian's bio.

She plugged in her earbuds and dialed his number.

"Brian Phelps, please."

He wasn't in, but she did get his voice box.

She left a message, explaining the connection, and asking about potential writing positions.

She dropped her phone to the table and leaned in on her hands.

Finally, something good.

It worked! Getting out of her house really did accomplish something.

She might have a lead for work.

She might actually get paid.

And right now, it's exactly what she needed.

24

"Hi." Annette dropped her purse and her keys on the counter. She kissed Curt quickly as she handed him several reusable bags filled with food from the market. "I have several more bags in the car. Can you take these?"

He didn't say anything, just took the bags and turned back around to place the bags on the counter and started putting things away.

"I had a great day today. Let me grab the rest and I'll tell you all about it."

He grunted.

She grabbed the bags and closed the trunk of her car. She slowed her stance as she walked back into the house.

When Curt was quiet, she knew he had something on his mind. And the only thing on his mind as of late was the fact that she didn't have a job.

"I decided to set up my office at Peet's this morning. I needed a change of scenery."

"I saw the charge come through our account."

Okay ...

"And you're never going to believe who I ran into."

"Did they offer you a job?"

"Jeez, Curt, what the hell? Do all our conversations have to begin and end with me getting a job? I get it. But you're turning into a broken record. I'm working on it, okay?"

He scrapped his hand over his face and turned, leaning into the counter. He crossed his arms and legs and looked at her intently. "Okay, you're right. I'm sorry. Who did you run into?"

She huffed out her breath.

She wasn't going to let him ruin her mood. She'd felt too good all day. She launched into her story.

"And as I was picking up the groceries, Brian called. I have a meeting with him at the end of the week. He doesn't hire; he takes writers on as freelancers. We'd start out small, but if he likes what I do, it could lead to bigger things."

"That sounds promising."

"It is. He liked the fact I was a teacher. He asked to see some of my work before our meeting. It's a good thing I have that website up and have posted a few articles on it."

She'd been feeling good about having that built all day too.

She beamed. She really was excited about the opportunity.

If Brian would give her a chance, she knew she'd do a great job. And if he needed high quality writers, she knew there must be even more Brians out there. She intended to find them.

But one step at a time.

"It might turn into something. But even if it doesn't, it's given me a new idea. I'm going to spend tomorrow seeing if I can find more companies like Brian's to talk to. He also suggested a couple of meetups in the city I might want to attend. He told me he regularly finds new business that way, so I'm going to look for some networking events as well."

She wouldn't call it a smile, but Curt's face changed a little. Maybe not quite so tense.

"That's my story. Now what's wrong? I can tell you're upset."

He leaned in and kissed her before settling back against the counter. His body language changed. He relaxed a little. "I'm sorry about what I said. I really am excited for you. This is the first good news we've had since you quit."

"But …"

"But I ran over a piece of metal when I was on the job today. It ripped a hole in my tire. And I can't just buy one tire, I've got to buy two. And even at Costco, they're expensive. It's several hundred dollars I wasn't planning on spending."

"I'm assuming it's done?"

"Yes. I stopped on my way home. Even the spare didn't have much left on it. I had to get it done today."

"And you charged it?"

"Yes. But that ate up almost all of what was left on the card. If we have any other emergencies …"

Yeah, she got it. It was always something.

But maybe this was their wall. Maybe this was their low. She'd felt too good all day to think that she wasn't on the right track.

"Then we won't. If I get this job, *when* I get this job, I'll start bringing in something. And we can pay that off and get the card back down, okay?"

He nodded.

"And we still have some in savings. It's not like we're in big trouble."

"I know. But …"

"But nothing, Curt." She moved in and linked her fingers with his. "I know it's been rough. I really do see a light at the end of the tunnel. I feel good about this. I actually have a plan with potential. I know it'll work, okay?"

She could tell he was skeptical, but he nodded his head.

"I bought stuff to make your favorite dinner."

"Yeah?"

"Wanna help?"

He kissed her.

Today's crisis averted.

Now if she could just get the job.

She didn't. At least not right away.

Brian liked what he saw on her website. He promised to keep her in mind as work became available. But for the moment, he didn't have anything to outsource to her.

He gave her names of a couple of friends operating other digital ad agencies, and she'd left messages with each of the contacts. She'd also taken his suggestions to heart about networking events she should attend.

She'd done her research and marked them all on the calendar.

She was disappointed.

But what she'd dreaded the most was telling Curt. She knew he'd be mad. She just didn't know how frustrated he'd become. She sat and stewed until she heard him pull into the garage.

Curt did what he always did when he got home from a day in the garden. He kicked his boots off and placed them in a tray by the door. He hung his jacket on a hook.

Annette watched him move to the sink where he could scrub his hands. The dirt flowed.

"Hi."

Curt jumped, looking back over his shoulder. "Hi. I didn't see you there."

"I know. You seemed lost in thought."

He nodded. "I'm working up the budget for next year. I'm debating on trying for a couple of new projects. It's due in a couple of days, so it's crunch time."

She was used to his schedule. He'd been doing it long enough she knew how much time he put into his budgeting. A bigger budget meant more work. And he loved to improve his gardens.

"How was your day?"

She could hear the tenseness in his voice. Or was she imagining it?

She knew what he was asking. She could see it by the way he glanced back over his shoulder. The way he squinted his eyes.

He wanted good news.

And she had none to give.

"I didn't get anything. Brian didn't have any work at the moment. But he likes my style and said he'll keep me in mind as work comes up."

He turned back to the sink, added more soap, scrubbed harder. He grabbed a towel, rubbed his hands as he turned and leaned into the counter. "That means no job."

She chose to ignore the implications. "But he did give me a couple of other companies who might have work. I left messages. And I put a few networking events on my calendar. Something will turn up."

"Sure it will." He threw the towel towards the back of the counter before marching past her, heading into the living room and up the stairs to the bedroom.

Oh, she heard him alright. She was in hot pursuit.

"What the hell, Curt? Are you really that pissed with me?"

He didn't say a word.

He stepped into their master bath and closed the door.

She heard him. She paced by the door as she heard the shower turn on, turn off.

She yelped and jumped as he threw open the door, banging into the wall.

Without a word, he pushed past her and into their closet. He jumped into a pair of jeans and grabbed a t-shirt, pulling it on without looking. He ran his fingers through his cropped hair before heading back out and down the stairs.

"Goddammit, Curt. Talk to me. You're just going to ignore me now? I can't help it it's taking longer than I thought. I can't help it I haven't earned any money. I'm working on it. I'm trying so hard ..."

She jumped back as he turned and went all up in her face. She didn't even get a chance to finish before he started in on her again.

"I believe you. I know you're trying. But that's just it, you're trying to pick up jobs that won't bring in more than grocery money. You had a great job, one that paid the bills and had insurance. And you quit it without even talking to me. You just left. If you would have kept it at least through the summer, you could have spent the summer on salary. We could have talked about it. Made plans. Maybe even decided you should keep it, at least for now. Instead, we're left watching all of our savings disappear." His voice trailed off as he turned and made his way towards the kitchen. "As if we had any to begin with."

She followed. And just as she was about to say something, he whipped back around. His eyes glared and his finger shot up, pointing at her.

"Oh, I get it. I'm the cause of a lot of this. If we hadn't spent thousands on all the crap with an incorrect diagnosis, we wouldn't be in this mess. But it happened. And now we have bills. And I'm working desperately to right all that. I'm even looking at going with a larger corporate job again. I'm giving you your time. But we have to find something fast. You have to get something, or I don't know how much longer we can handle this."

"Do you think I'm just sitting around doing nothing?"

"I didn't say that."

"Because I'm not. I'm trying, Curt."

"I get that. But we really can't focus on that. We just need money."

She doubled over, biting back a scream, before standing up to look him square in the eye. "This isn't easy for me. Don't you think I know what I gave up? But I can't do that shit anymore. I can't. I won't. *Please.*"

She didn't care how desperate she sounded. She didn't care that her words trailed off into a shrill wail. She felt like bursting into tears. She felt like escaping, one and for all. She felt like ... she just felt like hell. She'd expected stress. But this?

She watched as he slid on his Nikes and headed out the door.

Not one word. Nothing. He didn't say he'd be back. He didn't stay to finish the conversation.

He just left.

How could he leave? How could he tell her he wished she still had her old job?

Had he really forgotten how upset she was when she'd been on the inside with an active shooter in place?

She knew it was the money affecting his judgment. But how could he forget all of that so easily?

He'd felt it too, it wasn't just her that had been impacted.

The more she paced around her house, the more pissed off she got.

They were supposed to work this out together. They were supposed to talk.

And he just leaves?

Well, two could play at that game.

She knew her favorite coffee house was open late into the night. She grabbed her laptop and hurried out the door.

25

Why had she agreed to this?

Oh yeah, she kind of liked him.

Sherri padded back and forth between her bedroom and bathroom to check how she looked in her mirror. She'd never cared much about how she looked with any other date. But thinking of Wesley, it was different.

And that confused the hell out of her.

She'd never been a woman to pine after a guy. Especially after her divorce.

She'd always taken the if-they-don't-like-what-they-see-they-can-leave approach with her other dates. But this one made her nervous. In a giddy sort of way.

After settling on a skirt and a t-shirt, she grabbed her favorite jean jacket and rolled up the sleeves. She put on two of her favorite bracelets, slid a ring on her right hand, and pulled her favorite sandals from the back of her closet. The weather had finally turned warmer, and she was going to dress the part.

She was putting the finishing touches with her lipstick just as the doorbell rang.

She answered it to a bouquet of flowers and a sexy smile.

"I thought you deserved something as beautiful as you."

And she melted just a little more.

"Thank you. Come in." She kissed him lightly on the lips, then led him into the kitchen.

They chatted about their days as she found a vase and put the flowers on her table. She locked up, and they were on their way.

She'd made reservations at Joe's, a local restaurant that was becoming the talk of the town. After winning Iron Chef, people were driving from all over the state to sample the head chef's dishes. He never disappointed. And that was making it more difficult to snag a table. But she knew Joe personally, so she pulled a few strings and got reservations.

She'd requested a table by the window. They sat, ordered wine. Relaxed.

And just like after the painting class, they settled into good conversation.

They talked about family one minute and interwove it with politics the next.

They chatted about books they enjoyed, and swapped recipes for their favorite meals-for-one.

That's what she found she liked the most about him. Any subject they touched on, he had a story to tell.

She'd never met a man so comfortable in his own skin. A man who was just as happy showing his knack for the arts as he was talking about sports.

Scratch that; he didn't really want to talk sports. He found everything else more interesting. And though she didn't say so, she really like that.

"You know what I'm doing this summer," she teased. "What are you up to?"

"It looks like I'll be traveling a bit too. I told you my daughters live in Hawaii with my ex and her husband."

"Um hm."

"They're sixteen, and apparently that's too old to come and stay with dad for the summer. They both have jobs, and feel it would *put them out* too much to visit the mainland. I guess that means I'm heading to Hawaii for a couple of weeks."

"Sounds brutal."

"I know." He shuddered. "But someone's got to do it." He grinned.

"Actually, I think the timing is off. You're supposed to go to Hawaii in the winter, not the summer. Not when a million other tourists will be there too."

"I wouldn't be going if it weren't for them. Especially to the Big Island. My only consolation is I'll be in the suburbs, away from the normal hangouts. I found a house on Airbnb to rent close to my girls' neighborhood. It has a great space to paint, so I'm going to bring along some basic supplies and get a few ideas going."

"Do you do that a lot? Travel with supplies?" She was genuinely curious.

She loved visiting art museums and galleries when she traveled. But she wondered if she'd feel the same way if she did it for a living. Would she ever want to bring her job along?

"Yeah, actually I do. For short trips, I only bring along sketch books. But for two weeks, I'm packing more. I have the room. And I know I won't see the girls all day every day. If they're working or with friends, it'll give me something to do."

"As if you'll need something to do in Hawaii. I can think of other things to do in paradise." She caught her breath. It came out way more flirtatious than she'd meant it. But watching his face, the way his grin rolled into place, she changed her mind.

Why shouldn't she flirt with him?

She felt comfortable with him. She enjoyed being with him. And wherever that led, she suddenly felt ready.

He studied her for what felt like minutes. She didn't back down.

Her eyes held his. She studied his features for what felt like the hundredth time. She never got tired of trying to figure out how many gold specs highlighted his eyes. Or how the curls in his hair always seemed to find the perfect way to fall in front of his ear.

She was starting to dream about ways she could finger those curls, wrap them around her pinky as she straddled him and …

"Italy's coming up fast. Are you counting down the days?"

She shook her head lightly, bringing herself back into the conversation.

"I'm glad I'm finishing up work next week. I still have to get a few things from the workshop list your friend sent over. I'm glad she provides most of the stuff. Even with her list I'm wondering how I'm going to fit it all into two bags."

"Go with the *less is more* philosophy. You'll find Tivoli is a pretty small town."

"But it's Italy. It's less than twenty miles from Rome! I have to be prepared for anything."

"I'm telling you, once you get to her villa, all you're going to want to do is paint."

"You keep saying that. I've seen the pictures on her site. But I can't imagine not exploring. It's what I do best."

"I know she'll have lots of field trips ready to keep you inspired. But even Italy is more casual these days. You can get by wearing anything."

"Said no woman ever. You do know men can show up in jeans to just about anything. But a woman has to analyze all of her outfits, and spend hours agonizing over making the right selection."

His eyes dropped to her hand on the table. He picked it up, linked her fingers with his. He touched her ring, twirled her bracelets, before returning his eyes to hers. "Did you do that tonight?"

She blushed. "Maybe."

"You look very nice." He pulled her fingers up and planted a gentle kiss.

"Thank you." She was happy he'd noticed. "And you chose your jeans in, what, two seconds?"

He snorted. "Alright, you made your point."

"Yeah, it's a guy thing. Remember, we were just talking about that."

"So we were."

She leaned over and fingered his shirt. He'd put on a soft blue linen shirt over a white t-shirt and rolled up the sleeves to show off a small tattoo on his wrist. "But I did notice no paint tonight."

"That's rare."

"You paint in everything?"

"Pretty much. I get a wild idea, and I can't help myself."

"A painter's life."

"Yep."

She ran her finger over the words on his wrist. She'd read them a hundred times: *love til the end of time.* She'd always wondered what they meant. They sounded personal, and she'd been afraid to go there.

His fingers moved over hers, as if reading her thoughts. It still spooked her when he did it, but she was getting used to it. It was as if he had a direct line, knowing exactly what she was thinking.

"I got this right after my girls were born. Everyone says kids change you. But you never know until you have your own. In my case, they were both so little. They were both under four pounds, so tiny, so fragile. I didn't think anything could ever be that little. And yet there they were."

"So small. Did they have to stay in the hospital long?"

"Four weeks. It broke our hearts to leave them there. But we spent every hour we could with them. Looking back, we should have gone home and slept."

She giggled. "Oh, man, I can't imagine two. My one almost did me in. He got his days and nights mixed up for the first year."

"Oh yeah. We'd get one down, and the other would wake up. I don't miss those days, and yet I do."

She nodded. "I get that. You wish it all away because you're so tired. And once it's gone, you want nothing more than to bring it back."

"Especially when they hang up on you because they don't want to talk. Their friends are more important."

"Just wait. At least you and your ex have some control. Once they leave for college, you can go weeks without hearing from them. You just have to trust that they're okay. That takes a while to work its way into your heart. To let go."

"And does it? You're telling me you still don't worry?"

She snorted. "Not in the least! I still call Tanner up all the time and quiz him about things. Once a mom …"

"Exactly. My mom still does that from time to time."

She lifted her glass. "Once a mom …" She drained the last of the wine and put it back on the table.

Wesley turned the key, letting the engine still. He hopped out and hustled to the other side.

He tucked Sherri's arm in his own as he walked her to her front door.

He turned, leaned in. He laid his hand along her face, caressing her cheek. "You're eyes just do me in. They're so expressive. I love watching what you're thinking."

His lips touched hers gently. Not pressing for anything more than a gentle kiss.

And right now, it's exactly what Sherri needed.

She could get lost in him. She already felt way more for him then she'd admit. And with all that was going on in her life, she wasn't sure what her next step should be.

"Wesley …" She didn't know where to begin.

But in the uncanny way he'd always surprised her in the past, he did it again.

"You're getting ready to leave for Italy. It's difficult to think about where this might take us."

"Exactly. How do you keep doing that?"

He chuckled. "I told you. It's in your eyes. I can tell exactly what you're thinking."

"Then do you know how confused I am? How I want this more than anything? And yet, I'm just not sure if it's wise to take the next step. Not right now."

He nodded. "You need to go to Italy. I need to go to Hawaii. And we'll see each other later this summer."

She agreed. That truly was what she was thinking. Though a tiny part of her wished she was a little bolder, a little more spontaneous.

He kissed her again, grabbed her fingers, took her keys and unlocked her front door. He turned and faced her. "We've got time. This'll happen when it's meant to be."

Her head fell to his chest. "Does it have to be this damn confusing?"

His arms pulled her in tight. Though it wasn't cold, she felt comforted by his warmth. She could get used to this.

"I'll be waiting when you get back. And maybe we can chat a time or two while you're away."

Just him saying that eased her mind.

She wanted this, she did. But so much had changed in her life in the previous few months, she wanted to take each step deliberately.

She needed to think.

And she was glad he got that.

She kissed him goodnight, then shut the door tight before she changed her mind.

She needed to find herself first, before she let Wesley - or any other man - enter her life.

26

Sherri stood at Annette's door, chocolate cupcakes in hand. She knew Annette would never say no to chocolate, even it was ten-thirty in the morning.

"Hi." Annette answered the door, a little wary.

"I come bearing gifts." She held up the box with Nina's Cupcakes' distinctive packaging.

"Is it chocolate?"

"Is there anything else?"

That brought the smile Sherri had hoped for. Annette invited her in. "I was just putting the teapot on. Want some tea?"

"Sure, sounds great."

Sherri followed behind Annette, placing the box on the counter. She helped herself to plates and forks from the cupboard, one for each of them.

Then she flopped down in her familiar chair. It felt good to be back, inside her second home.

Annette placed tea bags in two mugs, filled each with hot water, and pushed one across the counter to her friend. She leaned in and with a slight quiver in her voice, whispered, "I missed you."

Sherri grasped Annette's hands. "I missed you, too."

"I'm sorry I yelled the other day."

"I'm sorry I walked out."

"No, you had every right to. I can't believe I acted like that."

"You were right. Everything you said was true."

"But that didn't give me the right …"

"It did. You got me thinking."

"I've been through so much, stuck in my own head lately. It's just me here, and I'm going a little crazy."

"And I should have been a little more sympathetic."

"But I shouldn't have pushed."

"I'm glad you did. Everything you said, it's all I could think about on the way home. That night. The next day. You were right."

"No, I wasn't. What we went through, nobody should go through. We each process it differently."

"True. But I am the one who wanted change."

"And you will. In your own time."

"If you hadn't pushed, I might not have gone back to my painting class over the weekend."

"I should just listen and be there for you instead of -" Annette stopped and pushed her mug out of the way. She leaned in a little closer. "Wait, what did you say?"

"I went to my class on Saturday."

"You did?"

"Yep. And I'm going to Italy this summer."

"Wait. What?!" Annette moved around the counter and dropped into the chair next to Sherri's. She turned, leaned on her arm she'd placed on the counter. "You did *what*? Italy? How? When? Start at the beginning."

Sherri launched into the story of how Wesley had taken her by surprise when he suggested Italy. And just like she knew Wesley's class was perfect, she knew she was meant to go to Italy just from the brochure.

"I know it seems like a spontaneous decision. But after I left here, I really started thinking. I *have* been the one to push these past few months. And somehow, I'd let all that go after the *event*. I know I stormed out of here, but you really shook me." Then she grinned. "Thank you for that."

Annette sat back in her chair, pulled her hands through her hair, wound it around her finger before throwing it back over her shoulder. She eyed Sherri, "Wow. I'm shocked. I can't believe you did all that."

"There's more." Sherri almost whispered it. "I kind of went on a date with Wesley."

"You what! Ohmigod, you did all that and you didn't call me?" Annette hopped out of her chair and went back around the kitchen island to the stove. She turned the knob to start the kettle up again, before opening Nina's box and taking out another cupcake. She bit into it, chocolate oozing down onto her chin.

She swiped at it with her finger before putting it into her mouth and sucking.

She grinned. "You sooo have to start at the beginning."

Sherri chuckled. She grabbed a second cupcake of her own. She swiped at the frosting around the edge, sucked it into her mouth. "Not much to tell."

"Oh, no. You're not getting by with that. I knew you liked his class. I know you think he's gorgeous. You said you felt connected to him. But you never said you were attracted to him, or that you remotely, possibly wanted to date him. How did that happen?"

"I honestly don't know. Everything you just said is true. I felt all of that. But somehow, I'd always separated all of that in my mind. I was learning from him, and that was that. Maybe that's the teacher in me."

Annette nodded. She got that. "So …"

"I went to class, and I'm sad I didn't go back before. Not one person came up to me and asked me what it was like, or to explain what happened. Nobody said a word. The most they did is pull me in and give me a hug. I love that group so much."

Sherri swiped at a tear running down her cheek. She dabbed her eyes with her napkin. Their new normal really sucked. "Do you feel like you cry at anything now?"

Annette rolled her eyes and groaned. "I had to hang up the phone yesterday talking with Clara. She mentioned ice cream. All I could see was her when she was a little girl - remember that blue ice cream she always got when we went out? How she'd get it all over her cheeks and grin? I started sobbing so hard, I had to call her back."

"After class, Wesley and I fell into our normal pattern of a tea and conversation. And something hit me, looking at him, watching him." Sherri turned her attention down to the half-eaten cupcake in front of her. She poked at it, thinking about that moment. Her voice quieted down as she continued. "I suddenly felt bold. I moved from my chair, next to him on the loveseat. And we started talking, and …"

When she didn't continue, Annette cackled, "Ha! You *bad* girl. Did you …"

Sherri jumped and swatted at Annette before her next words. "Jeez, no, he just leaned in and kissed me."

"That's it? Just a kiss?"

Sherri fell back in her seat, remembering the feeling. "It was some kiss." Her face heated at the thought.

"Wow. That good?"

Sherri looked up at her friend. "You have no idea. I've *never* had a kiss like that."

"Seriously? Do tell."

Sherri touched her lips, eyes fell out of focus. "It must be the artist in him. We kissed for what felt like hours, with no intention of doing more. But he literally blew my mind." She giggled. "Let's just say he's *very* good at paying attention to detail."

Annette screamed the way teenagers do when they're talking conquests. Which made Sherri laugh harder.

And just like that, the tears were back. She dabbed at them with the back of her hand. "I missed you so much."

Annette's eyes filled with tears as she moved back around the island and in front of her friend. "Me too. Let's never do that again."

"Ever."

And with a tight hug between them, they both whispered, "Deal."

"You went out with him last night."

"Yes."

"And all you did is kiss."

"Yep."

"You agreed to nothing more until you get back."

"That's the agreement."

"Are you crazy?" Annette reached up and grabbed a curl right by Sherri's ear. She gave it a friendly tug. "Now you'll have to remain *unsatisfied* until after Italy. And that, my friend, is going to be very difficult. It's Italy. The most romantic place on earth!"

"Oh, don't think for a moment I can't take care of that myself."

Annette rolled her eyes. "You learned too much in L.A. Having someone with you is so much more fun."

"I'll get there, we'll get there. If it's meant to be." Sherri shuffled her feet underneath her. "And I'm really thinking it is."

"And he was okay with all that?"

"Sure. Call it age, but we both know this is complicated at best. We're not horny teenagers who jump at anything that walks by."

"True."

"And I really needed the time to think. We went from zero to all-in so quickly, I hadn't considered being with him until a few days ago. It's going to take a lot longer to wrap my head around all this."

"Him too, I imagine."

"Yes, he's heading off to Hawaii this summer. His girls are sixteen and no longer want to come for the summer to visit. He's heading out there instead."

"Hawaii in the summer?"

"I know. That's what I said. Italy sounds far more fabulous."

"That'd get my vote."

"Wow. I'm impressed. Sounds like I gotta meet this guy."

"I would really like that. Maybe the four of us can go out after I get back."

"Consider it scheduled. We can do something here, grill, eat outside."

"Perfect, your backyard should be in full bloom by then."

Sherri loved Annette's backyard. She often told her how envious she was of her having the perfect spouse who could build a secret garden the way he had.

She'd tried to plant flowers in her tiny rental. But even with her landlord's help, it never had the same charm and brilliance.

"Enough about me. How are you?"

Sherri had often thought about her friend since their fight. She knew how much stress Annette was under. She knew not working had to be ramping it up even more.

"Oh, you know. I'm trying. My website is up and running. I've been adding posts to it."

"I've read them."

"You have?"

Sherri nodded. "I check every day. I like what you're writing."

Annette rolled her eyes. "I don't even know what it is yet. I just write. I have to come up with a theme."

"Yeah, but you're talking about your experience. I especially like the post you did on today's education system."

"Yeah?"

"It's spot on."

"I spoke with a guy last week who owns a digital marketing company. He's looking for writers. He said he'd keep me in mind."

"Well, that sounds promising."

"I've been contacting other firms this week. I've spoken with a couple ad managers. We'll see."

Sherri could hear the stress in her voice. She reached over and grabbed her hand again. "How's Curt?"

Annette snorted. "Curt's Curt. He was fine with all of this. But last week he blew out a tire. He filled our credit card up with two new tires. He's had a couple of meltdowns since then."

"How are you?"

Annette bit her lip, shaking her head, as the tears began to fall again. "What have I done?"

Sherri pulled her friend in for a hug. She let her cry.

After minutes - or hours - Annette dried her tears. "As much as I hated my job, at least I got a paycheck at the end of the week. I thought I'd be able to get something faster than this."

"It hasn't been that long."

"I know. But I'm going to have to figure something else out if a job doesn't come through soon."

"It will."

Annette just nodded, not looking like she believed.

"Weren't you always the one who told me you have to believe?"

"Yeah, but you don't have a husband who frowns at everything you do."

"Curt? He's never been like that before."

"I know. He's just under so much stress. He took two extra jobs with the city this week. He'll be working this weekend for a special event. Sometimes I wonder if it's more to get away from me rather than the money."

"Have things gotten that bad?"

"I don't know. We haven't talked much this past week. I only know he's here because he's on the other side of the bed at night. I hate this."

"Then do something about it."

"I'm trying," Annette covered her eyes, breathed in. She scraped her hands through her hair, bringing it back to a ponytail before releasing it down her back. "Shit. I'm not happy about me, how can I expect him to be happy? If just something would come through."

"It will."

Though in the back of Sherri's mind, she was worried.

How had the two of them gone so wrong so quickly? She knew they were stressed about money. She'd tried to offer her friend a loan in the past, to no avail. She knew there was no way she'd accept it now.

She might not be able to do anything about their marriage, but she could do something to cheer up her friend.

"I came over here with chocolate as a peace offering. And also to see if I could bribe you into coming with me to buy what I need for my trip."

Annette sat up a little straighter. "Shopping?"

Sherri winced, teasing her friend. "Yes, shopping. As much as I hate it, I need some new things to take with me. And I have no idea what to get. I can't do this without you."

Annette smiled. "When would you like this help?"

"Are you doing anything now?"

Annette hesitated. "No. I have absolutely nothing to do other than sulk. I'm game if you are."

"Perfect! We could do lunch. We could hit our favorite stores. I also need to run to the art store if you're game. Most everything is supplied, but I do want to bring the recommended brushes along."

"Curt's working late tonight. I don't think he'd miss me much anyway. I have all the time in the world."

A little piece of Sherri's heart ached for her friend. She hated seeing the two of them this way. But there was little she could do, other than support her friend. And she intended to do that as well as she could.

"Are you ready? Maybe we could hit a couple of stores and then do lunch."

"Okay. Just let me change. I'll be down in a minute."

Sherri pulled her list out, contemplating their afternoon together.

She'd used shopping as a way to reconnect, and after talking with Annette, she was grateful she'd come over when she did. She loved both Annette and Curt, would do anything to help them. But this was out of her hands.

She turned her attention to her budding relationship with Wesley.

With her first marriage, they'd done everything wrong. He was all spend-spend as if tomorrow would never come. She preferred to save for a rainy day. When they started fighting, they were both too headstrong to try and correct it. Not that there was much to correct by that point. They were to people on very different paths.

They both had wanted to be right. And in the end, they both had lost.

The biggest loss, of course, had been on the part of their son. He was a great kid, was doing well. But they'd weathered more than a couple of teenage tantrums as he tested the boundaries. She hoped he wouldn't have relationship problems based on the way her and her ex had handled the situation.

She was older now. And though she had a lot of thinking to do, she was beginning to realize how bright her future could be. Though she hadn't decided what she wanted her second act to look like, she was growing more certain she wanted someone in it.

Was Wesley the one?

She wasn't sure. They had a long way to go.

But he was interesting. She found herself wondering what he was up to. If she could see him before she left.

She took a chance and pulled out her phone.

Are you free tomorrow night?

She'd barely clicked her phone off when she heard the familiar ding.

Yes. What are you thinking?

Well I did promise you a home cooked meal.

I'll bring flowers. And wine. What time?

How about seven?

Perfect. See you then.

She dropped her phone back into her purse. Perfect. Yep, she couldn't agree more.

27

Sherri stood in front of her full-length mirror. She smoothed down the front of her skirt.

She slipped on her new pair of sandals, then twirled once again. She still wasn't used to frills.

She hadn't had so many dresses in years. She supposed she could thank Annette for that. Annette was the girly-girl, always choosing pink when she had the choice.

Sherri preferred her jeans. Always would.

But standing in front of the mirror, hooking her bracelet into place, she kind of liked what she saw.

She swiped on a touch of lipstick a deep rose Annette promised she could wear in any situation. She had two; enough to last her throughout her trip. She only had to remember to pack it.

She smiled one last time as she clicked off the light in her bathroom and made her way back into the kitchen.

Everything was in place. The table was set. The eggplant was warming. All she needed to do was throw the spaghetti into the boiling water, and her eggplant parmesan would be ready in just a few minutes.

She turned up the volume on her favorite playlist just as the doorbell rang.

"You clean up nicely" she said in greeting.

He glanced down. Jeans. A dark t-shirt. A jacket slipped over the top. Italian loafers. He returned his eyes to hers with an eyebrow raised.

"No paint." She grinned before touching her lips to his. She motioned for him to come in.

"Ah," he nodded, understanding. He handed her the flowers and leaned in for a different sort of kiss.

A kiss that wiped the grin right off her face.

It was his turn to smile. "You look beautiful."

"Thank you, come in."

She led him into the kitchen and put the flowers in a vase. She moved it to the table, giving it the finishing touch.

She dropped the pasta into water while he served the wine. As she leaned into the counter waiting for it to cook, he handed her a glass.

He touched it lightly with his. "To a fantastic summer."

"To possibilities."

She served them both, then sat next to him to eat.

They chatted about their summer plans. She told him about her adventures shopping with Annette. He told her about his most recent conversation with his girls. They were more excited about him visiting Hawaii than they'd originally let on.

She poured the last of the wine into their glasses and asked him to follow her into her family room.

A cool breeze flowed in from the back door. The sun was just starting to drop in the sky. She clicked on a lamp beside the loveseat before she sat down.

He dropped by her, turning to watch her. He always gave her his undivided attention. It seemed to be a natural thing for him to do.

And she didn't mind.

"I'm leaving next week."

"I know. I'm leaving the week after that."

"I'm excited to meet your friend."

"You're going to love Francesca."

"How did you meet her?" Sherri had wondered that often since she'd booked the trip. She always forgot to ask.

"I met her about ten years ago. We taught a retreat together near Sedona, and we connected instantly. It was one of those weeklong passion-finding events, where each day pushed the attendee in a different direction. I was the morning session; she was the afternoon. We sat in each other's classes, and we couldn't stop talking after."

"Instant friendship?" *Or more?* Sherri kept the last part to herself.

"Friendship, and that's all," he said with a smirk.

She blushed.

"She still lived in the states at that point, so I saw her from time to time. We taught several more retreats together, they were very popular. She divorced and remarried. They settled in Italy four or five years ago. I stopped in for a couple of nights two years ago when I was touring Italy with my girls."

"What made you think of Francesca for me?"

"I trust her. I know her style. I love what she does in her classes. I know how she pushes her attendees. And I thought she'd be perfect for you."

"Really? I'd barely mentioned wanting something more. And you popped out with her name."

"But I'd been thinking about you since the *event*. You were in my thoughts, every day. Even though I hadn't connected you up with Francesca at that point, I'd given you a lot of consideration."

He had? She felt a little flustered, warm inside.

This man. He kept saying everything right.

"Are you ready?"

She blinked. She could take that in so many directions. She settled by focusing on packing for her trip.

"I finished getting all my supplies. I'm a little surprised at how good it feels to have art materials in my home again."

"Why'd you stop?" He sat his wine glass on the table, turned and gave her his undivided attention.

She shook her head. "I don't really know. Life, I guess. I've always been creative. And a lot of that went into the school. First to volunteer for committees. Always in charge of the creative programs. Teachers know if they have trouble making flyers, I'm the one to turn to."

"You're the one they visit for design?"

"Yeah, I have turned into *that* person. I got the Illustrator software years ago, and I've loved playing with it ever since."

"Do you like that better than the real thing? Then playing with paints and canvas?"

"I always thought so. But the last few weeks have been exciting. I hadn't realized how much I missed getting dirty."

Her words caught in her throat. They came out a little more sensual than she'd intended.

She was getting bolder; she'd noticed that. At least where he was concerned.

Had she changed that much?

She still wasn't ready to jump into a relationship with the man in front of her, not yet. But she definitely saw her life changing.

She'd been alone for so long, never questioned it. She'd been happy with her decision.

Until now.

He stirred something in her that had been dormant far too long.

She'd always assumed relationships were for other people. She was the one that tagged along.

But dammit, she was only fifty. And she wanted more.

She wanted to touch a man. She wanted to *be* touched by a man.

She wanted to come home to someone who cared about her.

She wanted to cook dinner for someone. Eat next to him. Sit with him and just be.

Make plans with someone. Travel with someone.

Climb into bed with someone …

"Sherri?"

She looked up into his eyes and felt heat spread to her cheeks.

Oh yeah, she had it bad. And she'd been caught.

She could tell by the smirk on his face he knew *exactly* what she'd been thinking.

She should hate the fact that he was so intuitive.

But somehow she found it … a turn on. The fact that she was an open book with him, and he'd only been drawn in closer was a good thing.

"Should we talk about this?" He said it as a question, but she saw the emotion cross over his face.

She put her glass on the table next to his. She moved in closer. Pulled her legs up underneath her, so she could lean into him. She placed her hand alongside his face. "I'm really going to miss you."

Her lips touched his lightly, just tasting.

He tasted like wine, the deep smoky sauce she'd whipped up for her entree.

She felt his hands wrap around her waist. His fingers spreading, touching, moving, learning as they went.

She was grateful she'd chosen the dress with the full skirt. She moved, straddled him, before diving in for more kisses.

And just like before, he didn't disappoint.

His hands continued to wander, touching the curve of her breast. Running across her ass. Slow, achingly slow.

Part of her could do this forever.

He was never in a hurry, not with anything he did. She noticed that early on, how he was content, and rarely paid attention to time.

She seemed to focus on nothing but.

But she was learning. With him, time seemed like the best thing in the world to lose track of.

All she wanted was to feel the warmth he spread throughout her body. To feel as if he had nothing else to do, nowhere else to be, other than right here, with her. As if they had all the time in the world.

Some part of her wanted to dive in, right now, and move forward in their relationship.

But the other part of her said no, wait. And that's the part that moved her into action.

"Wesley," she let her forehead rest against his as he nipped at her nose.

"We should wait." He took a deep breath in.

She nodded. "I want to."

"We should make this perfect. When we're both ready." His words said one thing. His hands were saying something else entirely.

She sat up taller, staring into his beautiful eyes. She really could look at them forever.

"Honestly, ready isn't really what's going on. I *am* ready." She wiggled against him, feeling his hardness brush against her core. "*So* ready..." she whispered.

He groaned, and turned it into a chuckle as he gently touched her cheeks, pulled her in for a quick kiss. "We're going to stop now."

"Yes." She tried to sound convincing.

"We're both leaving. We're both busy this summer."

"And I'm anything but sure of what's happening in my life."

"A lot has happened in the past few weeks."

"And my trip and all ..."

"Italy's calling."

"And you need to think about your trip."

"My girls."

Sherri was having a hard time focusing. She placed both hands alongside his face, kissed him before moving back to his side.

They lingered at her front door.

"This is for the best." She tried to sound convincing.

She knew it was. They'd both agreed. But letting him go, knowing she wouldn't see him for several weeks, that was turning out to be harder than she'd imagined.

"We'll talk."

"We can FaceTime."

"And you're going to be busy. I know Francesca's going to fill your head with all sorts of ideas."

"And I know you'll be busy with your girls." She was already starting to imagine going days without hearing from him. They'd be busy, after all.

"Maybe we should set a date for our first call."

She glanced at his eyes, seeing the humor there once again. "How do you keep doing that?" It was a little unnerving.

"Maybe I see it, because I feel it too."

She nodded. "I can call once I'm settled in. When I have a little time."

"That sounds perfect."

His kisses were doing very little to make her want to unlock the door and turn him away.

He sensed that too. He reached out, turned the key and pushed.

"How about dinner with me when you return in August?"

She nodded, "That's a little far out to plan."

"It'll give us something to focus on."

He grabbed her hands, pulled them up to his lips. "Bye for now." He turned and disappeared.

She closed the door, leaning against it, trying to catch her breath.

So much to think about.

She heard the familiar ding coming from her phone. She crossed the room and grabbed her mobile. With a swipe, she saw it was from him.

"Start packing."

She giggled. Yep, he knew her well.

Another ding.

"I miss you already."

She did too.

28

"You got everything?" Tanner placed two bags in the trunk of his car.

"Uh huh." Sherri tucked her tote bag into the back seat before climbing into the front. She'd been up half the night making sure everything was in its place.

She'd always been a last-minute packer. But this time had proved to be even more of a challenge, knowing she would be gone for weeks.

Tanner climbed in behind the wheel. "You have your boarding pass?" He knew her patterns well. He'd scrambled one too many times back for odds and ends she'd mistakenly forgot to pack. Even as a teenager, he'd started running through his mental checklist before pulling away from home.

Sherri nodded. She knew his questions were coming. She was ready. "Yep, right here on my phone." She held it for him to see.

"How about your painting supplies? The ones you told me you were bringing?"

"Yep. They're in the bag I'm checking."

"Your shoes? Your clothes?"

Sherri turned to him with a scowl on her face. But burst into laughter when she saw the grin on his face. She playfully punched him in the arm. "Yes. I have everything."

"Just checking. I know how you are." He pulled away, stopped at the stop sign at the end of the street, and moved into traffic.

They settled into a familiar conversation, one Sherri loved having with her son. They were comfortable with each other; they were just as happy talking about the weather as they were diving into difficult subjects, debating controversial topics.

Today, he knew she'd be nervous, so he had a topic ready. Something to keep her mind off the long trip, and the home she was leaving behind.

Traffic was heavy, but Tanner had made sure they'd have plenty of time. She loved that about him. She'd raised him well. He was a great kid; she was lucky to have him.

"What?" He glanced at her as he pulled up to the terminal - just shy of two hours to spare. Time to check her bags, make it through security, and grab a bite to eat.

She merely shook her head. "Nothing." She reached over and gave his hand a quick squeeze. "I just love you. That's all." She hopped out of the car.

Tanner popped the trunk lever and opened his own door. He pushed open the trunk, pulled out her bags, hugged her tight.

"Have fun, Mom. Live it up."

She did her mom duty, making him promise to check in. "You know my mobile plan works in Italy, so if I don't hear from you, I'll call."

"I'll *call*." It rolled off his tongue, a promise she knew he'd never keep.

They looked at each other and laughed. "No, you won't." "No, I won't."

"Okay, at least text me. Let me know you're doing okay."

"That I can do." He hugged her one last time. "I love you."

She stood on the curb, watched him jump behind the wheel, and head away, back to his own life.

She grabbed her suitcases and started pulling them towards the door. She was off to hers.

She should be tired.

Sherri hadn't slept well on the plane. She never could.

She'd been up almost twenty-four hours with only a nap here and there.

But she was in Italy - Italy! - how could she sleep?

She was sitting in a van next to another woman just a few years older than herself. They'd met at the airport, waiting for their ride.

Marlee had signed up for much the same reason. She'd lost her husband to cancer a few years before. Her kids were all grown. She retired from her job and had too much time on her hands. Renewing her interest in her painting had seemed like the right thing to do.

Marlee was from Tennessee, a little town just outside of Nashville.

Sherri smiled, listening to her slow, Southern drawl. Something the van driver was having a difficult time understanding. Marlee didn't seem to notice; she just kept rambling on.

She spoke of everything. The flight. The cars. The people.

"Have you visited Europe before, Marlee?"

"Nope. Never been much further than Tennessee."

It was difficult not getting caught up in her enthusiasm. For a woman closing in on sixty, Marlee's excitement mirrored that of a small child at Christmas. Sherri humored her and played along.

But even Marlee sucked in her breath and stopped for a moment as they rounded the corner and inched up the driveway to their *home* for the next month.

"Wow."

"Double wow ..." Sherri whispered. She twisted her finger lightly, as if ensuring she wasn't dreaming.

This was *her* life. She was here, in Italy!

All around her were fields of green. Grape vines. Trees. Flowering bushes.

Rolling hills transformed the landscape. The yellows mixed with the greens, which led to the blues and whites of the sky. And the buildings. Everywhere she looked, she saw structures she knew were hundreds of years old.

The gravel road meandered through hundred-year-old trees. Far off in the distance, she saw what she assumed to be the main house - Francesca's house - with several buildings popping up around the property.

She'd studied the map Francesca had provided. She knew one of them was the sleeping quarters for the artists staying onsite. Her home away from home for the next month.

As the van pulled up to the front door, a beautiful woman stepped out, smiling.

Francesca looked exactly as Sherri had pictured. She knew a lot about her from Wesley. And her website had added more details.

Marlee and Sherri dropped their bags in the entryway, then followed Francesca as she gave them the grand tour.

Each turn brought new "oohs and aahs" from both women.

Sherri eyed the infinity pool with an excitement she hadn't felt in years. Swimming wasn't her thing, not anymore. Not since Tanner was younger and on the swim team. But she was glad she'd thrown her suit in at the last minute.

The gardens were lush and filled with all sorts of temptations. Pear trees, grape vines, tomatoes, herbs, even the vegetables were all there for the picking. Francesca assured them they could eat whatever they wanted. She regularly visited her garden in the morning to plan out her meal.

Down a hill were the residences. Both women would be staying together in a six-bedroom farmhouse, with a common living area and kitchen.

Though Francesca would provide most meals, having a kitchen would be nice for morning coffee and for snacks. And for the occasional lunch or dinner when they didn't feel like dining with the group. The city center was a short drive away, and there were numerous opportunities for shopping at the market to fill their kitchen with anything they liked.

With a three-hour break before meeting the rest of the attendees for cocktails, Sherri shut herself in her room. She put her things away in the closet and the drawers, before lying down for a nap.

Her phone gently nudged her awake with twenty minutes to spare. She replaced her travel wear with one of her new dresses and made her way back outside.

She stopped halfway back to the main house to took in the view. She snapped a quick photo and texted it to let people know she'd made it.

One to Tanner. One to Annette. One to Wesley.

She barely had her phone back in her pocket when she felt the familiar buzz. The answers came in as she expected, a thumbs up from her son, a smiley and a note of encouragement from her friend.

And then as she was looking at her screen, the one she'd been holding her breath for.

Told you it was gorgeous. Have you met the cat?

Before she could consider his question, a very large and very friendly feline looped her tail around her leg, purring as she moved.

Sherri leaned down and scratched behind her ear.

She found a small bench and sat down.

Thanks for recommending this place, she typed out. She was in love with it and she'd only been here a couple of hours.

A million things ran through her mind. Like a fast-running movie, she saw herself over the course of the past year. Turning fifty. Making the decision she wanted something more. Her trip with Annette to California. School. Her painting. Her life.

Wesley.

How had she gotten here so quickly?

And yet, it felt like it was so long - forever since she'd made the choice and taken the first steps.

She wondered if this was the thing they called midlife crisis, the feeling of wanting things to speed up and slow down at the same time. The feeling of emptiness, like she didn't have a clue what she wanted to do. Yet on so many levels, she was enjoying every moment she had, loving everything she was doing.

She loved her life. Every minute of it.

Okay, maybe not the few very bad moments in the past couple of months. But everything else, she was really enjoying.

She wanted more. And yet she felt like she had it all.

She wanted to dive deeper, to explore what her art meant to her now. What she wanted to do with it, she hadn't a clue.

And she wanted the man at the other end of this conversation.

But she had no idea what to tell him. Or even what that meant. Not really.

How could she put all of that into a text?

He was thousands of miles away. And she was here.

She needed to figure herself out first. To explore.

She decided to go with that.

I'll text later. Our opening night cocktail hour is about to start.

At least that was the truth. And it was … noncommittal.

She stood, following the sounds of voices down the hill. She could see several people lingering around the pool, cocktails in hand.

She was tucking her phone in her pocket when she felt the familiar buzz once again.

Have fun. Explore. You have so much to give.

She felt a ripple down her spine.
He kept doing it, reading her mind.
Maybe that's why their attraction continued to grow.

29

Annette read through the announcement with building anticipation.

We are looking for people ready to travel the world.

We're a small niche travel magazine that is published twelve times a year. Our reader base is over one million affluent and sophisticated travelers who comb the world for unique experiences; our job is to be their guide.

We're starting up a new column The Places You'll Go to feature our top travel picks for the year. These are places most only dream about; our readers want more.

You're a traveler, an explorer, someone who is ready to share. We know you're a writer; that's a given. But what we're looking for is that little something extra.

We are seeking a visually descriptive writer who is ready to tell a first-person account of what the road less traveled has to offer. The ideal candidate will have writing experience, yet it might not be in traditional standards. Do you write for your community newspaper? Are you an English teacher itching for something new? This may be your chance to bring destiny and destinations together.

Annette scrolled down the page, taking it all in. Yep, it sounded like a dream job. Yep, she met all the qualifications too. Even the optional qualifications were a fit.

Annette was quickly finding out that her definition of a job was expanding. She'd started out with a belief she'd write a book. Maybe pick up a few freelance jobs on the side to pay the bills. And though she'd started out with nothing more than a scattered approach, she was quickly finding her groove.

She knew it was going to take time to get her book written and selling. She knew she had to find something that paid for in between. Even the occasional freelance gig wasn't going to cut it.

And with just a little research, she'd come across a variety of ideas that were proving to have opportunity.

Like the connection she'd made the day before with a small company that was looking for someone to write their product descriptions for the website they were building. She had a meeting with the owner next week. But she knew the owner through a friend of a friend. She was sure she could convince him to take a chance on her.

Then today, when she'd grown bored, and started following a trail that led her to a travel magazine, she had no idea it could lead to opportunity.

Yet the more she read the job description, the more excited she became.

This is a one-year contract. Please don't apply if you aren't willing to travel every month in the coming year. This is a salaried position, all expenses paid. You'll also be doing guest appearances on our podcast, as well as remain active on our social sites answering questions about your experiences. Experience on Facebook, Twitter, and Instagram a bonus.

She clicked and read through the application. She also read what was expected for the cover letter.

She closed her other files, sat back, and thought for a moment. Then she dove in and roughed out her cover letter.

Thirty minutes later, she read it through. *Not half bad.*

She built an account on the magazine's website, filled in the spaces on the application, and hit save.

She heard Curt rustling around in the kitchen. She shut down her computer and called it a day.

"Hi," she kissed him as she walked into the kitchen and found him rinsing his lunch dishes and putting them into the dishwasher.

"Hi. How was your day?"

She tried to not read anything in his tone. Their *discussions* had become more frequent. She knew he was worried.

Hell, she was worried too. That's why she'd been doing everything she could to try and find work. She was determined to make this work. To not regret her decision to turn in her resignation.

She'd make it. She'd be the writer she'd longed to be.

She had no choice. She'd do it. Or else.

"Mine was good. How was yours?" She pulled down two wine glasses, while he reached into the fridge and grabbed their favorite chardonnay.

She'd promised herself she'd give up many of their old activities, now that she didn't have a paying job. Their nightly relaxing time wasn't one of them. They'd been performing the same ritual since their youngest had left for college.

They settled into their chairs at the bar in the kitchen. Side by side, facing one another, ready to talk about their days.

Curt launched into a story about an event they'd just booked. It would require him to work the next Sunday, the third that month. But given their current situation, he had been more than happy to pick up the extra hours.

"It's only a two-hour event. I'll have to be there an hour or so early to get the chairs set up. And then clean up afterward. But they're willing to pay time and a half."

She laid her hand on his arm. "Curt, I get it. Thank you. I know you hate working weekends. Especially how many you've been working. And I appreciate you stepping up so I can do this. I promise you, I'll have this all under control here in a few weeks."

"Does that mean you've had luck? Did you find anything promising? Another meeting?"

He had been excited the day before when she'd told him about the connection she'd made. She'd had several meetings, she knew it was only time before one of them turned into a paid gig.

But she never gave up. She was hoping to find a few more. Maybe if she got this job, she could use that to connect with others.

She swirled her wine in her glass, watching the red as it sparkled with each rotation. "Um, I did find an ad for a job with a magazine. A reporting job. It's only a year assignment, but it looks interesting. And I meet the qualifications."

"Did you apply?"

She looked at him, a bit annoyed. That seemed to be his only interest these days. The application process. That and getting paid.

"No. I have most of it filled out. I'll finish it in the morning. I wanted to think a bit and make sure I have everything on my cover letter before I hit submit."

He nodded.

She swallowed the rest of the liquid in her glass, then set it down a little harder than anticipated. "Don't you care what it is? Don't you want to know what the job entails?"

He slammed his down next to hers. "Will you get paid?"

"Yes, Curt, I'd get paid." She tried to bite back the frustration she knew was in her voice.

"Okay then."

She jumped out of her chair. "Jeez, Curt. Give me a break, will you? I've only been at this a short while. Do you expect miracles?"

"No, I don't. But ..." He walked over and set his glass down on the counter. Then corked the bottle and put it back into the fridge.

"What?" She leaned against the counter, crossed her arms, and watched him moving things here and there around the kitchen. He looked like a man on a mission. And yet he wasn't accomplishing anything. "I can see you have something to say. Say it."

He came closer to her, leaned into the counter facing her. He mimicked her posture, crossing his arms too. "I got another bill today. From the checkup and tests I had last month."

"What? Why didn't you say something? Where is it?" She turned and looked through the basket by the door, the place they dropped things in as they came in each night. She found the envelope from the doctor's office, yanked the paper out, and opened it up. "Eight thousand? For what? Where did this come from? I thought we had it all? This has got to be wrong."

"Well apparently not. If you read on, down here," he moved next to her and tapped the bottom of the page. "It says they've been *negotiating* the price."

"Negotiating? What the fuck does that mean?" She folded it back up, put it in the envelope, and moved back to the center of the kitchen. "Look, forget about this for now."

He gave her a look. The look that said: *How can I? How are we going to pay for this?* And a little of: *I hate the fact that I put us in this situation in the first place.*

That was the look she hated the most. It's the one that broke her heart, just a little, every time. He'd felt bad after all the tests and procedures had revealed it wasn't as bad as they had first suspected. Even worse now that they wanted to continue testing every six months. What should have been a good thing, just made him feel bad that they'd wasted so much money.

She'd been trying to knock that out of his head since the first bill had arrived in their mailbox.

"I'll call tomorrow. You know all of this is senseless. The last time I called up, they dropped the charges to almost nothing. I swear sometimes I think they do this just to see if you're paying attention."

"Yeah, well I'd much rather let you do what you need to do, then to worry about how we're going to pay the next medical bill. I've been looking at the premiums now that we don't have your insurance. I'm checking with the city, but I think we're going to have to go out on our own. And …"

She grabbed him by his collar and pulled him in, planting her lips on his. "Just, stop. None of this is going to change anything tonight. Let's just celebrate I have a few potentials that look really good, okay?"

He dropped his forehead to hers. Closed his eyes. Then pulled her in for a bear hug, the kind she just melted into whenever she could.

She loved that he was several inches taller. And when she pressed against his chest, and he circled her with his arms, she felt warm, safe, and secure. It was a feeling like no other. One she'd fell in love with only a few weeks after they started dating, and it never had changed.

"I made your favorite tonight," she mumbled into his chest.

"Is that what smells so good?" He loved her lasagna.

"Mm, hmm. I even ran up to the bakery for fresh bread."

"Is it ready?"

She glanced up and grinned. The twinkle in his eye had returned.

She vowed right then and there that she would do her damnedest to keep it there, make it even better, in the very short term.

"Why don't you grab two waters and the silverware. I'll fill our plates."

30

Sherri dipped her paintbrush into the paint. She swirled the deep red onto her canvas, stood back and admired the color. How her work had changed in the weeks she'd been here.

She saw the confidence. Her work from before lacked definition. But with every conversation she'd had with Francesca, every piece of art she completed, she'd seen a noticeable improvement in the way she painted.

"Hello," Francesca's low-keyed voice floated from behind.

Sherri turned and saw her walking up the path. Francesca gave a little wave as she moved to her side.

"I hadn't seen you this afternoon and wanted to check in with you." She stopped and stared. "Wow, you've come a long way. It's beautiful."

A true compliment coming from Francesca. Sherri had already witnessed she didn't give them easily. In fact, she'd only heard anything remotely as complimentary twice to the group since they'd arrived.

Sherri popped the tip of her brush into her mouth, nibbling on the corner. She'd been assessing it for the past hour, adding little bits here and there. "I've been focusing in on the details, adding depth and definition. I think I might set it aside for a day or two. But for the most part, it's done."

"I love how you've transitioned the mood from here to here," Francesca got in close, looking at the details. "And the color ... I have to say, I think that's been your biggest change while you were here. You were subdued when you got here. This boldness, this is the real you."

Sherri went eyebrows up. Had she really changed that much? Bold? She'd never used that adjective to describe herself before.

"What are you thinking of doing with your art when you return home? I know when you first got here, your sole goal was to explore. Any thoughts now?"

Sherri dropped her paintbrush into the bucket of water to soak. She folded her arms, thinking, considering her options.

Because she hadn't just been thinking about how she could include painting in her life. She'd been thinking about a whole lot more.

Like where Wesley fit in. They'd been talking several times a week by

FaceTime. She'd come to rely on their conversations more and more.

And her job, her school. Was teaching still in her heart?

She'd always wanted to explore painting more. But what did that look like? "I have no idea." She blew out her breath, looking at her new friend. "Does this make you happy? Are you glad you transitioned away from corporate? Do you ever miss America?"

Sherri knew Francesca's story well. Born in Florence, she'd moved to the US as a small child. She'd studied art in college and worked for several art galleries in New York City. It was only after she'd divorced and met her current husband that she'd questioned everything. When they'd decided to marry, they'd concocted a plan of moving to Italy as a part of the package. That had been five years before, and they'd never looked back.

"I don't miss it at all. In fact, the last time I went back to New York to see my family, I counted the days until I could return home. We've only owned this place for four years, but I can't imagine what I ever did without it."

"But what made you leave? You were successful in New York. This is an extension of what you did there, and yet it's so different. Did you have any idea *this* is what you wanted to do?"

Francesca motioned back to main house. "Would you like to join me for some tea?"

Together they walked back up to the kitchen. Francesca filled a pot with hot water, then led Sherri back out to a little table for two in her gardens.

"Can I ask, are you and Wesley together?"

Sherri nodded, then shook her head, then laughed at her own indecision. "I took his class back home."

Francesca nodded.

"And somehow, we wound up talking after class. From the first class, we chatted over tea long after the class had ended. And over time that morphed into a few dinners out. We've talked several nights a week since I've been here." She took a deep breath and let it out. "And I have no idea where it's leading."

"Sometimes you don't have to define it. What happens, happens."

"Spoken from experience?"

"Yeah, I guess it is." Francesca stopped as her husband walked out with a plate of freshly baked muffins. He gave them both a plate before retreating towards the house.

Francesca watched him disappear into the kitchen, her eyes clearly giving away the love she had for him. "Our love affair was fast. We both have been married before, and we'd been single for years. We'd both decided we wanted to change that, so that may have made things easier. But when we met, something clicked. I suddenly could see my future, with him by my side. Everything fell into place pretty quickly after that. And here we are."

"Was it easier? At your age?"

Francesca snorted. "Oh, God no. We're both fiercely independent and have our own way of doing things. I think the one thing that helped us is we were both looking for a change in our lives. And we both were willing to work on a relationship as top priority. We made us first. And we planned our lives together second. I don't think that's something I could have ever done back in my twenties, or even thirties. This is more of my second act. And it works. My kids are back home, happy and healthy. His too. We probably see them more now because they love to come and visit."

"How did you know that this is what you wanted?"

"I can't say I ever would have pictured this, not before I married. I'd always loved running an art gallery, hosting classes, painting. Doing my own thing. I saw myself doing that forever. But I also enjoyed having my own creative outlet. I loved when I got out and explored and played. I loved teaching classes; I'd been doing it on the side since my kids were little."

"Wesley told me he taught alongside you in Sedona."

"Yep. It was one of those weeklong retreats where people came to *find* themselves. I attended as a student and loved the results. And by the third year they asked me to present."

"Was that the start of this?" Sherri motioned with her shoulder to the workshop behind them.

"Maybe?" Francesca twisted her mouth, squinted, thinking. "Honestly, it was a lot more spur of the moment than that. I've always loved Italy. I was born here, but don't remember living here; I was too small. But we used to come here all the time when I was growing up. My mom named me after one of her favorite authors, someone she'd found on one of her trips before I was born. I continued the tradition and brought my own kids here multiple times. I'd always said I wanted to live in Italy. As I was planning life with my new husband-to-be, we finally said to one another: why not?"

"So it wasn't a smack over the head. Or something falling out of the sky that said: pick me, pick me!"

Francesca laughed. "Oh, no. I was too dense for that. I swear, the signs were there, over and over again. I missed them all. In fact, I'd had a chance to do this long ago, when my youngest left for college. I ignored it. That's when I was having trouble with my ex. It would have been perfect for me to leave that old life and start something new. But, alas, I was too stubborn. I thought I could fix anything. And in retrospect, if I hadn't stayed, I wouldn't have met Nick."

"Everything for a reason?"

"The universe speaks in mysterious ways."

Sherri knew that. In more ways than one. She felt the universe had been screaming at her lately. And yet, here she was, still moving at a snail's pace.

"I was hoping something would fall from the sky soon and hit me over the head. That it would tell me what to do with my life." Sherri had wished for that on numerous occasions. "But ..."

"But you've pushed your painting skills to new levels. Your latest is fabulous."

Sherri nodded. "Thank you. I have pushed. And I love what I'm doing."

"Where do you see yourself going from here?"

"That's what I don't know. This is so difficult. You know, my friend back home, the one I've taught school with for years, she just up and quit. In some ways, I think that's easier. Sink or swim. Instead, I feel like I'm floundering, not sure what I want to do next."

"Do you like teaching?"

"I love it."

"But you're tired of what you do?"

"Yes, I'm tired of the red tape. I'm sick of the mandates on teaching performance. And now my anxiety about safety is going to be sky high. I love the kids though. And I love staying busy. I never thought I'd find it so difficult trying to move forward."

"My best advice to you is to stop trying so hard. Things tend to work out best if you just try one thing at a time. Say yes to more. Try new things. But then you don't need me to tell you all of that. You're here; that says it all. Let me go grab something for you."

Everything she said was true.

Sherri thought back to how far she'd come since the beginning of the year.

Her fiftieth birthday had taken her by surprise. Tanner had baked her a cake. She'd been surrounded by her friends. As she blew out the candles, she knew she needed something new in her life.

And looking back, she could see how much she'd changed.

Maybe she had set things in motion when she'd convinced Annette to go to California with her. She thought about her plans before she'd left, and how things had changed since she'd been back.

Francesca returned through the kitchen door, flipping through a binder as she walked. She laid it in front of her before returning to her seat.

"This is a life journey workbook I use in one of my other retreats."

Francesca flipped the book to the table of contents and started pointing out sections. She provided a brief description of each. "We've covered a lot of this in our talks every morning. And in some ways, this is a little more simplistic than the level we're at in this class. But it might help spawn some ideas."

Francesca picked it up, flipped to the back of the book. She returned it in front of Sherri. "This is the biggest reason I'm giving this to you. This is an interesting exercise, one you might not have done before. The purpose is to see in writing things you want to do for the rest of your life.

"We all have a bucket list. But this exercise takes it a step further. Your goal is to create a list of one hundred to-do's you wish to complete in the next few years. It sounds easy enough, but trust me, it's not. One hundred is a lot."

Sherri nodded. She'd never written down one hundred items before. But she did have a mental bucket list. And she'd vision boarded a time or two.

"Once you have your list, you start to break it down by category. The next few pages I offer advice on how to help you weave through your wants and desires. How to look at it in different ways. I promise you if you spend an hour or two with this exercise, you'll see your life in new ways."

Sherri glanced at her watch. She had a little over two hours before they met for dinner. She picked up her workbook, thanked Francesca, and made her way down to the flower garden to fill in the answers.

Life. Love. Happiness. She had so much on her mind.

She'd never really believed she'd change her life for the better. She'd been traveling the same road for so long, she didn't know anything else was out there. But maybe it was time to think about the answers.

Maybe it was time she put her own needs and desires first. Instead of accepting her life the way it was, maybe it was time she did something about it.

She was only fifty. She had so much left to do.

If she could just figure out how the pieces fit together.

31

Sherri rose to another beautiful day. She found herself longing to take a walk, to find the perfect place to paint.

It had become somewhat of a habit, one that she was thoroughly enjoying.

She made her way to the shared kitchen and turned the coffeepot on. Then made her way back to her room to get ready for the day. With her bag packed with her paint gear, she returned to the kitchen to pick up her to-go cup.

She stopped by the big picture window, stood looking out at the horizon and sighed.

With only two days until the retreat was over, she found herself already grieving. Soon it would be back to the States, back to her life.

Back to a life without painting on a regular basis.

As much as it hadn't been a part of her life before this year, she'd already discovered it was no longer an option.

In the course of one summer - four weeks of time - painting was in her, heart and soul.

Or maybe it was Italy. She snickered as she took a sip of coffee. Italy was *definitely* in her soul. *Oh, what it would be like to live here forever ...*

She shook her head, coming back to reality. As much as she loved Italy, America was her home. She wanted to see her son again, her friends. She even missed her home.

And some part of her missed her kids. Not the school, not the red tape, not the politics of teaching; her kids. The mere act of helping them learn and grow.

She wanted that again. But another part of her was ready to add in more creativity.

And with Francesca's help, she was starting to see it all come together.

Funny, how life had a way of showing the way.

She sipped her coffee as she dropped her bag to the ground. She balanced her cup on a rock, then opened her portable easel.

She pulled out the canvas she'd worked up the night before. A few pencil marks covered the white space here and there to act as her guide. She'd roughed in her ideas, knowing this location well. She'd painted in this very spot a handful of times. The colors left her in awe.

She glanced at the horizon; it was a very good spot.

She smiled as she stood straight, allowing her hands to come together above her head, reaching for the sky. She balanced, took a few deep breaths, and did a few twists to help her relax.

Then she grabbed her coffee, ready to finish it before she began. She stared out at the scenery, as if memorizing it before she left.

She'd miss this place.

But part of her was ready to move forward. She had ideas. She was ready to take some action.

She'd already sent an email exploring the possibility of teaching an art class after school. Several other teachers offered similar classes to supplement their income, including teaching a piano class and drawing. Why not painting too? She'd already come up with some ideas for what she would offer.

She'd been doing research every night, looking at what was offered for kids. A lot of them were good, but she'd been contemplating more.

Her class with Wesley had given her ideas. A painting class to allow personal expression. An art class that helped build self-awareness, self-confidence, and made them feel good about their own inner creativity.

She'd spin it, of course, for something tweens would love. But she knew there were a lot of eight- and ten-year-olds like she'd been. All she'd wanted to do was get her hands dirty with paint and clay. And since the school systems no longer offered it, she was going to do something about it.

She'd pulled together her ideas and had a pretty good approach. She'd talked with Wesley about it several times to get his input. But now that it was in final format, strong enough for her to have sent an email to the school board, she'd also sent something to Wesley, to gain his final approval.

She hadn't heard from him in two days. She was starting to wonder why.

She'd pulled up her email before she'd left her room. But he hadn't responded yet. She wondered what he was doing.

She hadn't seen him in a month, and yet she felt closer to him than ever.

They'd been talking on FaceTime several nights a week. They texted all the time. She could hardly wait to get back and see where this relationship took her.

He was everything her ex wasn't. Burt had wanted to live fast and furious; Wesley loved calm and simplified. Her ex had never listened, even when things were important. Wesley listened so intently, she often was a little unnerved at what he heard in her voice.

She'd always chosen bad boys, and now at fifty she was thinking she'd found the error in her ways. And luckily, Wesley had been there waiting for her, without her even realizing she was looking.

She picked up several tubes of paint and added color to her palette. The sun danced across the sky, sending shockwaves of yellows, blues, and pinks bursting from the gardens. She knew she'd remember the sweet fragrance the rest of her life. It would always remind her of her time in Italy, when she changed her life for the better.

Though she still wasn't quite sure what that would all entail.

She picked up her paintbrush, then turned to move behind her easel.

And ran right into Wesley's chest. Paint palette and all.

They both looked down at his shirt, until he started to laugh.

"I guess you're right. I just can't avoid being covered in paint."

"Wesley. I'm sorry." Sherri dropped her palette to the ground, reached in her bag for the rag she'd tucked in earlier. She started dabbing at the paint on his shirt.

"I'm not. Now I feel like I'm at home." He grabbed her hands, pulled the rag from her fingers and dropped it to the ground. Then hauled her up into his arms.

She was a little shellshocked. Why was he here? How was he here? What did it mean?

But as she watched his eyes dance, watching her, she felt everything slip away. All she'd been thinking about. Her work. Her life. What did it matter if he was in her life?

This - whatever it was between them - could be good.

And with his arms wrapped around her, she decided she wanted nothing more than all of it. Every last bit of him from his head to his toes.

He chuckled as he tightened his grip. "Yes, I think you should do it."

He didn't wait for her answer. He kissed her, letting his tongue taste everything he'd missed for the past few weeks.

Sherri didn't mind. She reached higher, letting her fingers tangle in his hair. "How'd you know I wanted to kiss you?" She grinned.

"I can always read your mind."

He did it so well. As much as she loved seeing him, wanted to pull him in closer and never come up for air, curiosity got the better of her.

"Why *are* you here?" Her brain was finally putting together the pieces that he was here, standing in front of her.

"To see you." He leaned in to kiss her again, and lingered, breathing her in. "And to tell you that you should do it."

She went eyebrows up.

What the hell was he talking about?

"Your email. Yes, I think you should offer more classes. I think you should expand beyond the school. And if we work the times out, you can use my space too."

"Really?" She could hear her voice getting a little higher than she'd anticipated. She always did that when she was excited. "Are you sure?"

"Perfectly. Think about it. It's a win/win for both of us. If parents drop their kids off and see my facilities, they may book a class or two of their own. It could be a big boost for me too."

She draped her arms around his neck. "Look at you. Always the entrepreneur."

He just grinned.

"But why *are* you here? You could have emailed me back. It's cheaper." But she couldn't hide her delight. She was glad to see him.

"I missed you. And since you don't have to be back at school for a couple of weeks, I was hoping to talk you in to staying here a few extra days. With me."

"Really?" Her mind quickly scanned her mental to-do list. Most of it was getting ready to start school. But since she still had a couple of weeks before her first day, none of it was pressing.

She already planned on spending a couple of days with him when she returned. Did it matter if it was in Italy? "And where would we go?"

"I have a room booked in Cinque Terre, it's a place I've been to before. I promise you'll have a view from your balcony. And a comfy bed to share with me. If you want it. I'm not pushing."

His eyes heated as he searched her eyes, waiting for her confirmation.

She couldn't say no to this man. What's more, she didn't want to. "Yes. To all of it."

No more waiting on the sidelines for her life to begin.

No more wondering what direction she should take.

He was here. He came for her. And just watching him, she knew he was meant to be in her life for a long time.

Best they get started on living it, together, right here in Italy.

"But I have one more night here. I suppose I could leave early." She said it more to herself, thinking.

"Nope. I know tonight's your last night. I'm staying a few miles from here. I don't want to pull you away from here. I just wanted to catch you before you started packing to go home."

"I'm spending the afternoon boxing up my paintings and sending them home. Wanna see?"

But she didn't wait for his response. She left her stuff right where it was, knowing she'd return to get it later.

She linked her fingers with his and walked backwards towards her room, pulling him as she went.

She found her door, and pushed him inside.

As the door shut behind her, he took her breath away as they fell onto her bed.

Hungry wasn't the word for what either of them felt.

She wanted to devour him.

So she touched, and played.

"I'm not quite sure how this happened," she said between kisses. "We weren't even really together when I left. And yet, here we are."

"I knew this was happening, from the second time you joined me after class."

"You did?" She went elbows up on his chest, looking deep into his eyes. "How? I didn't even look at you *that way* until after the *event*."

"It wasn't what you said, but how you said it." He flipped her over, so he was on top. "You started telling me about your son, about a trip you'd taken the previous summer."

"When we went to San Francisco."

"Uh huh. You take care of your people. And they love you for it. That works for me. *You* work for me."

Her eyes narrowed, revealing a sensual smile. She pushed him, once again taking top position. "Now it's time for me to take care of *you*."

32

Annette sat at her desk, tapping her fingers as she read.

Really?

Could they get any more precise?

She'd read through a zillion job descriptions in the past four hours, and she was getting a little drunk on their language.

Who has all of this experience?

Where do they find people with these specific skills?

She printed the latest off and added it to her pile. She'd started accumulating some of the goofiest in a folder. *Maybe I'll write an article on it later.*

She clicked and scanned through another one.

Like five years of social media experience to help design Pinterest campaigns.

What the fuck did that even mean?

She knew what Pinterest was. But designing campaigns? How did one even go about that? *Why* would they go about that? Was it even possible to have five years of experience with this? And when had she gotten so old she didn't know what this all meant?

Annette took a deep breath, trying to relieve the stress she could feel building.

She never expected all of this when she'd been sitting in the classroom dreaming of bigger and better things. She hadn't realized how different the real world was. How freelancing was. How crazy the job hunt had become.

How little she felt she knew. How small the whole process was making her feel.

She was a smart, intelligent woman. She had a master's degree in education. She'd taught school for twenty-five years. People trusted their kids to her.

And yet nobody would trust her with a Pinterest campaign?

She typed *Pinterest* into her browser window. She logged into her account and saw the one lonely pinboard she'd created two years before, when she'd decided she wanted to redo their kitchen. She'd pinned exactly eight pictures of kitchen designs she'd decided she loved.

She glanced at them now. *Hmm, not bad.*

At least her tastes hadn't changed.

Not that she'd ever gotten that kitchen. Cancer scare, and all.

She rubbed her eyes.

That was her world now. Before. After.

Before Curt got sick. After.

Before an active shooter changed her world. After.

Before she quit her job. After.

Before she went crazy …

Buzz.

She jumped at the sound of her phone vibrating on her desk. Feeling a little annoyed, angry she felt a little annoyed, she picked it up and answered.

"Hello?"

"Hi, is this Annette Hinton?"

Annette pushed her chair back and sat up a little straighter. "Yes, this is she."

"Oh, hi, I'm so glad I reached you. This is Wendy Tavish, the editor at Escape Magazine."

"Hi, Wendy." Annette swallowed, trying to force her nerves back down.

"Congratulations! We loved your submission."

"Thank you!" Annette tried to hold back her excitement. She jumped up, and ran into the kitchen, trying to hold in her squeals.

"Is this a good time to talk?"

As if I had anything else to do …

She had trouble finding her voice. She didn't want to sound to desperate, her voice too squeaky. "Give me one second."

She covered the mouthpiece with her hand and took three deep breaths to control the butterflies fluttering inside. "Thanks for holding."

"Sure. I'm excited to reach you. We'd like to welcome you to take the next step with the travel writing position, if you're still interested. And I'd like to talk with you a bit about your submission. Make sure you're a good fit."

"I'd love to hear more about the opportunity. And yes, I'm definitely interested." Annette shut her eyes, trying to tone down the excitement she knew was in her voice. "What's next?"

Wendy laughed. "I love when people are excited about this. And rightfully so. This is an exciting opportunity. It's one of my favorite columns, actually."

"I agree. I couldn't believe it when I found the ad. It … I was excited to apply."

"Well, we're really glad you did. We loved your article, your cover letter, and your application. It was a bit different than our other applicants. We've been doing this for four years now, and I'll have to say we've pretty much attracted journalists and bloggers before. But your application, it was … refreshing."

Refreshing. That was a good thing, right? Annette held her breath, not sure what to say. Before she got the chance, Wendy jumped back in.

"Tell me, why did you apply? Your job history says you were a teacher until a few weeks ago."

Annette took a deep breath. She'd been rehearsing this in her mind. She didn't want to scare anyone off by talking about the impact of the shooting. But it wasn't something she could hide.

"I loved teaching. It's all I wanted to do when I was younger. But over the years, it's lost some of its magic. My own children are adults now, which means I have more time to explore what I want to do. And my English background is finally catching up with me. I always said I wanted to write the epic novel someday. I guess I consider this my time to blossom and discover the writer that's been hidden deep inside. And while I still have hopes of writing my novel someday, I'm also reaching out in other ways and exploring how to grow my writing skills. That's what led me to your announcement."

"Have you started your novel yet?"

"Um, well, I have a lot of notes." Annette was thrown a bit of guard. But she recovered quickly. "I've been writing short stories for the past couple of years, just for myself. I've submitted a few this past year, trying to get them published. And now that I'm free to write full time, I'm trying my hand at both fiction and nonfiction work."

"I would imagine this is different than the writing you did with your elementary kids."

Annette laughed. "Yes. Definitely. But the kids I taught still had imaginations. They hadn't lost that flair for making up wild stories."

She stopped for a minute, swallowing, pushing down the mixed emotions she'd had over the past few weeks. "I loved teaching. But I always kept writing as a creative outlet, just for me. While I've never been serious about turning it into a career in the past, I've always journaled and written stories. I took a lot of creative writing courses in school, so it's a side of me that I'll never give up. And now I like to think I can take that in all sorts of different directions. I'm excited about discovering what this new path brings."

"As far as traveling goes, this job does entail quite a bit of travel. If you're selected, you'll travel to each of our twelve locations for a week each. They are all over the world, so travel will be a big part of your job. Plus we'll need you here in San Francisco for meetings. Our columnists have also done promotional tours, expos, travel events, things like that. Nothing too hectic, but you might be required to be in New York or L.A. on occasion. Otherwise the rest of it can be done on location. That's not a problem?"

Annette didn't even hesitate. "Nope, not at all. As I mentioned, my kids are grown. I'm looking for new adventures. This could be just what I need to kickstart my new direction."

"I agree. That's one of the reasons I was excited about your submission. Obviously, our writers are mostly journalists and travel bloggers. They do this stuff for a living, and you can feel it in their write ups. Something was different with your approach. It was more of an a-ha moment when I read what you wrote. And I think a lot of our readers will pick up on that too."

"I would love to give it a try."

"Good. Well, then I guess we'll move on to the next step. We'd like to see what you can do under deadline."

"Okay. I'm ready. What's next?"

"As we mentioned in our ad, this is a two-step process. You've passed the first hurdle. We've selected ten finalists whom we all feel have the potential to be a good fit. So now we move on to round two. Another assignment. I have the details in an email I'll send over to you now."

Annette could do round two. She could do anything. It was the first bite she'd had. And this job had caught her interest from the start. It was way out of her comfort zone. Something she'd never experienced in the past. But a dream job - yep, she could definitely define it as that.

"There, I just sent it. Did you receive it?"

Annette ran back to her office, tapped on her inbox, and waited for her new messages to load. When she found the one from Wendy, she clicked. "Yes, it's here."

"Good. The second phase is pretty simple. We want to see how well you work under pressure. There's ten of you in the running. We're speaking with all of you this afternoon. You'll have until the end of this week to write a thousand-word article using the content in the email as your guidance. What we need from you is to write a story and sell us on your home town. What makes it special? Why do you live where you do? What do you think our readers would enjoy reading about your city? And you must do it all in a very succinct thousand-word article. While we won't publish it in our magazine, we will use it online. We'll see what our readers think. It'll help us determine which person to offer the job."

That sounded simple enough. She quickly scanned the email, noting the bullet items that had to be included. "I see it says pictures are a bonus. Do you need anything special? Size? Content?" *Yep, that sounded like a good question.* Annette was so nervous, but she wanted to come off as if this was simple, her norm.

"Great question. I should have clarified that a bit." Wendy stopped as if she were making a note. "Really, it can be anything you want it to be. If you get the job, we have requirements there too. We want photos with your stories. But for this, we're looking at possibilities, not specifics. We want to see what you take, how it relates to your story, what it contributes to the overall feel of the article."

"Okay. I'm glad they don't have to be professional. I don't have any equipment. I love taking pictures, but any more, they're usually with my phone."

"And that's all we need for now. Again, if you're our *one*, we'll train you on the details. But this will only go online, so whatever you take with your phone will be sufficient."

Annette quickly scanned the rest of the notes. Mostly content suggestions, what they liked and didn't, things to include in her write up. Nothing out of the ordinary. "I think everything else sounds easy enough. I shouldn't have any problems."

"Good. This storyline is fairly easy; it's not meant to trip you up. We know you should be an expert in your own location, that's why we've made that the focus. Your deadline is this Friday. Then we put all ten submissions up online to let our readers help us out. We'll be watching analytics for the ten, see which ones are read more, shared more, commented on. Of course, that's only part of the process. We'll have the ultimate say. We want someone for the job we feel is a good fit for our magazine. We should be able to make our final selection in about a week. And from there, we finalize the contracts and get everything in place. We'd expect you to leave on your first trip," Wendy hesitated.

Annette could here flipping in the background, as if Wendy was consulting her calendar. Annette took the time to pull up her calendar too, though she knew there was nothing as important. If she got the job, she'd do it. No ifs, ands or buts.

"Probably in about six weeks. Do you have a passport?"

"Yes. I just renewed it about a couple of years ago for a trip we took to Mexico."

"Perfect. That makes things easier. Any other questions?"

"No, not that I can think of." Annette's eyes still scanned the documents Wendy had sent over. Her mind churned.

"Okay then. I'll watch for your article by Friday and confirm when I receive it. And if you have any other questions for me, let me know."

They hung up, and Annette dropped her phone to her desk and let out a squeal.

"Yes!"

She created a new file and started typing out a few of her ideas. She had several days to put together the best article of her life, and she had no intention of failing.

This was her first chance at a real job - a job she was very excited about.

To travel for a year? It was something she and Curt had talked about in retirement.

She opened a browser window and glanced back at the column over the last four years. Many of the places she had no idea where they were.

What would the destinations be like? Would she really get to go there?

It really would be a dream come true.

Maybe Curt could tag along.

Her mind itched to share her news.

She glanced at the clock in the corner of her computer screen. Curt wouldn't be home for several more hours. Her news would have to wait. She didn't want to call him, so she settled in and decided her news could keep.

33

One hour later, Annette grabbed her bag and her car keys. There was no way she could hold her news for later that evening.

And she decided calling wouldn't be good enough. She wanted to see her husband's reaction when she gave him the news.

She hopped into her car and drove to the park where she knew he would be. She remembered him saying something about pruning, so she figured he'd be there most of the day. She saw his truck parked in the far corner of the lot. She pulled forward and found a front space.

She loved this park. It had always been one of her favorites. The views were to die for, with the river following along the path, and hills on both sides of the river. It never lost its charm, no matter what time of the year she visited.

She thought back to the long walks they used to take as a couple. *Why don't we do that anymore?*

She snorted, then looked around to make sure nobody was around. Work. Life. They'd simply become too busy to enjoy the simple things, like walks. Something she vowed right then to change.

She knew he'd be somewhere along the path. She got out of the car and listened. She heard a generator off in the distance. And there he was.

Annette was giddy as she watched her husband work. Somehow, seeing him in action always took her breath away.

He was up on a ladder, trimming away at the vines that were growing above the arbor. It was one of the more popular parks in town. They'd planned it well, with a rentable shelter that could be used year-round.

And the way the vines covered the sides, the structure made it a beautiful sight, every time she saw it. Even at the holidays, they followed the vines with sparkling lights, interweaving white stars every few feet. The glow was something you could see for miles, especially as you walked along the river.

She locked her car and followed the trail over to where he worked. She leaned against a railing and waited for him to come down off the ladder.

He was intent on his work. He was like that at home too. Let him loose in the garden, and you wouldn't see him again until he was through. He was in his zone, the place he loved to go. Headphones on, probably listening to an audio book.

Luckily, she didn't mind the view. He was still a good-looking man. His jeans fit him well; almost as well as when she'd first met him in college. His job kept him active, so he hadn't changed much in all the years. His shirt pulled up as he stretched above him working to trim every branch. She caught a glimpse of his skin, just enough to send shivers down her spine.

Sure, they fought. They'd been married forever. But that was just where they were; the stress of trying to make sure it all stayed together. She knew in the end, when everything was on track again, they'd still be there for each other.

Life was good. If she'd ever needed reminding, this was her sign.

She watched as he stepped down, bending to drop his equipment on the ground.

She moved behind him and tapped him on his shoulder. "Hi."

He jumped, took off his headphones, and switched off the power generator. The sound died, leaving nothing but silence, with only the wind rippling through the leaves, and the birds tweeting in the background. "Jeez, you scared me. I didn't see you." He leaned in and brushed his lips against hers. "What are you doing here?"

"I have some good news. And I didn't want to wait until you got home tonight."

"Yeah?"

"Yep," she nodded. "Do you remember I told you about the job with the travel magazine, the one where I'd write up an article a month based on different places I'd travel to?"

He nodded. "You talked about that the other night."

"They called today. I'm a finalist."

"Really?" His eyes got wide. "Wonderful!" He picked her up and kissed her hard. He set her down and backed away as her words caught up with him. "What does that mean, a finalist?"

"I guess they have ten people that met all of their requirements. They're having a write-off contest. And the best wins the job."

He crossed his arms.

Which was only mildly annoying. She knew what that look meant.

But today, she was just too happy to care. She was on the right track, she just knew it.

"Okay. What does that mean?"

"The woman who called me is the editor. I'd be working for her. This is the fourth year they've hired someone like this, so they have a pattern. They narrow the applicants down to ten. Then they send over an assignment. We have until the end of the week to turn in our article. Then they post them to help determine which they like best."

Curt scratched his head. "Online?"

"Yes, online. Curt, you really have to come up to modern times." She laughed. "Anything that doesn't have dirt attached to it is complicated to you."

"Hey," he tried to sound wounded, but they both knew it was true. When it came to technology in the house, Annette was the one that set everything up. If he touched it, it seemed to go awry.

"I'm going to have to dig your iPad out again and download the magazine's app. That way you can read my articles," she kidded. Mind over matter, she was thoroughly convincing herself she'd get the job.

"But the good news is she told me my application intrigued her. She said she found it refreshing. They normally look for reporters and travel bloggers, but the way I wrote up my application made her think I could have a unique approach to the project. It's only a one-year assignment, so they like to change things up a bit."

She saw his eyes narrow at her last comment.

"Just a one-year assignment?"

"Look, if I get this, it's a full year of pay. And it'll give me time to work on my book, plus try and find other assignments too. If I can add this to my resume, that'll give me credibility as well. This really could be a launching pad for future assignments."

He nodded. "I can see that." And for once his mood improved rather than looking at the downside.

"What is it you have to do?"

"I have to write up an article selling my hometown. With a unique approach."

"What are you going to do?"

"I haven't completely decided yet. I'm throwing around some ideas. I've read every article written in that column since it first started. I think I've read several of them a dozen times. So I have the feel down. I know what they want. I'm just trying to find my approach. I'll write some this afternoon. Get my thoughts down. Then I'll blast through it in the morning. That still gives me another day for editing and rewriting. I've lived here forever. This'll be a piece of cake."

He grabbed her hand and pulled her in for a quick kiss.

His lips turned up in a grin, but she could still see the stress behind his eyes.

She vowed right then to do whatever it took to make that go away, forever.

"They post all ten online? You'll get to see your competition?"

"Yes. They want to get their readers reactions too. They're going to see what comments come in, what articles are shared, what people like."

"And how do they know what they like?"

"From the like counts. From analytics. From the number of posts shared on Facebook, Twitter, places like that."

Curt swiped his hand through his hair, a blank look crossed his face. She laughed. Clearly, he didn't have a clue.

"When I get this job, we'll sit down and have a class. I'll get your iPad ready so you can read. And I'll teach you how to like my posts, and maybe we'll get you an Instagram account. That way you can keep up with me when I'm traveling around the world."

It was as if it hit him for the first time that she'd be traveling if she got this job. "How much travel again?"

She bit back a sigh. They'd been over this the other night. Before she'd applied for the job. "Maybe a week or two each month. We talked about this. We decided that you could come with me once or twice."

He nodded. He shook his head.

A small glimmer came back to his eyes. "I'll help any way I can."

She hip-bumped him. "You'll like my article?"

"Of course!"

She saw it on his face. He still had no idea what she meant. That was okay. She'd teach him. "Thank you."

"For what?"

"For letting me do this. For letting me go down this road. I know it's not going to be easy. I know this is all a big adjustment. It's not like teaching. But I really think this is going to be great. It's what I need, what we need. We're going to come out of this in a much better place."

She saw a hint of doubt. But he recovered quick. "I trust you, and that's all that matters. I know I haven't made life exactly easy the past couple of years. The kids are gone. We really don't have any huge commitments riding on us. If this is what you need to do, I'm behind you all the way. We'll make it work. As long as you're happy, I'm happy."

"I'm happy."

"Good." He pulled her in again, kissing her hard. Then he turned her around and gave her a playful push towards her car. "Go. I have to get back to my pruning."

"Before the boss comes around and sees you're not clipping the way you should?"

"Exactly." He grinned.

"I was thinking, maybe we could go out tonight. We haven't been to Thai Basil in forever. Maybe we could celebrate."

"Sounds like a plan."

"Can you be home by five?"

"Sure. I want to take a shower first."

"Perfect. I was thinking I'd wear a dress." She'd turned back around, but was walking backwards, away from him. She sashayed, flirting just a little.

"Oh yeah?" His eyebrows went up, as his eyes did a quick scan down.

She felt a tingle. She loved making an effort, for him. Especially when there was something to celebrate. "Plus we have something else to celebrate."

"We do?"

She lowered her head and gave him one of her looks. "We got a box this morning."

"Yeah?"

Yep, that got his attention.

He looked left, then right. Then in a low voice, "And what's in this box?"

"I'm not quite sure. I thought we'd open it together."

"Five?"

"Five."

"I'll be there."

"I'll be ready."

"Now how the hell am I going to do *this* the rest of the day?" He motioned over his shoulder, towards the ladder that he'd abandoned.

She smirked. "Not my problem." She giggled when he took two quick steps towards her and pulled her into him. He grabbed her around the waist, bumping against her.

Oh yeah, she could feel he had a *big* problem.

"I'll take care of you tonight." She laid her hands along his face and pulled him in for one last kiss. "I love you."

"I love you, too."

"See you tonight."

34

Annette stood in front of her closet trying to decide what to wear. She didn't want to go too fancy. It was just out for dinner. And most people at the restaurant considered blue jeans to be the fanciest they'd get.

She finally selected a dark blue knit dress she'd picked up on clearance at JJill the previous year. It fit her well and was comfortable too. She matched it with a pair of two-inch heels.

She piled her hair up, then pulled a few strands back down. She added a few curls and fingered them into place, going for a tousled beach look.

She'd noodled through her lingerie drawer for several minutes, before deciding the best way to go was nothing at all. Yep, she'd surprise Curt with that too. When the time was right.

Then she went back to the box that had arrived earlier in the day. She placed it on the bedside table for later.

Who said love gets boring with age? Curt kept surprising her every year they were together. No matter what she threw at him, no matter how crazy some of her ideas became, he almost always nodded in agreement and went with the flow.

Maybe that's why they'd been together for so long.

She heard the door bang shut; Curt was home.

She made her way back into the kitchen and found him dropping off his things. "Hi."

He turned and let his eyes drop down, back up. "Wow. I thought it was a casual dinner out?"

"It is." She moved in closer and placed her hands on his chest, leaning in so she could kiss him. "But I felt like dressing up."

He moved back a step. "Don't touch, I'm a mess. I had a tough time removing a dead bush, and I think I lost the fight." As if to make a point, he shook his head and a few leaves and clumps of dirt fell to the floor.

"Curt ..." she leaned over to pick them up.

"Sorry." He grinned.

Yeah, she was used to it. It was their normal. She squinted at him in reprimand, but her true feelings spread across her face. "Go. Shower. Now."

"Yes, ma'am," he saluted her, and strolled back towards their bedroom, whistling.

"God, I love their pad Thai. It's got to be the best." Annette opened the fridge and started moving dishes aside to make room for the leftovers.

"Nope, sorry, the pumpkin curry has it beat."

She slid two takeout containers on the shelf and closed the door. She cocked her head to the side, considering for a moment, "Yeah, that was good. I've never had that before."

"Well, don't think about stealing my leftovers. I'm saving it for the weekend."

"I don't know about that. What's in the fridge is fair game."

"Since when?" He folded his arms around her waist and walked her back against the counter.

"Since I started working at home." She laced her fingers together around his neck.

"You think that gives you priority?"

She nodded. She leaned in close, breathing him in. Just a hint of the cologne she'd given him for Christmas. And just underneath, an earthy, woodsy scent that never seemed to leave.

She bit down on his earlobe gently, before whispering, "What are you going to do about it?"

He pressed into her, before shutting his eyes and getting lost in her. He cupped her face with his hands, and let his tongue explore.

She melted into him, letting her senses run wild.

The bottle of wine they'd shared left her a little giddy. The extra chocolate they'd ordered for dessert left her happy and satisfied.

And now, it was time for the two of them to explore. She suddenly remembered the box. And the fact that there was nothing between her and her dress. A fact that he hadn't figured out quite yet.

She revved up the heat just a little, to get his hands moving.

Her hands moved to his shirt, the one she hadn't seen in quite a few months. He'd pulled it out, just for her. She pulled away, then started undoing his buttons, one by one. She placed tiny kisses as his skin was revealed.

"I. Like. This. Shirt." She whispered as her tongue traced over each mark.

He responded with a soft moan. And pushed his hips closer to hers.

And as she reached the bottom, she worked to pull his shirt out. Then ran her fingers just below his belt. She felt a small shudder ripple through him.

She knew that's all it would take.

His hands began roaming down her back, around her, finding her breasts. His thumbs went to work pressing in her. She leaned into his touch.

His hands continued to trail down, over her hips, pulling her in close. He cupped her ass, rubbing, feeling. Then he pulled away, looking deep into her eyes, questioning.

He reached down, grabbed the hem of her dress and pulled up. He sucked in as he saw her, commando, standing before him.

She couldn't help but giggle at his wide eyes. "See something you like?"

His eyes narrowed with a heat she recognized well. A look that said he wanted her, and he wanted her bad. "You were commando all night?"

She gave him a friendly push, and he fell back to the counter behind him. "Maybe," and she skipped towards the door.

"Holy shit," he said under his breath, and he was in hot pursuit.

She squealed as she ran down the hall, and into their bedroom. She only stopped when she was a few feet from their bed, turning, holding her arms out to make him stop.

He skidded to a halt inches from her. But his hands reached out, trying to get his fill.

She held him off by slipping her dress over her head. Then carefully releasing her breasts from her bra and dropping it to the floor. She turned, raised her eyebrows, then moved back against the bed.

He was on her in an instant, continuing where they'd left off.

His eyes nearly set her on fire.

His hands sent chills down her spine.

His mouth started by fucking hers, before he continued moving down, frenzied, as if they'd been celibate for months.

She wrapped her arms around him enjoying every nibble, every lick, every bite. He knew how to wind her up.

As he shimmied back up to unbuckle his belt, he nudged the box that was on the night table. "What's in there?"

She leaned on her elbow and looked over her shoulder. "I have no idea. I was waiting for you."

He stood for a second, dropped his pants to the floor, grabbed the box, dropped it between them. "Let's find out."

She giggled. "You're like an overgrown kid. I honestly didn't know if you'd like these boxes."

He stared at her as if she'd sprouted two heads. "You're kidding, right? You bought something that makes us have more sex? Something that prolongs all of *this*?" He pressed her to the bed with a big, wet kiss. "And you have to question if I like it or not? What's not to love?"

She reached down,and wrapped a hand around him. "I forgot. You're a guy."

"No, no, no." He pulled away with a groan. "Stay back. We have to investigate what's in here first."

She sat up, tucked her feet underneath her, as they slid the top off the box.

"Well, what do we have here?" Curt pulled out a box with Love Ties written across the front. The photo clearly depicted its intended use. He popped off the seal and let them fall to the bed. He picked them up and stretched the soft nylon ropes, then wiggled his eyebrows, "I think these could be fun."

She smiled as she reached in and pulled out a jar, with *wicked passion fruit lube* written across the side. She flipped it over, then read out loud, "Designed to heat up at just the right moment." She unscrewed the cap and brought it close to her nose. It was sweet, without being obnoxious. She held it up for him to sniff.

"Mmm. I think we can put that to good use."

They continued going through the box one item at a time. A larger vibrator than what they'd received in their last shipment. One that promised multiple stimulators in multiple places at the same time. Annette squirmed at the thought.

And finally, a deck of cards, with intimate suggestions. *Simply pull one from the deck and let the fun begin,* the back suggested. They both agreed that could be interesting.

"Now, you're all mine." Curt picked up the ties and stretched them in his hands. "Get up there, near the headboard." He had a wild look in his eyes.

She scooted back, thrilled, and held her hands above her head, positioned close together, right next to the metal frame they'd selected years ago when they'd redecorated.

She watched as he crawled forward on his knees, his shaft jutting out in front of him. She couldn't help but watch him grow closer, and larger, as she licked her lips in anticipation.

He straddled her, watched as his tip danced across her lips. Then leaned down to secure the tie around her wrists. He moaned softly, pressed his palm against the wall as he enjoyed the sensation.

He straightened, then carefully, pushed his tip between her wide-open lips. Just a short rhythmic pulse as she flicked her tongue over him again and again. She sucked, enjoying the look on his face.

"Oh, God, as good as this feels, we're not going there just yet." He crawled back down and dove into the pile of goodies they unpacked.

He opened the jar and dipped a finger in. Then swirled it around her, covering her most sensitive spots.

He went back for the vibrator and played with the buttons before finding what seemed like a good place to start. He rubbed it on her tummy, before moving it down.

When he hit a sensitive spot, she jumped. She moaned. And as she arched her back, he pulled back, just for a moment.

Over.

And over again.

Until she was half mad.

"Now. Curt. Stop. I *need.*"

He dropped the vibrator beside her, then moved his tongue into position. And played. And played. Until he heard her familiar sound. A release that said she was sailing over the top.

He moved back up her body, trailing kisses as he went. He found her tongue and played some more.

"You taste like passion fruit."

"That's all you, baby." He positioned himself at her entrance, then pushed deep within. They both sighed. "You're beautiful. You make me so happy."

She wrapped her legs around him, pulling him deeper, deeper. And felt the heat set in.

"Ohmigod, warm."

He looked down. "You okay?"

"Yes. More please." She latched on tighter, feeling it build again.

As she kissed him, she felt his familiar pulse, the one that told her he was close, oh so close. Up and over. They flew together.

And as he dropped to her, reaching up to release her hands, he snuggled into her side. "I love you."

35

"Flight attendants, take your seats."

Sherri sat back, clenching her fingers together. No matter how many times she flew, it was the takeoff that worried her most.

Wesley sensed it, pulled her clenched fists into his lap. With just a gentle pat, she felt herself relax.

"What's the first thing you're going to do when you get home?"

She knew he was trying to take her mind off the roaring engines. But she played along. She started making a mental checklist of things she needed to do upon returning home.

"Well, since we're getting home early afternoon, I want to run to the market, so I can eat outside in my gardens. I bet everything is in full bloom. I can't wait to see it." She'd received an email the week before from her landlord, telling her how beautiful everything was.

"Sounds perfect."

"What about you?"

Wesley pulled his phone out of his pocket and tapped until he found what he wanted. Then he held up the screen for her to see. "You know the new water feature I'm having installed at the entrance? They sent this to me this morning. It should be done by the time I get in."

"Wow, that's gorgeous." Sherri touched the screen and moved through the images. "I love this tree here. What's going in this empty space?"

Wesley glanced at his phone. "They're going to plant annuals for some color. I might add perennials this fall, but annuals will be good for the next couple of months. It'll give it a finished look as my classes start up again at the end of the month."

"I can't wait to see it."

"I can't wait to show it to you."

"Did you see it's supposed to be in the nineties all next week?" Unusual weather for the Pacific Northwest. But she found herself longing for it; it would remind her of Italy.

"I read online we've already had a week of the heatwave and there's no end in sight. The fires are kicking up again."

"They've done that for the past two years. It's bad enough now, but I'm dreading going back to school. Not all the buildings are air conditioned, and we rely on windows for a breeze. But with the smoke, that'll be out of the question." At least the kids wouldn't be back for a couple of weeks.

When they were at cruising altitude, she opened her bag and pulled out her workbook, the one she'd received from Francesca a couple of weeks before.

She'd been diligent in filling it out every day.

And now, paging through it, she saw how things were coming together.

She'd sent in her request to the school board, to start up an after-school art program for the kids. She was waiting to hear back.

She'd also been working on the curricula for it since she'd come up with the idea.

She didn't want it to be an average arts and crafts class. She wanted to use a lot of the skills she'd learned from Wesley and Francesca. She had so many ideas, she knew they'd be perfect for upper elementary kids. And she knew several kids she was going to target and convince their parents to let them be in her class.

If approved, it was going to be a trial run, from the fall into the holiday break. And as she perfected the program, she'd already spoken with Wesley about using his space for a more advanced class in the spring.

He, of course, was all over it. Anything to get her closer to him daily.

She glanced over, watching as he rubbed her fingers with his thumb while he read his book. Just a small gesture, but one filled with love.

What amazed her the most was how in tune they were with one another. They had this unspoken language between them, and she wasn't sure where it had come from.

It's like they'd known each other all along.

According to Wesley, maybe they had. She still wasn't quite sure she believed in that sort of thing. But she did admit that it was uncanny how well they got along.

"Your son's coming over this weekend?" He said without looking up from the pages.

"Yes. He confirmed he can do dinner on Saturday night. He's bringing his girlfriend."

"I'll bring the wine."

She chatted at length with her son over the summer. They'd started a ritual of Skyping one day a week, before she started her day.

It helped that she rose early, and her son stayed up late. With the time difference, their weekly meetings had worked out perfectly. She'd told him about Wesley; he was excited to meet him. She'd never asked him to meet a guy before, so he knew this was different.

She hoped they'd hit it off, that the four of them did well together. Sherri had a funny feeling Noah's latest girlfriend was *the one*. It was the way he spoke about her the past few weeks. She already had it in the back of her mind she was going to spend time getting to know her better. What she already knew, she loved.

She flipped through her workbook, eyeing her class once again.

She had her proposal fully written. Yet still she lingered, holding back from submitting it. She wasn't sure what was holding her back. She'd told herself she was waiting until she went back to school. Now with only a few days left, she found herself rethinking her strategy.

"Do you think it would be better if I went in and talked about my idea once I'm back?"

Without missing a beat, Wesley responded. It was like they'd been married forever, aware of each other's thoughts. It never ceased to amaze her.

"I think you should do what you think is best for protocol. How do others do it when they teach extracurricular activities?"

She didn't know if there was a protocol. Only a few teachers did it, and most of them had been teaching classes for years. It was more assumed than by chance. She'd emailed a friend who taught an after-school music class, but she hadn't heard back.

"Do you think ten kids is too many? Maybe I should reduce the numbers to eight."

"You're giving this for fourth and fifth graders. You know they're independent enough to work on their own. You're their guide."

"I know. But I want to make sure I have control. I need to learn before I take on too much."

"You'll be fine."

"Maybe I should back off and think about this some more. I could always start it up next year and plan a bit more."

She was cut off mid thought. He hooked his fingers around her neck and pulled her in for a kiss. His eyes held hers as he backed slightly away, nipping at her lip. "Stop already. You're worrying yourself sick. It'll be great. You've been teaching for years. What's your biggest worry?"

That was the question. What was her concern?

She was good at her job. She'd been doing the same job, living in the same house, etching out her single life in the same manner for years.

She'd wanted change, had gone searching for it after her last birthday. She'd jumped at so many things these past few months.

But somehow this all felt different.

She'd left for a summer vacation - a few weeks of fun in a faraway land.

But she was coming home with a plan. A plan that might potentially change her life forever.

Her future looked nothing like she'd thought about even just a few short months before.

And that scared her.

Her life had been … safe.

And now. Now she wasn't sure.

Teaching, she could do that with her hands tied behind her back. She'd always assumed she'd do it until she retired.

Then Annette went and quit on her, and now she just wasn't so sure.

She liked teaching, didn't love it. And that was the real problem.

Suddenly, she was seeing that liking her life wasn't a good thing. She was too young for like. What she wanted was to fall in love.

And she knew what it could look like because she was seeing it fall together, right in front of her.

If she was just brave enough to reach out and take it.

She knew it. And yet she still backed away.

Could this be possible? Could she really make these kinds of changes, and make them work too?

She'd tried love and failed. Would it work a second time?

She'd always wanted art in her life. But could she really turn it into a career?

She continued to flip though her notes, the ones she'd been creating for the past few weeks. The ones that told her yes, she could do whatever she pleased.

"I can do this, right?" She said it out loud, just enough for Wesley to hear.

"Yes, you can." He gave her fingers a little squeeze. Just enough to make her breathe deeply, and once again put her fears at bay.

She looked at him again. "Thanks."

"Of course. Now, I've been thinking."

She raised an eyebrow, curious at the expression on his face.

"Your place or mine when we land later today?"

36

Annette read through her article once again.

She liked it; it was good. At least she thought it was.

She'd rewritten it several times. She'd pushed Curt down to her chair in her office and made him read it too. And just when she'd thought about submitting it, she'd called up her daughter and had her read through it.

And finally, with the deadline looming, she'd tucked it into an email and hit send. She'd waited patiently to hear back from Wendy, giving her a heads up on the next phase.

That had been three days ago. Waiting had made it a weekend filled with stress. All that went through her mind was: would Wendy like it? Would it pass the next test?

As she sat in her chair, waiting for action, the familiar ding came through, and she clicked on her email.

A link to a page on the Escape Magazine site, where her photograph was neatly displayed with nine others, links to their articles below.

She sat back in her chair, clicked and read.

Every article was different. Every post shined a different light on unique places throughout the world, places where each writer currently lived. She was amazed at the diversification between the writers, and how differently they each thought.

They were all good in their own unique way. She couldn't say one was better; they all held their own unique approach to the story.

She clicked on her link and brought her article up. She copied the link from where her article resided on Escape Magazine's website and started forwarding it to her friends. To her mom and dad. To her daughter and son.

Annette went back to the email from Wendy and read it through from top to bottom. She knew this final phase was important. It was a matter of getting the job ... or not. If there was a way she could sway the odds in her favor, she'd find it. She read through the email, paying attention to each of the specifics.

The editorial staff at Escape Magazine would read through every post. They'd all voice their own opinions and have a meeting about who would be a good fit.

But there was more.

Wendy had told her they'd rely on social media too to determine the final winner. They were looking for likes and shares. They would be watching how many people liked each article. They would watch the statistics for how many people shared it on their Facebook accounts, or attached the link to Twitter. Down at the bottom of the email, Wendi offered suggestions for increasing the odds.

"Feel free to share this link with those you know. Ask them to like and share. We're looking for clear winners here, for content people are willing to share. A reporter's job is to get his or her audience to connect and follow. We're ready to give your application a boost if you show us how it's done."

Annette blew out her breath. She was so far out of her comfort zone with all of this. She knew her own son and daughter could manage this without thinking twice. But herself? How would she ever figure out how to use likes and shares herself?

Her thoughts were interrupted when her phone vibrated across her desk. Her daughter.

"Hey."

"Mom, I love it! It looks even better online. I like the picture you chose to go with it."

"You think it looks professional? I didn't really have something business-like." It's not as though she needed something as a teacher.

"It's perfect. I haven't read through the others yet, but I'll do that later on my lunch break. Oh, Mom, this is so exciting! What's the next step?"

She smiled. Clara, her go-getter. The two of them were so much alike. To the rest of the world, the two of them were quiet and reserved. But with the ones they loved, they were wild and passionate. She loved hearing it in her voice, even if she was scared shitless herself.

Annette read through Wendy's email, clarifying in her own mind what it all meant. "Do you think I stand a chance? I don't have a *following*." She said it with authority, though in truth she really didn't know what it meant.

Her daughter just giggled. "I'm going to help you."

"Yeah?"

"Yep."

Millennials. Her kids were always online, texting, bringing their phones to the dinner table. They knew it was off limits; they'd never allowed devices at the table. But that didn't prevent them from trying. And as adults, her and Curt found it harder to hold the rule.

"You're going to be glad I work for MonkeyBusiness."

Clara had moved up to Seattle the year before, taking a job with an app building company. Though Annette still struggled to understand all her daughter did, Clara enjoyed her job. And that's all that mattered in the end.

"I've already talked with my boss. That's why I'm calling. I'm going to give you a little love, from my friends here, to you."

That got Annette's heart pumping. Though she wasn't quite sure what it meant. "Okay. Do I need to do something? Give you the article? Or set up a new account?"

"Just say *thanks*."

Annette could hear her daughter giggling, with click-clicking in the background. Why argue if it meant she'd be one step closer to getting the job? "Thanks."

"You're welcome! I've told several people here about your story, and we're going to like and share. Give your results a boost. Plus I can share it through my social sites. With any luck, you'll shoot forward quickly. When is the deadline?"

That, she knew well. "I have four days. They make their final selection by the end of the week. They'll let everyone know by the close of business Friday."

"Then you better get to work."

"Clara, I don't even know what that means."

Annette heard more clicking in the background.

"I just sent you something. Check your email."

Annette did. She found a message from her daughter. "Okay. It's here."

"Copy what I have written there. Start emailing it to everyone you know. Tell them it's under deadline, and you're really hoping to win."

"To everyone I know?" She wasn't sure she was ready for that.

"Yes, Mom. Don't think. Just do. You want this job, don't you?"

"Yes." More than she'd let on to anybody.

"Email your old bookclub, your teachers, why don't you email Robert?"

"As in my old boss?"

"Yes. You said he wished you luck and told you he'd help you out in any way."

"Well, yeah, but …"

"But nothing. If you can get him on board, maybe he'll send it to everyone on staff."

She was touched her daughter was so invested in her success. And she did have a point. "Okay."

"I gotta go. I'm starting the process. We'll talk later. And we'll celebrate next time I'm in town."

As Clara hung up, Annette chuckled at her assurance. She'd raised one hell of a daughter; maybe they'd celebrate that.

She could do this. She could. She would!

She copied her daughter's words and pasted it into an email. She started sending it to all of her friends.

And as promised, she sent it to her old boss too. *What the hell?*

What's the worst that could happen? He ignored it?

He didn't.

After lunch, Annette sat back down at her computer, thinking of ways she could increase her odds.

She opened her email and was surprised to see something from Robert: an email telling her how happy he was she'd been given an opportunity to write for Escape Magazine, and he'd do what he could to help.

He'd forwarded it to everyone at school. He'd even forwarded it to the head of the district; they'd become a close-knit community since the shooting.

She kept clicking through her emails, one more exciting than the next. She'd received one from a friend she hadn't spoken to in years; a friend of a friend had forwarded her the link and she was happy to help.

And still another, from a reporter at their local news. They'd included a link in their daily emails and wanted to chat with her for a special feature. If she had the time, they'd be willing to put her on their homepage for the next day. She called. She chatted with the reporter. And hung up feeling giddy.

She was going to be top news the next morning!

She clicked again and found an email from her sister. She owned a small restaurant and sent her a photograph of the flyer she'd just put up in her window. She'd been sharing Annette's story with all her patrons. She didn't know how much it would help, but she wanted Annette to know she was doing her part.

Annette felt the tears sting her eyes. It was all too good to be true.

She clicked back to the magazine's website and navigated to her article page. She scrolled to the bottom, where the analytics showed current statistics. Her likes already registered in the hundreds. The shares weren't too far behind.

She backed out and clicked to several of the other articles, all of who barely registered on the scale.

If this kept going …

Could she dare think she might win?

She might get the job!

And a whole different set of emotions filled her mind.

She'd been so busy thinking about getting a job, she hadn't considered what would happen if she did.

She'd be traveling. All over the world. For the next year!

"Hey." Curt leaned into her office, saw her tears and moved beside her, bending down and taking her into his arms. Tears quickly wetted his shirt. "What's wrong?"

"I didn't know you were home."

"I just walked in. I called out. You didn't answer. I figured this is where you'd be."

She stood and pushed him into her chair.

She clicked. She showed him her numbers. She told him all the wonderful things that had happened throughout the day.

She turned and sat on the edge of her desk, biting her lip as she peered into his eyes.

"What if I get it?" She said with a shaky voice, the tears still flowing down her face.

"Then I guess you better pack up your bag."

"You'll be okay?"

He just shook his head, his eyes brimming with his own tears. "Have I told you how proud I am of you?"

"You are?"

He pulled her in and gave her a kiss. "Yeah. I am. All of this?" He motioned around him. "You've done a lot these past few months. I'm sorry if I've been such a pain. Just my nerves getting the better of me. But all this work you've done, it's incredible."

"Thanks. But that still doesn't help me. What if I get it?"

"You're scared?"

"Yes! I've never done anything like this before."

"Weren't you the one who said you wanted to write?"

"Yes."

"If you get this, you obviously have proven yourself."

She nodded.

"And weren't you the one that said you wanted, *needed* a change?"

She nodded again.

"Well, consider this your answer. If you get it, it's meant to be."

In a low voice, she whispered, "Will *you* be all right?"

That's what she'd missed in her excitement about this job. If she got it, she'd have to leave. They'd be apart. And that was something rare in their married life before.

He fell back into her chair, smiling at her. "If - *when* you get this, think of this as your way of planning out where we're going in our retirement. You always said you wanted to travel the world."

"With you."

"Take notes. We can go back."

She grinned through her tears. "You'll be okay?"

He gave her his smart-ass look. The look that said: *really?*

She took a deep breath.

He moved the chair so he could pull her between his legs. He settled his hand on either side of her hips. "I love you."

She laid her hands on his shoulders, looked down into his eyes. "I love you."

"They have this little thing called the internet now. Someone taught me that."

She giggled as he cocked his head and rolled his eyes at her.

"*When* you get this job, we'll talk every day."

"And you'll be okay with that?"

"Why do you keep asking me that? Yes, I can manage."

"But we've never been apart. Not really."

"This is about you. This is what you need. You've said so yourself."

"Yes." He'd listened; she'd give him that. Even when she'd convinced herself he'd done more ignoring than hearing.

"It's not forever. And we're solid. Besides, I'm going to be so proud, and so in awe of who you are …"

She heard the catch in his voice. Her eyes bounced as she watched him, reading the emotion that spread across his face.

His voice was scratchy, almost a whisper. "I almost lost you, Annette." His forehead fell into her chest. A small sob escaped. "This is nothing. Not compared to that."

She wrapped her arms around him, pulled him close.

He was right. She'd gotten here because of the chaos that existed in the world. She wouldn't be here if something inside her hadn't clicked.

And now, she'd found something that changed her for good, and made her want more. She *wanted* this.

They'd be okay. She'd make sure they were.

This was her time to shine. And she was going to shine as brightly as she could.

37

"Hey, stranger." Sherri wrapped her arm around Annette's shoulders and pulled her in for a sideways hug.

"Where'd you come from? I've been here for ten minutes. I didn't see you come in." Annette moved both of their cups, giving Sherri room to drop her stuff and settle in.

"I was in back," she pointed to the small room behind the barista station. "I had to drop off some supplies with a woman in my painting class. I figured meeting here would kill two birds."

Annette chuckled. "Always the master of multitasking, aren't you?"

Sherri shrugged her shoulders, making a funny grin.

Yep, some things never change.

Annette hadn't realized how much she missed seeing her friend. Or how lonely she'd become working at home by herself. She shook her head, clearing her thoughts.

"You okay?" Sherri grabbed her mug and took a sip.

"Oh, yes. Of course. It's just," Annette sighed. "I've missed you. And I can't wait to hear all about Italy."

So Sherri talked. She pulled up her iPad and showed Annette photographs of the Italian countryside. She tapped on a folder and shared pictures of her paintings.

She spoke about Francesca and her retreat. She had Annette drooling after describing the lay of the land.

And finally, she got to the part where Wesley had shown up.

"He just walked up? You had no idea?"

"None. I was shocked."

"I didn't realize you two were that close before he left."

Sherri huffed out her breath. Where did she begin?

"Honestly, I'm not quite sure what we were before I left. This whole thing has hit me like nothing I've ever felt before. It's like he *knows* me, *gets* me. That might not make sense, but there was just something different about him - us - from the moment we kissed."

Annette nodded. "I get that. Love should be easy, not difficult. And when you know, you know."

"Exactly. And maybe I've never understood that before, but I've never met anyone like Wesley before."

"He's different, isn't he? I can see it in the way you talk about him." Annette shook her head. "No, it's more than that. You've changed. And I know there are a lot of reasons for that, a lot has happened this year, but I get the sense you're more settled somehow. Not that you need a man for that."

"I've thought a lot about the way I've dated since my divorce. I always said I wanted more … someday. But what I really meant was that I was happy with the way things were. I was never serious about looking. First, I blamed it on Tanner, that I wanted to wait until he was on his own. Then it was work. I always had an excuse for not pursuing something further."

"I get that. Why add more headaches? We have busy lives."

"Busy? Yes. Stuck is more like it."

Annette snorted. "That's how we got where we are today. Maybe that's synonymous with *fiftieth birthday*. Stuck. That's all we've focused on for this past year."

'Exactly. That's why we went to San Diego. That's why you quit your job."

"Can't say we've been smart about a lot of this. But we have changed."

"And maybe that's good. You know, I've really envied you. Quitting like you did. Maybe even bordered on jealous."

"Jealous?"

"Um, hmm. You were so gung-ho about changing. You knew you wanted to write, and nothing would stop you. And you did something; you quit. You dropped everything and gave yourself the space you needed to move on."

"Yeah, but I wouldn't say that was a smart thing. More of a gut reaction."

"Still, I envied it. Because you had something to move towards. And I still had no idea what I wanted."

"How does Wesley fit into all of this?"

"That's just it. I didn't see the connection either. He just sort of happened, like everything else in my life. And when he showed up in Italy, something sparked inside. I realized that I've been a reactor. I accept things without ever reaching for them. Sure, Wesley was there. But it was up to me to decide I wanted him in my life."

"And you do? You're ready for him to be more?"

"Believe it or not, yes. Me, the one who swore she'd never jump into a relationship quickly ever again. I jumped. And it's moving quickly."

Sherri giggled when she heard Annette's gasp.

"Okay, not *that* quickly. I'm not doing anything stupid like getting married. But we're going to build a life. We're going to spend more time together. I'm going to start teaching youth art classes, first at the school, and if it works out, at his place."

"Wow."

"I know. I discovered on my trip that I don't want to give up teaching. I just want to change how I teach. I'm not going to give up my paycheck anytime soon. But if I can build a successful side gig and make that grow, who knows in a year or two."

"Interesting. I can't wait to hear more about it."

"I have the whole thing mapped out. I was hoping you'd look at it. See what you think of the curriculum, from a teaching standpoint." Sherri handed her a file.

"Sure. I'll look it over tonight. When are you starting?"

"I'm hoping this fall. I've submitted the paperwork to start an after-school session in September. I figure I'll use that as my test."

Annette tapped the folder in her hand. She opened it, looked briefly at the notes Sherri had made. "Just breezing through it, it looks good. And fun! I think you're going to have a hit on your hands." She closed it, placed it in her bag.

"Now I really want to meet him. Want to bring him over this weekend for dinner?"

They agreed on a time. Sherri promised to bring a salad. Then she dug into her bag and pulled out a piece of paper.

"I see you've been busy too." She placed Robert's email about voting for Annette's article between them.

Annette picked it up and read through it. "Wow. Robert emailed me and said he'd send something to everyone. I wasn't quite sure if he meant it. I'm still kind of nervous about quitting. I was afraid he was still mad at me."

"Don't worry about it. He isn't. I don't think anyone could be, not after everything that's happened."

"He seemed upset when I left. But he understood."

"He did. We all do. This is a crazy time for schools and teachers. And Robert gets that more than anyone. He knows how much time we put into all of this, and how much we get out of it. You want to hear something?" Sherri leaned forward, looking to both sides to make sure nobody was listening.

Annette leaned forward too. "Just like the old days." She grinned.

"Robert's wife quit too." Robert Neil had accepted the principal's job three years before, moving in from a school district close to Seattle. It was on the condition his wife, Nancy, could also have a job teaching at the local high school. The school district willingly obliged.

Annette couldn't hide her shock. "You're kidding? She quit?"

"Yep. I think they were both a little more freaked out then they let on. They have three kids, and supposedly she told him she wasn't willing to chance orphaning them. She's had it and she's looking for something else."

Annette put her hand up to her mouth. "I had no idea. Poor Robert. Maybe I'll touch base with him again. I'd be happy to chat with his wife. Maybe that's how I can thank him for this email."

"He'll probably take you up on that. That might be why he was so excited about your opportunity. He knows what we're all facing. Maybe this is his way of trying to figure things out for himself."

The two spent a few minutes with the familiar gossip they'd always shared when at the school. Annette still kept in close contact with many of them, even if it was just through email

"Okay, back to your article. Tell me all about it."

Annette launched into her story about finding the job, applying, and the notification she'd made the top ten. She told Sherri how her daughter had made a few recommendations for increasing her likes and shares. And how she'd emailed everyone she knew, hoping to push her chances higher than the others in the running.

"When do you find out if the job is yours?"

"Friday."

"I'll bring champagne too. Since we're going to have something to celebrate." Sherri could see the nervousness in her friends eyes. She leaned in and grabbed her hand.

"It's a great article. But if I know you, it was hard, hitting the send button."

Annette sat back, blew a breath to push her bangs out of her eyes. Then she sipped at her coffee for a moment, reflecting. Sherri had seen that look a million times. She also recognized the satisfaction in her eyes. Something she realized she hadn't seen on her face in quite a while.

Annette scooted forward and placed her cup in front of her. "You know, it wasn't at all. I mean, I read and reread it a hundred times. But I liked it. I had a good feeling when I hit send. I still do. And the numbers …"

"I noticed that. I went over there earlier, just to check. Your numbers are zooming, way higher than the others I looked at." She hadn't clicked through to them all, but it wasn't even a close competition with the ones she had.

Annette tapped her fingers nervously on the table. "I check them several times every day. I'm glad it's fixed where only one vote per account, or I'd be the one inflating them."

"What happens when you get the job?" Sherri had no doubt her friend would be the one to pull into first place.

"Then I pack my bags."

"Where to first?"

"Puerto Rico is the first. Then I zigzag all over the world."

"You're really going to be a jetsetter, aren't you?"

Annette grinned. "I am. It's crazy. I never expected something like this. But now that it's a little closer to reality, I'm getting excited."

"How's Curt?"

"Good. He's excited about the paycheck," Annette couldn't help but chuckle. "I can't believe I can say that so easily anymore. He's become a bit neurotic about it."

"Still?"

"Yep. We got another bill."

"Another one?"

"I don't even want to talk about it. I called them. They're *looking into it*. I'm sure I can get it lowered. I'll pay it eventually."

"He'll be okay when you're away?"

"Actually, it won't be that bad. Each month is two weeks out, and then home. I'll have to go into the main office occasionally. And I might have meetings for promotional purposes. But it sounds like I should be home two weeks or so each month. And it's only a one-year assignment."

"Who knows where it will lead?"

"Exactly. I'm just going to enjoy it. At first, anyway. But I am thinking more about where this road will lead. There are all kinds of opportunities in the travel industry. I might pursue some of them too. After I get through this year."

Sherri reached across the table, and linked fingers. "I'm proud of you. You've come a long way."

"I could say the same about you."

"It's amazing, isn't it? How far we've come?"

"Thank you. I mean that. I'm sure I'd still be teaching, dreaming of writing if you hadn't given me that nudge, and asked me to come to California with you."

"You would have done it. Eventually."

"Yeah, but not as quickly as this. I'd been dreaming about this for *two years*."

"But you're here now."

"Yep."

Sherri grinned. "We're doing this. We're making changes, and it's good! It's really good." She could feel the tears well up in her eyes.

She'd missed her friend so much. They'd been so close for so long.

Being away put everything in perspective. What she wanted most. What she was going to strive for from now on.

Her friends. Her family.

Loving what she did. Having fun in the process.

And she was happy it was all happening so fast.

38

Today was officially the longest day of her life.

Wendy had told her she'd hear about the job by the end of the week. All the paperwork she'd received had said Friday was the day they'd let everyone know.

Today was Friday, as if anyone would let her forget it.

"Today's the day." Curt had grinned at her as she'd handed him his coffee mug, kissed him, and shooed him out the door.

"Let's not talk about it. Not yet. I don't want to jinx it." She'd said that - almost screeched that - as he climbed into his car, waving goodbye.

"Today's the day." Her son's text had been waiting for her when she'd hopped out of the shower.

She'd answer with nothing more than a "Yep, I'll let you know."

Then her daughter had sent the very same words right before lunch. Along with, "Have you heard?"

No!

She was on the Pacific coast. Three hours *behind* East Standard time, where it was currently mid-afternoon. *So why hadn't she heard by now?*

She was driving herself crazy. She paced back and forth, from her kitchen to her office, with her phone attached to her hip.

She kept pulling it out of her pocket, making sure it hadn't somehow gone dead.

For the umpteenth time, she yanked on the refrigerator door, pulled out a pitcher of iced tea, and filled up her glass. Then set it down next to her computer before dropping into her chair once again.

She didn't even have to type in the URL anymore. The magazine's website was there, blinking at her as she opened her laptop. She hit refresh and watched as her article remained at the top of the list. She knew this was far beyond what her little community could do. It might have started the ball rolling, but it took a lot more that to keep her numbers growing every day.

Two others were close behind, only a few likes separated them.

But she'd done it. It was Friday, and she was still in the lead.

If she didn't get this job, she'd given it all she had.

Who knew she'd learn so much about social media in such a short time?

If she *did* get the job, she knew her newest skill was going to help her a lot.

She grabbed her phone, lifted it to make sure it lit up. Then laid it down near her glass once again.

If she *did* get the job, she'd have to invest in new luggage. The old luggage they'd used since the kids were little just wasn't going to cut it.

Maybe a new backpack? Something she could carry on and not check. Maybe she should invest in a new outfit or two, something that was easily washed. And wouldn't wrinkle.

She opened a new browser window and started Googling for ideas. Best luggage for traveling, backpacks, how to pack lightly: she'd Googled it all in the past few hours as she'd been sitting, fidgeting, waiting for a call.

She found a navy blue backpack that might be the perfect …

And jumped as her phone vibrated next to her.

She picked it up and … New York area code. *This was it!*

She clicked and held it up to her ear. "Hello, this is Annette."

"Hi, Annette. This is Wendy Tavish from Escape Magazine."

Her voice sounded amazing, happy. Annette crossed her fingers and her toes. "Hi, Wendy."

"I don't want to keep you in suspense, so I'm just going to blurt it out. We'd like to offer you the job!"

Annette felt so many things at once, she wasn't sure what to do.

Laugh. Scream. Collapse in her chair.

Her feet did a little happy dance under her desk. Her fist shot up to the sky. A grin spread across her face.

She did it! She got the job! A job that would let her write and travel the world.

Shit, a job where she'd write and travel the world …

She was thrilled - ecstatic. Yet somehow terrified too. Her mind whirled to all she'd be doing in the coming weeks and months. And to what she was about to leave behind.

Annette shook her head slightly, hearing Wendy's laughter.

"Did I leave you speechless?"

Annette chuckled. "You did in fact." She blew out a breath. "Thank you! I'm really delighted. Excited. Thrilled!"

"And maybe a little overwhelmed too?"

"You have no idea."

Wendy laughed. "I can't wait to meet you in person. And for the record, I totally understand. We picked you in part because of your honesty. Your approach for explaining your feelings is what we liked about your articles. They were so different from what we normally print. I know I mentioned that last time we spoke, but your style carried through to this one. And obviously our readers loved it. Your sharing numbers took us by surprise. Have you been watching?"

"Uh huh. I can't believe how many people liked what I had to say."

"We knew within hours that you were going to be our winner. It was hard for us to wait for today to announce. We made up our minds officially two days ago."

Wow. "Thank you."

"I have a package for you I'd like to send over. It has the contract, an onboarding file, an itinerary, a schedule. We'd like to have you fly in here so we can firm everything up. Possibly the week after next."

"Yes, of course. Just let me know when."

"I'll have my assistant get in touch with you shortly. We'll use the week in our offices to get everything on track. Then from that point forward, we should be able to do most of it virtually. Except for the occasional meetings, which we talked about."

"Perfect."

"Oh, and I forgot the most important part. Your salary."

When Wendy told her how much she'd be making, she nearly fell of her chair.

A whole lot more than what she'd made as a teacher, even after a master's degree and twenty-five years in the business.

"Plus we cover expenses too. I have a guide to walk you through how you'll make your reservations. We'll be giving you a business credit card for all the incidentals. When you're here, we'll go over it all in more detail."

Wendy kept talking about policies and procedures. But Annette's mind had stopped at the mention of money. An incredible salary *and* more for expenses? She felt like she'd hit the lottery.

The last of her stress and worry melted away. And she couldn't wait to tell Curt. She knew it would do the same for him.

Annette tried to pay attention, tried to listen to the rest of the details. She promised she'd fill out the forms Wendy was sending over in the next few days.

They concluded by scheduling a Skype call for early Monday morning.

As she hung up, Annette refreshed her inbox.

The documents popped in. She downloaded everything to her desktop. She breezed through them, looking for what she wanted.

The itinerary captivated her from the moment she opened the file. In the next twelve months she'd be visiting the Danish Riviera, Nairobi, Kenya, and Santiago, Chile. She'd be covering the restaurant scene in Panama City and the undiscovered wine industry in Etyek, Hungary. The potential of discovery at each destination made her giddy.

But it all started with her first assignment; a trip to Puerto Rico to report on the best hidden-gem beaches. An assignment she'd be leaving for in just a few weeks.

She printed off the list, grabbed it and her car keys and headed out the door.

She saw him in the rose garden, digging in the dirt. He'd told her the night before he'd purchased a dozen new bushes and was excited to plant them the next day.

His back was turned as she raced across the grass yelling his name. He turned just in time to catch her as she launched herself at him.

She wrapped her arms around his neck and kissed him on the lips. "I. Got. The. Job." She hummed between kisses.

He wrapped around tighter and spun her once around before putting her down and stepping away. "You got it!"

"I got it!" She couldn't quit bouncing. "They want me in New York the week after next to finalize everything. But that's it; it's me. They picked me!"

She held out the list, pointing out each place she'd be visiting in the weeks and months to come. And as she reached the bottom of her list, she let out a tiny sob.

"I'm going to miss you. We're going to do this well, right?" Now that reality was starting to set in, she was trying to imagine their new lives without each other in it daily. "We're going to be okay, right?"

He laid both hands along her cheeks and pulled her in for pure passion. His tongue played. His teeth nibbled. His lips were pure magic.

Annette got lost in it. He hadn't done that in … "Years," she whispered.

She nervously glanced around, glad to see no one was nearby to witness their heat.

"Nothing will ever stop this. I love you too much." His voice was rough, filled with emotion.

And she knew he was right.

Because nobody else had been through what the two of them had faced and conquered together. They were going to be all right.

"I love you."

"I love you too."

Annette started backing away. Her playful mood had returned.

"You didn't ask me how much I'd make."

He just shook his head. "I didn't. You got the job. No matter what it is, we'll make it work."

She couldn't help but grin from ear to ear. She pulled a folded piece of paper from her pocket.

"I'm on salary. Plus an expense account for while I travel. I have to be fairly conservative, but it has wiggle room for me to explore."

She unfolded it slowly, turned it and handed it to him.

She'd printed only one thing on the sheet - the amount she'd be making for the year. Twenty-five percent more than she made as a teacher.

His eyes moved from the paper back to her eyes. "Are you serious?"

"Yep."

He was in hot pursuit. He scooped her up for another hug.

He whispered into her ear. "I think we need to celebrate tonight."

"Sounds good to me." She pushed away, backing up, moving back towards her car. "Oh, and by the way, right before I left, they delivered a new box."

39

Annette pulled her good dishes from the shelf. She set the table for four.

She went into the dining room and pulled out her good crystal too. Four wine glasses made the perfect addition to the table.

She found some old candles in her closet. And after a few minutes rummaging through her china cabinet, she found holders for them too.

She stood back and assessed the table. Perfect.

She went back to the stove and stirred, checking on things in the oven.

"Hi, gorgeous." Curt strode in from the backyard, with dirt all over his hands. He placed his hands on the side of her face and pulled her in for a kiss.

"Curt," she mumbled, lips against his. But she couldn't hide the laughter that bubbled up from within. "They'll be here any minute."

"Give me five minutes." He raced up the stairs to shower and change his clothes.

Give the man five minutes in a garden, and he can't keep his hands out of the dirt.

Not that she expected him too. It's what he did. It's what he'd done since they'd married. And she never wanted him to change.

She removed several serving dishes, and placed them on the counter, ready to fill.

She pulled out her corkscrew and pulled the cork from their favorite Barbera to let it breathe. The one she'd found at Trader Joe's several months before. She'd gone back for several bottles more.

A knock at the door had her scrambling to take off her apron, stowing it in the laundry room on her way to the door.

"Sherri!"

Nothing could deter her from being the happiest person in the world. Not tonight.

Or sharing that happiness with her best friend; the one who'd been with her through thick and thin.

"Congratulations!" Sherri thrust a bottle of champagne into her hands, then followed it up with a bouquet. "To celebrate."

"Thank you! Come in."

Sherri introduced Wesley, and they followed her into the kitchen. Curt joined them, more introductions, and they made a toast to Annette's success.

"I don't want to take away from your success, but I have an announcement too." With all eyes on her, Sherri held up her glass. "The board accepted my proposal. I'll be teaching my first art class in the fall!"

Another round of congratulations, more wine was served, and the four settled in to a night of toasting, sharing, and expanding their friendships.

"Hey, you shouldn't be doing the dishes alone." Sherri found a towel in the drawer by the sink and picked up a dish to dry it off.

"You don't have to do that. I just wanted to get a few of them out of the way before I served dessert. I was waiting for the coffee to finish brewing anyway and thought I'd get some of them out of here."

Sherri grabbed another dish. "If I help, we can get twice as many done. Besides, this gives the guys a chance to talk."

"I really like him."

"Do you?"

"Mm, hmm. And Curt does too. He usually doesn't open up quite like this with someone new."

"I guess it was all that talk about planting a garden outside his studio."

Annette giggled. "I don't know if Wesley was serious, but it was definitely the right topic to bring up. Curt lit up. Of course, I hope Wesley really meant he'd like Curt's help. Because now that Curt knows about it, he'll be over offering his opinions all the time."

"It'll give them both something to do."

"As if they don't have enough on their plates. I think we've both done enough changing this year to keep them guessing for a long time to come."

"I have a confession to make." Sherri paused for effect.

"Do tell." Annette dropped her dish rag into the water and turned to face her friend.

"Burt came over earlier this week. Knocked and tried to worm his way inside."

"You didn't let him in …"

Sherri shook her head. "I told him he was no longer welcome in my home. And I wouldn't be investing in any more of his ideas. He had the gall to blame my new boyfriend as the problem."

"No."

"Yes! I told him it was time to get a life. From now on, he has to find a way to fund his own ideas; he no longer had access to my bank account. He marched out and I haven't heard from him since."

"Good for you!" Annette hugged her friend. "I'm so proud of you."

Sherri leaned back into the counter, threw the dishtowel over her shoulder. "I'm proud of me too." She sighed. "I can't believe all we've done this year. I can't believe the summer's coming to an end."

"I can't believe how busy we're both going to be this fall."

"Or the fact that you'll be leaving here soon. I'm proud of you, too. But I'm going to miss you! Galivanting all over the world and all."

"Now I'll have a list of places the four of us can travel to together."

"We might just have to do that. It might be the only way I get to see you. After this year, you'll probably find you want to do this full time."

"It's funny you mentioned that. Curt and I have been talking a lot more about retirement. Not that we're anywhere near that point. But we have started the conversation about where we want to go and what we want to do."

"And?"

"Nothing serious yet, obviously. But we always talked about traveling more. And we never really defined it, you know?"

"I do. I think if I've learned anything this year, it's about being clear with what I want."

"Wishes never amount to anything."

"But goals and plans bring everything to light."

Annette pulled the drain plug and watched the water drain from the sink. She pulled four mugs from the cabinet, filled two and handed one to her friend. She leaned back against the counter, across from Sherri.

"Wesley and I have been talking more about combining our talents and creating classes. I feel bad in that he's so much more talented than I am."

"Excuse me? I've seen your work. You're very talented."

"Said my best friend …"

"Yeah, but it's true. You just haven't been recognized for it yet."

Sherri thought for a moment, then spoke up again. "Wesley says that too. It's been his career for two decades. I'm a little nervous stepping in at his level, considering I haven't even sold a piece."

"You'll get there. And if Wesley's asking you to be a part of it, obviously he thinks you're ready."

"Maybe."

"What kind of classes?"

Sherri bit back her nerves. She still had doubts about her talent, but their plans excited her. "We've been planning week long retreats next summer. Kind of like what I did in Italy only on a smaller scale. If he works with parents, I could handle the kids. That way families could come together and both get proper instruction."

"What a great idea! I really love it. I think that will be a winner. I know I'd have been all over that when CJ was younger. That would have been a great way to bond with my little artist."

Sherri and Annette looked up as the two men entered the kitchen, chatting like old friends. They gave each other a knowing glance, happy to see them getting along.

"Hey, there you guys are. We thought you forgot about us." Curt leaned in and pulled his wife into him, placed a kiss on the top of her head. "We're hungry."

"How can you be hungry?" Annette gazed up at him.

"Because you made your homemade apple pie."

Annette swatted at Curt's hands, grabbed the pie from the stove top.

Sherri dug into freezer and pulled out vanilla ice cream, while Curt took four plates from the cabinet. Wesley filled the mugs with coffee, and they all sat down at the kitchen island and consumed four pieces of apple pie.

"I'm going to miss this when you're traveling," Sherri said again. She swiped at a tear, something she'd been doing all night.

Curt noticed, and interjected a little humor. "I'm going to miss the pie."

Which made them all giggle.

"It's ridiculous, isn't it? We've been talking about making changes for months. That's why I dragged you down to California. But now that everything has changed, I kind of miss the old us."

They all cocked their heads, staring at Sherri.

"Okay, I realize we wouldn't all be together like this if we were all still stuck in the past."

"Thank you," Wesley leaned in for a kiss.

"It's just that ..." Sherri held her finger up to her nose, biting back the tears.

Annette just smiled. "I get it. It's a little *be careful what you wish for*. We've spent so much time together wanting something new, and only now are we truly appreciating what we had in the past."

"At least the good stuff."

Annette nodded. "It's the bad stuff we're replacing. Remember that."

Curt piped in. "I think that's really what this is all about. I fought this; I'm surprised you put up with me." He looked gratefully at his wife. "But in the end, we ended up in a better place. And I know this is going to change everything; we're going to have to adjust everything we do. But I have to believe the journey we're on now is going to take us to the very best places."

Annette sat there in awe. Her husband had always been so tailored in his thoughts lately; always looking for one result: money. She hadn't realized he'd thought deeper about where they were going. "This isn't going to change what we mean to one another. It'll just change what we're putting out into the world."

"And we'll have to play harder because we'll be working harder." Curt looked at his wife. "Maybe the three of us can meet you somewhere and spend a long weekend together."

"Sounds like a perfect plan to me."

40

"How is everyone today?" The host of the Fabulous at Fifty Conference adjusted the microphone, then waited for the audience to quiet down.

Excitement bubbled in the air. And for good reason. They'd never had a panel quite like this one; one where each of the four panelists had all sat in this very audience just a year before.

"I see you're all here to learn from these four fabulous women."

A roar filled the standing-room-only audience, as everyone clapped and cheered.

This was the most talked about presentation of the weekend. And now every woman in attendance was trying desperately to get in. To hear how these four women had moved mountains to change their lives once and for all.

And they wouldn't be disappointed.

The moderator continued, "One year ago, each of these lovely ladies came here with a hope and a dream. They were all stuck, not sure what to do next. They used this conference as their wakeup call. They used these few days to refocus and relaunch themselves once again.

"And these women are experts at setting the world on fire. I know we hinted at their successes in our course description, but just wait till you hear what they've accomplished. Want to meet them?"

The roar was deafening.

"Let me bring them on stage."

In moments, she'd introduced them. Each woman sat, while the moderator moved to the side. She waited for the applause to die down.

"I have a series of questions for our four panelists. You'll also get a chance to speak. If you want to ask one or more of our panelists something, we'll have an open mic session ten minutes before the end. Sound good?"

The audience bobbed their heads, moving to the edge of their seats. She continued, "Before my first question, I want to give each woman two minutes to introduce themselves and tell you why she's now sitting here on stage, instead of sitting in the audience with all of you."

She passed the microphone to the first panelist, who gave a quick speech. Then she handed the microphone to panelist number two.

Sherri glanced at her best friend, who was sitting next to her. She saw it in Annette's eyes. The excitement of being here once again. The thrill of being on stage, not just in the audience.

But it was more than that.

One year before, they'd had a dream. Sherri wanted to change her life, and she'd brought Annette along.

From the moment they'd arrived, they knew something was different. That they were changing their lives for good.

But call her crazy, she never once would have believed they'd both be sitting here, ready to answer questions in front of several hundred women who were looking for the same thing. It brought a tear to her eye.

Annette nodded. She fully understood. It was her turn. She took the microphone and turned to the audience. With a brief pause to catch her breath, she began.

"Hi, everyone, I'm Annette Hinton. Why am I here? Why am I on this stage? Because one year ago I had a dream, and this lovely woman on my left dragged me here kicking and screaming."

The audience laughed.

"We both taught school and we'd done so together since our twenties. We're besties in the best way; I can't imagine life without her. So, of course, I tagged along when she offered me a chance at a fabulous fifties convention. We'd both turned fifty months before. We both desperately needed a change."

She watched as the nods and murmurs rippled across the rows of people.

"I wanted to write professionally. I'd been trying to get started for years. But nothing ever quite worked."

She breathed deep. Now came the part that was always difficult.

"Then the unthinkable happened. We had an active shooter on campus."

A hush fell across the crowd.

"Luckily, nobody was hurt. Not physically. But something snapped in me, and my life changed forever. The day we were all supposed to get back to work, I marched in and turned in my resignation. And I set out on an incredibly difficult journey to replace my income with freelance writing. I'm not going to lie; it was often a struggle. I fought with my husband. I snapped at my bestie."

Annette glanced over to Sherri and gave her a smile.

"But in the end, it all worked out. I was rewarded with a one-year contract through Escape Magazine to be their Twelve Months of Travel columnist. I'm now traveling the world, blogging about my journey, and having the time of my life. I'm doing things I never would have imagined one year ago. And I have to say, a lot of it came from the courage I gained while attending these classes, right here. One presenter spoke of dreams. How most of us never fully believe we can dream big. I didn't truly understand back then, but now I'm a firm believer. Dreaming big is stopping yourself from saying no. Dreaming big means saying yes, even when you can't fathom yourself taking one more step. Because if you're willing to do that, the future can look amazing."

The audience went wild.

Annette passed the microphone to Sherri, and she waited for quiet to return.

"Hi, I'm Sherri Egan. I have to say, it feels surreal being on this stage today. And listening to the three other ladies here with me, I have a slightly different experience to share with you. Unlike these three, I had no idea what I wanted to do. I was somewhat happy with my life. Bored? Maybe. Wanting something more? That too. But I honestly had no idea what any of that meant when I signed up to come last year."

Sherri saw the nods from quite a few women in the audience.

"But I was itching for something more. Maybe that's the midlife crisis part of it."

Sherri waited for the laughter to die down.

"The biggest takeaway I can give all of you is to make it a priority to do something, anything, when you get home. That's what my BFF here and I did, even before we left for home. We made a commitment to taking specific steps, and we held each other accountable throughout the process. We said *yes* to new things. We jumped instead of just thinking about it. We moved forward in big ways.

"My story starts with looking for an art class, to let my creative soul come back to life. I'd always wanted to explore the arts, but life, marriage, a family, teaching, a home, a divorce … that all got in the way."

She heard the snickers from the audience. "You've all been through all that too?"

A resounding "Yes" echoed through the room.

"I found an art program near my home shortly after I returned. I not only found my love for painting returned with a vengeance, but it also opened a whole new world to me. My instructor told me to keep pursuing it. He recommended a summer program in Italy. That morphed into creating a children's course on expressional painting. I have six offerings of that course this coming summer, and they filled up in six hours."

She felt her breath catch just a little. She still couldn't believe it herself. It all seemed to happen so quickly. Why had she ever doubted?

"And that's not all. The reason I'm sitting here today. That first instructor I had shortly after I left here last year? He submitted my work for a grant from one of the largest painting educational programs. I won the Rising Artist award from the Holliss Foundation and received a one-year residence where I'll continue learning and receiving coaching from the best in the business. And a New York City gallery show at the conclusion of my stay."

The chatter flew at her from every direction. She knew the applause was for her; she still had a hard time believing it.

"Oh, and one more thing. I got the guy! That first painting instructor? We're dating!"

Annette leaned in, fanned herself with her hand, and spoke into the microphone. "And is he ever hot! And completely off the market. They look great together!"

It was hard to calm the crowd down after that much excitement. But the four women and the moderator worked quickly and passed the microphone back and forth to get as many answers out as they could.

They moved out of the meeting space when the next program had to start. They stood and talked with other attendees for almost an hour.

Finally, Annette and Sherri made their way out of the expo center, back to their room to drop off their stuff. They knew they'd be chatting for the rest of the afternoon, once they headed back down to find a place for lunch.

"Can you believe that audience?" Sherri dug for the room card in her bag.

"Can you believe those questions? There are a lot of very smart women here who have the potential to change the world."

"If we could only bottle belief. It would sell like hotcakes. We are our own worst enemies."

"Maybe we helped change some of them."

"Maybe we did."

Annette smiled and gave her friend a one-armed hug. "A year ago, we were them."

Sherri grinned. "And look at us now!"

ABOUT THE AUTHOR

After running several successful businesses, Lori Osterberg decided it was time to reinvent herself once again. Facing an empty nest and too much normal suburbia lifestyle in front of her, she talked her husband into selling off their 3300 square foot home, sell two-thirds of their stuff, all for the chance to slow travel the world. When not traveling, she finds a friend or two to share a good bottle of wine, visits tea factories, dances the night away at outdoor concerts, eats her way through farmers markets, and daydreams about the next set of characters she lives vicariously through. She's currently writing books and living the dream in the Pacific Northwest.

You can learn more at:
  http://LoriOsterberg.com
  Lori on Instagram: @LoriOsterberg
  Lori on Facebook: facebook.com/LoriOsterbergAuthor

Please turn the page for an exciting sneak peek of
Lori Osterberg's
The Creative Standalone Series

The Writer

1

She needed this workout. Bad.

He had her so mixed up. And so full of energy. She had no idea what to do with all of this pent up frustration.

Yeah, she was going with that. Frustration. She snorted knowing full well it wasn't just frustration.

She slid on her favorite workout shorts. Pulled the tank over her head and moved it into place. With a quick tie of her shoes, she was ready to go.

It was late; she was the only one in the gym. Tonight, intensity was her middle name.

One mile on the treadmill.

One hundred pull-ups.

One hundred pushups.

One hundred bodyweight squats.

Back to the treadmill for another mile.

She moved to the weights. And as she adjusted the barbell, she caught her breath. She knew he was there. Could feel him there.

She looked up, into the mirror, searching. Caught just a glimpse, in the corner, watching.

So he wanted to play that game?

She picked up the barbell, started in with the repetitions. Up. Down. Flexing. Moving.

She knew she looked good, standing there just a little sweaty, breathing hard.

Up. Down. Up. Down.

As she counted down ... seven, six, five, four ... she saw him move in.

He stepped to her side, searching for her eyes in the mirror.

He took her breath away. But she wasn't going to let him see how he impacted her. How bad she wanted him.

Three. Two. One.

She put the barbell back into place. And as she stood up, he was there. Behind her.

He wrapped an arm around her, pulled her in. He breathed deeply. "You're so fucking hot." He nibbled her neck, behind her ear, right where she liked it. Trailed his tongue down her spine.

She arched into him, moaned. How did he do that? How did he turn her into a quivering mess? How had she survived without him?

She pressed against him, feeling every last hard inch of him. Her hand traced down his abs, down his rock hard stomach. More. She wanted, oh, so much more ...

"Dammit." Kelly jumped as her phone rang next to her. She picked it up, turned the volume down. She glanced at the incoming call, hit accept.

"Hi, Beth. What's up?"

"Hey, you, whatcha doing?"

"Writing."

"You're kidding, right? It's eighty degrees. It's Friday. It's time to play."

Kelly Sorenson reached up with her free hand, pinched the bridge of her nose, trying to determine how to keep the conversation from turning the way she knew it was about to go. She loved her friend, but lately, Beth had been on a personal mission to get her a life. And it was driving her crazy.

"Beth..."

"Nope, don't *Beth* me. It's Friday. It's beautiful outside. It's festival time. Come on; we're going out to have some fun. Todd's gone this weekend, and I don't want to eat alone. So you're coming with me. Meet me at Henry's at six!"

Kelly glanced at her watch. Four. That gave her two hours. She could easily make it. She glanced back at her computer, looking at where she'd left off. She'd written at least five thousand words in the last couple of hours, more than enough to keep her on schedule. She could probably squeeze in a few hundred more before she left.

"I hear your brain churning, wondering if you should tell me no and stay at home and work. The answer is no. Shut your computer down. Get dressed in something cute and meet me at Henry's. Or I'll come get you."

Kelly dropped her head to her hand. Closed her eyes and counted to five. She loved her friend. Beth Watson had been there through the thick of things these past few years. They'd met three years earlier at a writing convention, became inseparable in their few days together. Even after they both returned home, they started a routine of talking once a day, met when they could. They were like soul sisters. They thought alike. They could finish each other's sentences. Hell, they even wrote alike, collaborating on three books to date. But Beth's current mission was truly driving her crazy.

"If I meet you, it'll just be you, right? You don't have an ulterior motive, do you?"

"Geez, I set you up with one bad date, and you're all over me. That was last week. Forget it already. I told you I was sorry."

"Beth, he felt me up. In the restaurant. With you and Todd on the other side of the table. I'd known him for all of twenty minutes. He was a first class creep with a capital C. Never again, you got it?"

"Hey, I didn't expect him to do *that*. He's really nice at the club. Todd's played squash with him for months. I have no idea what his problem was."

"Honestly, I'm okay. I don't need a man in my life. I'm really *okay*."

"Kelly, I know you are. But I just think you work way too much. Trust me; no other writer can dare keep up with your schedule. You're a writing maniac. But you have to live too. You're too young just to sit in your house and write. You need to get out and have fun. You're only fifty-three years old. I know life's been rough since Tom. I get that. Having someone in your life again would be good for you. You're too young not to have the time of your life. Tom would want that for you, you know."

Kelly swallowed, pushing the knot that always formed in her throat back down. Tom. She missed him so much.

Three years earlier, she and Tom had moved to Portland from San Francisco, partly to be nearer to their only daughter who had decided to make Portland home and partly for the opportunity Tom found to head a tech startup. They looked at it as their reinvention, their chance to do something fun and completely out of character.

And so Kelly wrote. She no longer needed a job - the startup bonus and stock option Tom had received ensured that. Her bucket list had always included a line item of becoming a famous novelist. So the move gave her the chance to write.

She nailed it. Killed it. Her first novel was an instant success. She'd hit Amazon and New York Times' best sellers lists within weeks.

They lived a fairytale life. They'd traveled every weekend, visiting Seattle, Vancouver, the coast. They explored the best restaurants. They found a quaint condo in the middle of the city center, remodeled it and called it home.

Then eighteen months later, Tom was on his way to a meeting. A young woman texted her friends, crossed the yellow line, and the fairytale ended, poof, in an instant.

Kelly couldn't have survived it without Beth.

Now she wasn't sure if she'd survive Beth. This dating thing truly was going to kill her. If she didn't kill Beth first.

"No, you can't kill me. It's against the law." Beth snickered, knowing full well what her friend had been thinking. "Come on. Let's meet at Henry's. You love it there. It's always lively, and they have great food. We can check out the latest happenings, watch the younger crowd hit on each other. It'll give us something to write about." If Beth knew anything, it was how to punch her friend's buttons.

"Well, when you put it like that ..." Kelly laughed. She loved Beth. And no matter what, she could never stay mad at her for more than a moment. Besides, the weather was truly beautiful. And since Henry's was only ten blocks from her condo, the walk would do her good. "Okay, six, I'll see you there in just a bit."

"Yeah. I'll see you there. Don't be late."